BURIED SECRETS

of BOIS BLANC

Murder in the Straits of Mackinac

Richard L. Baldwin

*To My friend, Chris,
Best wishes
Rich Baldwin*

Buttonwood Press
Haslett, Michigan

OTHER BOOKS BY
RICHARD L. BALDWIN

Fiction

Mysteries:

A Lesson Plan for Murder (1998)
ISBN: 0-9660685-0-5
Buttonwood Press

The Principal Cause of Death (1999)
ISBN: 0-9660685-2-1
Buttonwood Press

Administration Can Be Murder (2000)
ISBN: 0-9660685-4-8
Buttonwood Press

Spiritual:
Unity and the Children (2000)
ISBN: 0-9660685-3-X
Buttonwood Press

Non-Fiction

The Piano Recital (1999)
ISBN: 0-9660685-1-3
Buttonwood Press

*A Story to Tell: Special Education in
Michigan's Upper Peninsula 1902-1975* (1994)
ISBN: 932212-77-8
Lake Superior Press

Contribution Policy of Buttonwood Press

A portion of the profits from each book sold is contributed to three organizations chosen by the publisher. The organizations chosen for the *Buried Secrets of Bois Blanc: Murder in the Straits of Mackinac* include: The Bois Blanc Island Historical Society, the Citizens Alliance to Uphold Special Education (CAUSE), and the Michigan Association for Deaf, Hearing, and Speech Services. One dollar from each book sold goes to a fund to be equally shared by these three organizations.

This book is dedicated to the people of Bois Blanc Island, Jennie McGeen Brussow and Dianne Easterling, and to the CAUSE parent trainers who advocate for the children with disabilities.

This novel is a product of the imagination of the author. In many instances the actual names of people on the island are used, but only with their permission. If permission wasn't sought or given, a fictitious name is used even though residents and persons familiar with the island may know to whom the story refers. None of the events described in this story occurred. Though settings, buildings and businesses exist, liberties may have been taken as to their actual location and description. This story has no purpose other than to entertain the reader.

Published by Buttonwood Press
PO Box 716
Haslett, Michigan 48840
www.buttonwoodpress.com

Publisher's Cataloging-in-Publication Data
Baldwin, Richard L.
        The buried secrets of Bois Blanc : murder in the straits of Mackinac
/ by Richard L. Baldwin. -- 1st ed.

        p. cm -- (Louis Searing and Margaret McMillan mystery; 4)
        ISBN: 978-0-9660685-5-9

        1. Murder--Michigan--Mackinac Region--Fiction.
        2. Detective and mystery stories. I. Title.

PS3552.A451525B87 2001   813'.54
                        QB100-902083

Printed in the United States of America

ACKNOWLEDGMENTS

A book is a product of the joy that comes from telling a story. The drafts, the research, and meeting people who offer a piece of information are all part of the fun, and the magic that is experienced with most writers and assuredly, this one. I shall long remember with fond and vivid memories my visits to Bob-Lo and the hospitality of many wonderful people.

The Buttonwood Press team must be commended for hard work and believing in me to the extent of putting heart and soul into this story. Thank you to my editor, Gail Garber, who always seemed to see what was making sense and what needed revision; to Joyce Wagner, my long-time friend who proofread the book, finding hundreds of little "mistakes" that somehow flew by me when I was concentrating on the bigger picture, and to Marilyn "Sam" Nesbitt who designed the cover and typeset the book. Her calm demeanor and her willingness to try and accommodate all of my suggestions were appreciated. Sam and her husband took a trip to Bob-Lo in late summer of 2000 so she could get a feel for the island before designing the cover.

This book was reviewed by good friends who offered me honest opinions and advice. I am indebted to Anna L. Taylor of Charlevoix, a fan of the Louis Searing and Maggie McMillan Mystery Series and a student in Charlevoix Middle School, for giving me insightful revision suggestions; to Ben Hall, who rides with me on Tuesdays and Thursday mornings and who offered excellent words of advice about the plot and the characters; to Ann Saunders, whose eye for a good mystery led her to reinforce the positive aspects of the book and to encourage revisions in spots; and to Elaine Stanfield who took time to offer many helpful suggestions.

ACKNOWLEDGMENTS

Thank you to Suzette Cooley-Sanborn who for the past three years has always answered my questions via e-mail, has read the earliest draft of the book and who took the time to point out inaccuracies, offer suggestions, say the story was a good one and worthy of sharing with readers. Thanks to Suzette, I shall long remember talking with Su VanVorhees and listening to Jim Vosper tell stories of the island. During my visit in the summer of 2000, Suzette and John gave me a bed to rest my body and treated me to a hollow log fire on the shore of the south channel. With the full moon shining down on beautiful BobLo, we sat and talked till the embers were all but extinguished. Thanks, Suzette and John, for your hospitality and memories.

Thank you to Glenn and Judy Munro. Patty and I learned of a wonderful get-away on Bob-Lo from David and Holly Brock of Lansing, Michigan. We inquired of this place called Isle-A-While and spent a week there in 1995. We fell in love with Bob-Lo and spent countless hours hiking, noting wildlife, sleeping under the clearest sky with a bright moon and sparkling stars, really tasting food, enjoying the ships traversing the Straits, and listening to Glenn tell stories of the island. We returned for a week in 1999 to continue to enjoy all that makes Bob-Lo a vacation or summer home to many. Both weeks were shared with good friends from Overland Park, Kansas, Marc and Mary Lou Rottinghaus.

During my short visit in the summer of 2000, I was invited to share a gourmet meal in the Munro gazebo with Gary and Gail Wagner and Myrtle Hack, affectionately known to her grandchildren as "Grandma down the hatch." As we discussed the mystery, sailboats with colorful spinnakers were making their way to the finish line of the Port Huron to Mackinac Sailboat Race.

I wish to thank Elaine Stanfield of Williamston, Michigan. Elaine is a psychologist who serves as an advisor in character development. Elaine and I would meet at McDonald's in Williamston to talk about characters and their relationship to the plot. Her advice over coffee was always appreciated.

I shall long remember sitting and talking with Ray Plaunt about the development of the Plaunt Transportation Company now owned and operated by his son Curt. Ray suggested I go down the road a piece and chat with Glenn Gibbons who might have a story to tell. I did, and Glenn welcomed me into his home and told the story of being a young boy and getting a shooting lesson from one of John Dillinger's bodyguards. Dillinger and his entourage were on Bob-Lo while he was recovering from surgery. Glenn's father was responsible for the lumbering camp where the Dillinger group was staying. Glenn was a joy to listen to as he spun his yarn.

There were a number of people who were there for me when I needed a clarification, a question answered. In addition to the above mentioned people I sincerely thank a few more folks on Bois Blanc Island who helped me: Bunker Clark, Curt VanVorhees, and Sheila Godbold. Others who offered some advice or who answered a question or two include: Kurt R. Jones, Director of Public Safety and Chief of Police for the City of Cheboygan; Greg LaMore and Don Flagg, whose knowledge of yachting came in handy on more than one occasion; Jessica Fink, a freshman at Michigan State University and a major in Forensic Science who advised me on matters of evidence analysis; Byron Rogers who helped me with the helicopter scene; Greg Waller who clarified Coast Guard procedures; Jerry Wagner and Rudy, who taught me the anatomy of German shepherd paws, front and back; Greg Thornhill, who in real life is a great magician; Mary of the Mackinac Island Police who helped me understand their mode of operation in a missing person case., and finally to Eric Trap of Cortez, Colorado who answered questions about the police canine corps.

I would be remiss if I did not mention the legal assistance provided to me. Thank you to Lyn Beekman who gave me some good legal advice, Paul Zimmer who provided me with arraignment procedures at the district and circuit court level, Tom Anderson who answered some detailed questions about court room procedures and a special thanks to Fred Feleppa, Assistant Prosecuting Attorney for Mackinac County who truly went the extra mile to help me understand the procedures in the 92nd District Court and the 50th Circuit Court. Fred not only answered a host of questions, but gave me a tour of the courtrooms noting how my fictitious trial would play out and then offered to review the portion of this novel where the court scenes are presented. His advice was invaluable to the telling of this story.

This is the book that will have a lasting memory. Each book is like a child that is conceived, nurtured, and enjoyed. All of my books are unique in this way, but this book comes from fond memories of trips to Bois Blanc, from wonderful people who came into my life once I discovered this gem in the Straits of Mackinac.

Oh yes, a comment or two about the photo on the back cover. Lou enjoys riding his Harley-Davidson motorcycle. To try and understand Lou's passion for this form of transportation I wanted to actually sit on a Harley and have my picture taken. So, thanks to Steve Krusich, Superintendent of the Lenawee School District, who knew of Larry's Cycle Shop (Larry and Judy Ackley, owners) in Adrian and who made arrangements for me to live this dream. And, thanks to Judy, and to Randy Raper, the owner of the customized 1954 Harley-Davidson Panhead Motorcycle for an enjoyable photo shoot in front of Larry's Cycle Shop in full regalia.

As this book goes to print, I wish to thank Sheila Godbold for marketing my books in the Hawk's Landing General Store; Bunker Clark for announcing the pending arrival of this mystery in the *Bob-Lo Tatler*, and to Barb Schlund who offered to put a few books out for sale at her tavern.

Finally, I wish to thank Patty Baldwin, my loving wife, best friend, and best critic. Patty has supported my storytelling passion since its inception. She has read countless drafts and listened to many plot ideas, changes, and revisions. Her words always guided me to a better story. She said this one is my best yet. We'll see what you the reader thinks because after all, you are the only real judge of a good story.

W hen a visitor disembarks from the ferry service that brings them to Bob-Lo, he or she has the opportunity to read the front and back of a Michigan Historic Site marker which was erected by the Bois Blanc Historical Society and the Citizens of Bois Blanc Island in 1990. This two-sided historic marker reads:

Bois Blanc Island

Bois Blanc Island, known as "Bob-Lo" to area residents, is twelve miles long, six miles wide and has six lakes. In 1827 the United States government platted the island. The U.S. Coast Guard established a life-saving station at Walker's Point in 1890. The following year the Pointe Aux Pins Association was formed. In 1908, on behalf of the association, President Walter B. Webb hired the Mason L. Brown Company, a Detroit surveying firm, to plat and record the Pointe Aux Pins subdivision. Pointe Aux Pins was the first resort community on the island. Much of Bois Blanc Island is state-owned forest land containing White and Norway pines that tower 200 feet tall. As recently as the 1950s, Bois Blanc provided lumber to Mackinac Island where woodcutting is prohibited.

On June 3, 1795, Chippewa Chief Matchekewis ceded Bois Blanc to the United States as part of the Treaty of Greenville. The cession also included most of Ohio, part of Indiana, sixteen strategic sites on Michigan waterways and Mackinac Island. During the War of 1812, U.S. Navy Captain Arthur Sinclair's fleet took shelter at the Island while waiting to attack the British at Fort Mackinac. In 1880 the island provided a haven to alleged murderer Henry English who escaped from Pennsylvania authorities before his trial. He was apprehended on Bois Blanc by Pinkerton agents, returned to Pennsylvania and acquitted. During the twentieth century, Bois Blanc's wilderness supported a lucrative lumber industry before giving way to tourism. Although primarily a resort in 1990, the island had 45 permanent residents.

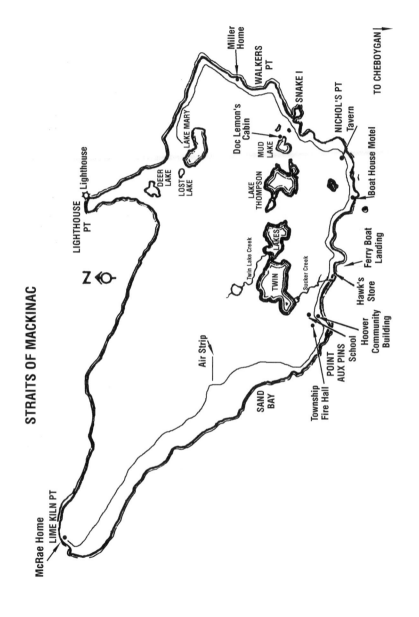

STRAITS OF MACKINAC

McRae Home
LIME KILN PT

Air Strip

SAND
BAY

Township
Fire Hall

POINT
AUX PINS

Hoover
Community
Building

School

Hawk's
Store

Ferry Boat
Landing

Sucker Creek

Twin Lake Creek

TWIN LAKES

LAKE THOMPSON

MUD LAKE

Doc Lemon's Cabin

LOST LAKE

DEER LAKE

Lighthouse

LIGHTHOUSE PT

LAKE MARY

Miller Home

WALKERS PT

SNAKE I

NICHOL'S PT

Tavern

Boat House Motel

TO CHEBOYGAN

N

CHAPTER ONE

Saturday Evening, June 1
The Straits of Mackinac

At approximately 10 p.m., Jessica Williams walked along the dock of the Mackinac Island Marina, hand in hand with her escort and friend Mike Miles. They were looking for the yacht, *Slinky*, to begin a short evening cruise in the Straits of Mackinac. They found the craft and Mike helped Jessica step into the cockpit of the forty-six foot Tiara. There appeared to be no one on board. Mike suggested they walk to the companionway where they would undoubtedly meet other guests. Jessica tapped on a door and said, "Hello. May we come in?"

"Yes, by all means. Welcome."

She entered and immediately was accosted by a woman with a gun. The gun was pointed directly at her. "Shut-up and get down! Now!"

Jessica, a strikingly beautiful thirty-nine-year-old advocate for children with disabilities, recognized her captor immediately. Mary Chandler was her old college roommate. She did as she was told with adrenaline coursing through her slim body. Mike assisted in gagging and blindfolding her. Her hands were tied behind her and her ankles were bound by rope. She was helped to stand and then Mary pushed her onto a berth. All of this took no more than a minute.

Jessica knew this was no joke, and she knew why it was happening.

The kidnap and departure from Mackinac Island went off without a hitch. Mary and Mike had planned to kill Jessica and dump her into the cold Straits of Mackinac, but as they headed west and south of Round Island, an argument ensued.

"Kill her and throw her overboard now!" Mary said with authority, while at the controls of her father's yacht the *Stinky*, so named because he had made his millions in the septic tank cleaning business in Ludington, Michigan.

"Are you crazy?" Mike asked. "With all of these boats around, someone's bound to see us!"

"I said, kill her and dump her—that was the plan. Do it!"

"That was the plan, but that was before this turned out to be a perfect evening for boating. Sound travels, people could have binoculars trained on us. It's stupid, Mary. Down-right stupid. We've got time to kill her. But, this isn't the time, not now."

"I want her dead and overboard. It's clean and done with. Walking off this boat and onto Bob-Lo is riskier than dumping her into the Straits."

"Trust me, Mary. Wait. You'll be glad we did."

"We'll regret this decision, Mike. Who's in charge here anyway? You or me? I planned this murder and you're not cooperating."

"I thought this was a joint venture. At least that's what I agreed to," Mike responded.

"I ought to put both of you in the Straits. I never should've brought you into my plan in the first place!" Mary snarled.

"You need me, Mary. You need me and you know it. Right now, I'm the one with common sense and if you know what's good for you and for us, you'll agree. No murder tonight. We're not going to take the risk."

꒛

My wife Carol and I learned that Jessica and Mike were missing while we were enjoying a conversation with friends in the ballroom of the world famous Grand Hotel. Erin O'Brien walked up and interrupted, "I think you're going to be needed, Lou. Jessica Williams and her escort are missing. They didn't come back from a boat ride in the Straits."

"Jessica Williams?" I asked, because I didn't recognize the name.

"She represented CAUSE, The Citizens Alliance to Uphold Special Education. They paid for four guests but said Jessica would be their official representative."

"Oh, I think I remember her. Pretty, late thirties, long hair, looks like a beauty contestant."

"Yes. She's beautiful."

"She appeared to be a delightful, intelligent, and charming woman. What's happening at the moment?" I asked.

"As I understand it, there's not much commotion. Some people in our group have gone off to town looking in bars, restaurants and shops in hopes of spotting them."

"Have the police been notified?" I asked Erin.

"Yes. I've been told the Island police are down at the marina talking to a few people."

"Guess I'll go down there and see what's going on." I excused myself from the group, gave Carol a light kiss and said I'd be back soon.

Still in tuxedo, I took the ten-minute walk to the marina. The night air was refreshing. The sky was aglow with a full moon and twinkling stars. I had a feeling that my next investigation was about to begin.

ॐ

"Excuse me, Officer. I'm Louis Searing."

"Tony Adams. Pleased to meet you. This is Betsy Bowers." I shook the officer's hand and nodded at the lady talking to him. "Nice to meet you, Betsy."

"You know something about this missing couple?" asked Officer Adams, a short, slightly pudgy, middle-aged officer.

"No, I heard that Jessica was missing. We were at the same party in the Grand. I decided to come down to see if I could help."

"I might be able to use a little help. Especially if you're the Louis Searing. A private investigator with your credentials could be of great assistance. Any police department would welcome your help, Lou."

"Thanks, I didn't know my reputation preceded me."

"I bought one of your books this afternoon at the Island Book Store. In fact, I was reading it when we got the call about this missing couple."

"Tell me, what do you know at the moment?" I asked.

"We got a call from Mrs. Bowers saying that Jessica and her escort, a man named Mike Miles, were missing. Mrs. Bowers says Jessica borrowed a shawl and was to return it when she got back. Apparently, the two didn't come back."

"Mr. Searing, I'm afraid that something terrible has happened to them," Betsy said with a tone of great concern. She pointed in the direction of the *Slinky* and said, "They got on that boat, went out for a half hour and then that boat came back but Jessica and Mike did not get off. I asked the owner where they were. He said he didn't know what I was talking about. I told him I was going to call the police. He must have thought I was crazy, but my friend was on that boat and she didn't come back. I was beside myself. I called the police and this officer came down."

I took my small notepad and pen from my pocket to record information. "Your relationship to Jessica is...?" I asked.

"I'm a friend. We shared the same table at the banquet. As I told this policeman, I offered her my shawl for the boat ride, she accepted and said she'd give it back when she returned."

"Can you describe this shawl?" I asked, hopefully not interfering with Officer Adams' line of questioning, but in case the shawl showed up, I wanted to be able to identify it.

"It was a white, wool Pashima."

"Okay, now, tell me, was Jessica staying at the Grand Hotel?"

"No, she was staying over there on Bois Blanc Island," Betsy said, pointing to the southeast where in the distance could be seen trees, a lengthy shoreline, and a few lights from summer homes.

"Does she own a cottage there?" I asked.

"No, she has a favorite place that she rents for a week each summer. It's a quiet island. This place is for fudgies and lots of tourists. That island is for a small group of year around residents, cottage owners and summer visitors. She came over for the banquet."

"How was she planning to get back?"

"She told me that she was to be picked up around twelve-thirty by the owner of the cottage she's renting."

I looked at my watch. It was eleven-fifteen. "Does the owner know she's missing?"

"I don't know. I don't know who he is," Betsy answered.

"How about Jessica's escort, Mike? Where's he staying?" I asked.

"I don't know where he was planning to stay tonight. Last night he was where we're staying, the Henderson Bed and Breakfast."

"Are search operations in place now?" I asked Officer Adams.

"We alerted the Coast Guard and because of the mention of Bob-Lo Island, we've called the Mackinac County Sheriff. They'll call the deputy assigned to the island. He'll probably ask Wags to go up and see if he can see something."

"Wags?"

"Yeah, a nickname for Bob-Lo's airport manager. He often helps when we need an additional pair of eyes from the air."

"How's the Coast Guard operation work?" I asked, because I wasn't familiar with their procedures.

"They'll put a 37 foot MLB into the area."

"MLB?"

"Motor Life Boat. That's what they use for search and rescue. The Soo, Cleveland, and Traverse City stations will be involved in planning and executing the search. They'll probably send up a helicopter from Traverse City."

"That would take awhile to get here, wouldn't it?"

"About fifteen minutes. That helicopter can make good time, believe me."

"How long will the search go on?"

"If they don't find any bodies, it could go on all night and into the morning I suppose. I don't know when they'd decide to call it off, but there is only so much you can do before you conclude there's no body to be found."

"You expect Jessica and Mike to appear out there?" I asked.

"If we're lucky, they'll surface; that is, if they did go in the boat, did encounter foul play, and did, in fact, drown."

"Lots of 'ifs' there, Officer," I said, thinking that he really didn't believe the couple was in great danger.

"Well, when you've been in the business as long as I have, you encounter a lot of stories. We've had missing persons on this island for hours and even a day or two. Most of them appear and were never in any harm, just a lack of communication, that's all. She may never have gotten on the boat. She may have asked the yachtsman to take her over to Bob-Lo to save her landlord the trip of coming over to get her. She may have come back on the Island and is talking with someone very innocently not realizing that we're lookin' for her. There are lots of things that could've happened."

"I don't mean to be such a fatalist, but they didn't come back and this is so unlike Jessica. If she came back, she'd find me and give me my shawl," Betsy said, sounding quite sure of herself. "While dining, Jessica said she wasn't feeling safe. She said something like 'I'm uncomfortable. I wish I weren't here.'"

"Are you sure you saw Jessica and Mike get on the boat?" Officer Adams asked.

"My husband and I followed them as they walked toward town. I saw them go into the marina walk along the dock and get onto a boat. I was at quite a distance, mind you, but yes, I did see them get on a boat. There is no question in my mind."

"Did you see the boat leave?" I asked.

"When we got to the marina, I looked at the back of the boat, the boat's name was *Slinky*. After I mentioned the name of the boat to my husband, we recognized some people from the party and stopped to chat with them."

"Did you see the city name under the name, *Slinky*?" I asked.

"I don't recall that."

"She said she'd give you your shawl when they got back?" I repeated.

"Yes, and since the cruise was to be about thirty minutes long, and we were enjoying our walk, we simply waited for the boat to come back."

"And?" I asked, pen above my notepad.

"Yes, it did; came right into the slip where it was when I saw Jessica and Mike step aboard."

"Did you talk with anyone on the *Slinky* after it came back?"

"As I said earlier, I asked a man on the boat if Jessica and Mike were on board."

"And he said?"

"He said, 'There must be some mistake. There was no one on my boat.' He excused himself and disappeared."

"That's when you called the police?"

"Yes. Officer Adams questioned the owner and even searched the yacht. He's convinced Jessica and Mike never set foot on that boat, but you'll never convince me of that. I saw it!"

"I think we've gotten all we need from you, Betsy. Let us know how we can reach you, if we need additional information," Officer Adams said.

"We're staying at the Henderson Bed and Breakfast in town. I don't know the phone number, but it's in the phone book. We'll be there tonight. We're going back to the mainland in the morning and then home to Jackson."

"Thank you, Betsy," Officer Adams said, continuing to jot notes on his pad of paper. "We'll let you know if we find your friend."

"One more question, Betsy," I said, thinking of Columbo, the detective who always needed one more question answered. "You said Jessica felt uncomfortable earlier this evening."

"Yes."

"Did she say anything more about that?"

"Well, she was not herself all evening. She seemed nervous, you know what I mean, you can tell when somebody isn't acting normally."

"Did she say anything more about what might have been

bothering her?"

"We went to the ladies room together and while there, I asked if she felt okay. She said she did but was nervous. All she said was something like, 'Should have kept some things to myself.'"

"She didn't say what she should have kept to herself?"

"No. I didn't want to pry. I expressed my concern for her and we went back to the table."

"Did Mike seem to be acting normally?"

"I don't know Mike. I never met him before tonight. He seemed reserved, quiet. They conversed, danced and seemed normal for a couple, I guess. Now that I think about it, there may have been an aura of tension." We thanked Betsy and assured her all would be done to find Jessica and Mike. She left with head bowed and looking quite worried.

"What will happen if you find the bodies?" I asked Officer Adams.

"Don't think we will. The Straits don't give up their dead, at least not for awhile. But, to answer your question, we'd work with the Coast Guard and the Michigan State Police. The body or bodies would be transported to St. Ignace."

"Let me know if you find them, will you?" I asked. "I'm staying at the Grand. You can leave a message at the desk. Here's my card."

"Thanks, Lou. Can I call you, Lou?"

"By all means."

"Talk with you later. Thanks for accepting me. Most officers are not enthused about private investigators walking onto their turf."

"You're the exception, Lou. We admire your skills. Enough said."

I thanked Tony and we parted. Officer Adams headed for the police station, and I went to the Grand Hotel.

ॐ

Prior to Erin's suggesting that I begin to look into the disappearance of Jessica and Mike, Carol and I were attending a dance in the Grand Hotel. The cause for the celebration was the 30th anniversary of the Michigan mandatory law for special education. The Society for the Preservation of Michigan Special Education History went all out in its planning for this evening. People were paying two hundred dollars a piece for the opportunity to attend a gala ball in the hotel's famous ballroom.

The room had been full of men in tuxedos and women in lavish evening gowns. There was an ambience of elegance. It was a wonderful night for a ball. People could stroll along the longest porch in the world. They could look into the sky and see a million stars; look to the west and see the lights outlining the unique and one-of-a-kind Mackinac Bridge, or hear the click-clack of the horse's hooves on the roads as people on the carless island moved about in carriages. The only flaw in the perfect evening was the rumor that Jessica Williams and Mike Miles were missing.

It was a little after eleven-thirty. As I walked back to the hotel, I stopped to admire the view of the Mackinac Bridge and took a moment to reflect on my many years in special education. A lot had been accomplished for children with disabilities. Many dedicated people had worked together and had created fine programs and excellent schools. Because of their efforts, life was a bit easier for more than two hundred thousand children and their families. Sure, there were still some negatives, but all in all, a fine effort had been expended for Michigan's recipients of special education.

I checked the front desk for messages. None. I didn't bother to locate Erin. I'd see her in the morning. I acknowledged some people talking in the parlor and went up to my room. Carol was in the bathroom preparing for bed. I told her what I had learned. It dawned on me that Jessica's landlord was about to arrive and may not know that she was missing.

"I'm going back to the marina. I might not be back for awhile. I'll call and let you know what's going on."

"Looks like you've got your next challenge, Lou," Carol said, wiping the cream off her youthful-looking face.

"I think so. You want to stroll down to the marina? I can wait a few minutes."

"No, I'm going to bed. My feet hurt from whirling around the dance floor."

"Be back soon," I said, lightly kissing Carol on the cheek.

I thought about changing out of my tux into something more comfortable, but decided not to as I didn't think I'd be long. As I approached the marina, a small boat was coming into the breakwaters. I looked at my watch and saw that it was twelve twenty-five. *If a boat was coming from Bois Blanc Island to get Jessica, this could be it,* I thought.

I watched as the boat slowly pulled up to the dock. A middle-aged, husky man with a full beard reached out for the large wooden piling. He wrapped a rope around it and secured his boat. I walked onto the short dock and said, "You're not from Bois Blanc Island by any chance, are you?"

"Yes, I am."

"Are you here to pick up a lady who's renting one of your A-frames?"

"Yes, Jessica Williams is supposed to meet me here in a couple of minutes."

"I've got some bad news."

"What's happened? Is she sick? She said she didn't feel well when I brought her over earlier."

"Apparently she and her friend went for a boat ride a couple of hours ago and they didn't come back."

"Oh God, no!"

"I talked with Tony Adams of the Island Police and he says a lot of missing people turn up in town or on one of these boats in the marina. But, Jessica's friend said she saw her and her date get on a boat named *Slinky*. When the boat came back, they weren't on it."

"I hope there's some mistake. Who are you, if you don't mind my asking?"

"Not at all. Sorry not to introduce myself. My name's Louis Searing. I was at a formal affair tonight which explains my tux. My partner Maggie McMillan and I have solved some mysteries involving education issues and people."

"Nice to meet you. My name's Gavin McRae. My wife Jenny and I live on Bob-Lo in the summertime. We have a couple of cottages that we rent. Jessica comes up each year about this time. She's a nice lady."

"Nice to meet you, Gavin," I said, reaching out to shake his hand. "I suggest you hang around for a little while. Jessica may appear momentarily."

"Yeah, I'll do that, but I've been bringing her to the Island for years. She appreciates a ride over and back and she would never think of being a minute late. Since she's not here now, she's not going to be."

We chatted until about a quarter to one. Jessica did not appear.

"Say, Mr. McRae, would it be too much trouble to take me back to Bois Blanc and allow me to look in Jessica's cabin? There could be a clue to her disappearance."

"Be glad to help. I took a nap this evening, so I feel good. The Straits are cooperating, waters are relatively calm. A storm is supposed to be coming, but not for awhile. Hop in, let's go."

I got into the boat, helped Gavin to get away, and within a few minutes we were out of the marina, and into the Straits. I called Carol on my cell phone. "My return will take a little while. I'm heading over to Bois Blanc Island. Jessica's landlord is taking me to her cabin. I might find a good clue or two. If Jessica is missing, I've got an opportunity to get right on the case. I'll be back in a few hours."

"I'll not be awake when you get here, Lou."

"Oh, I know."

"See you in the morning. Be careful. I love you."

"I will. Love you too," I said, and returned the phone to my pocket.

For twenty minutes the boat cut through the slightly rough waters. Gavin pulled up to the dock and secured his boat. We walked along the long dock and set foot on Bob-Lo.

"That's her place there, the west A-frame," Gavin said. A light was on anticipating Jessica's return.

"Beautiful setting for a getaway spot."

"Can't get any more peaceful than this, Lou. This island is the

11

exact opposite of Mackinac. There's no reason to come here except to stay in your home or cottage, hike, read, add birds to your life list, and relax with a capital R. The year-round residents number less than fifty. In the summer the island can have about two thousand at any given time. There's one bar and one general store at the southeast end of the island. There's also a four unit motel down there as well."

"Think the door is open?" I asked, as we approached the A-frame.

"Oh, sure, we never lock anything up here. Walk right in."

I knocked, opened the door, and quietly entered. Gavin flipped on the light. I felt a bit uncomfortable thinking Jessica might be inside.

"Jessica?" I said. Silence.

Gavin and I walked further into the cabin. "All seems quite orderly. Not a messy lady," I said.

"She's one of my best renters. Everything is always in its place. She keeps the cabin clean."

I didn't see anything that would help me. Jessica appeared to have brought very little with her. I looked into the wastebasket and pushed the trash around like a street person looking for a cigarette butt or an empty bottle to reclaim. My hand came upon a handwritten invitation. I picked it out of the wastebasket and read, "You and Mr. Miles are invited to an after the Special Education Gala Banquet Cruise in the Straits of Mackinac. Enjoy a short ride on the *Slinky*, viewing the famous Mackinac Bridge and the northern stars and moon. Ship sails at ten from the Mackinac Island Marina. An escort will greet you. Refreshments will be provided. Your captain and crew."

"Well, here's the invitation and just as her friend Betsy said, she and her escort were invited on a boat ride. Think I'll keep this." I looked into the wastebasket hoping to find an envelope. I was in luck. The envelope was there, but there was no return address. There was a postmark, however. It was mailed from Chicago and the date was May 22. The invitation was mailed to Traverse City.

"Did Jessica say something that would give you a clue that she was afraid of anything before going over to the Island?" I asked.

"She said she didn't feel good. I took that to mean she had an upset stomach, headache, or maybe she was coming down with a cold, but she never said anything that led me to think she was afraid of anyone or anything."

"I think I've overdone my welcome for this evening. I'd probably better be getting back to Mackinac Island."

"May I suggest you stay with us for what is left of the night?" Gavin said. "Maybe I'm being selfish, but the Straits are kicking up a bit. I see some lightening in the west. Daylight is only a few hours away, a long nap at our place would be good for you. It isn't the Grand Hotel, but you'll get a good breakfast and a comfortable bed."

"My wife is expecting me to return, but if you think it's not safe to cross given the weather, I'll call and let her know it'll be morning before I get back."

"I really think crossing now is not a good idea. Good captains don't take risks and I think it would be a risk."

"Sure. I appreciate your hospitality. I couldn't accomplish anything at the hotel tonight anyway. I'd like to call the Island police to see if they have any new information. I'll want to call the hotel to let my wife know I won't be coming back till morning, and to see if there are any messages for me."

"Not a problem. Our home is a couple hundred feet from here. My wife's name is Jenny. She probably went to bed an hour or so ago. You'll meet her in the morning. Jenny's mother, Myrtle, is living with us. She's delightful, you'll like her. Everyone does."

We walked out of the A-frame and Gavin's decision not to cross the Straits was a good one. We could see lightning and hear thunder off to the west. Even though it was late, we were still wide awake.

We entered the McRae home. Before me was my idea of an ideal summer home. While sitting in the living room, one could see the Straits, and off in the distance were the lights on Mackinac Island. The art was nautical with photos of ocean-going freighters on the walls. Their furniture seemed to beckon the visitor to get swallowed up in an old leather chair that looked like it had years of experience comforting people.

In the light, I could get a good look at Gavin. He was rugged, with a solid build, strong, and his face was covered by a heavy beard. His hair was long but only because he didn't want to make a trip to

Cheboygan to see a barber. "Want some coffee, Lou?"

"I'd never get to sleep with a shot of caffeine, but if you've a non-caffeine soft drink, I'd take that."

"Diet Pepsi OK?"

"Sure."

Gavin had a chance to get a good look at me. "You look like my uncle."

"Really?"

"Yeah, you must be around sixty-five. Right?"

"Fifty-nine."

"Sorry. Hope I didn't offend you?"

"Takes a lot more than that to offend me, Gavin."

"Good. Yeah, my uncle has your hairline."

"What hairline?" I said with a chuckle, as my male patterned baldness was textbook. "You think I'd get along well with this uncle?"

"Yeah you would, similar mannerisms, looks. You guys could be twins. He wears a couple of hearing aids, too. Sometimes I don't think they help him, but he wears 'em."

"Well, they help me. I can't function very well without 'em. I wear mine all the time."

"You always been a detective?" Gavin asked, putting a cold can of diet Pepsi in front of me.

"No, I used to be the State Director of Special Education for Michigan. Before that I was a teacher of children who were hearing impaired. In 1969 I went to the University of Kansas to earn a doctorate in deaf education. I finished that and went to teach at the university level for four years, two at Kent State and two at Texas Tech. Then I went to the Michigan Department of Education. Over twenty years I was a consultant, then a supervisor, and then the State Director. Late in that stretch I had a traumatic experience that led me to this work."

"Don't need to share it if it'll be upsetting to you."

"I can talk about it now, but it was traumatic for a long time. I still sometimes get cold sweats thinking about it. I was on a motorcycle camping trip with a good friend. He had convinced me that there was nothing like the freedom and the excitement of a trip on a motorcycle. I got myself a Harley and began taking short trips. I did some camping in state parks in mid-Michigan and then felt I was ready for an extended road trip."

"Not my kind of a vacation," Gavin interrupted. "I like to ride but I wouldn't be one for distant camping trips."

"I was skeptical, but I saw it as a chance to spend some time with my friend and I thought I might discover a great new hobby."

"Did you?"

"Well, the first day out was good. The long ride was invigorating. The new bikes are equipped with so much technology that you really might as well be in a car. You can talk with other riders. You can listen to the radio or to a CD as the sound gets piped into your helmet. The feeling is kinda like riding in a two-wheel convertible."

"You just stop where you want?"

"Yeah, you ride for a while and then like in a car, you need to stop and stretch, get something to drink, you know, no different than any other trip. But, it's an exciting way to travel. We were in black leather, heavy boots, and we had the latest equipment for a comfortable and safe trip."

"Motorcyclists always seem a bit threatening to people."

"Well, you know, not everyone inside all that leather has tattoos and beards. And, even if they do, people are people. Once you peel off the exterior, you get the same stuff."

"Yeah, guess you're right," Gavin replied. "I bike here on the island so I know you're right!"

"Anyway, the second night out we were in western Virginia at the first campground into the Appalachian Mountains. We had set up our lean-to, made a fire, had dinner, and washed the dishes. We talked into the evening and then called it a day. The next thing I remember was a lot of commotion and noise. By the time I became fully awake and realized what was happening, I discovered that we were being attacked. I didn't know it at the time, but my friend was dead. They told me later that my life was spared because I was wearing my heavy leather coat and the knife couldn't penetrate enough to mortally wound me. I got four or five stab wounds but they didn't go deep enough nor did they hit any vital organs. My friend had fatal wounds in his chest and back. It was brutal.

"I don't remember all of it. I'm told I called 911 from the phone on my bike. I don't remember that. I don't remember the police and ambulance crew at the scene. But I do remember the noise: the fighting, the feeling of being overwhelmed by force and the knife going in several times."

"Must have been like living a nightmare."

"Worse than a nightmare. I got sewn up, spent a couple of nights in the hospital. My wife Carol and my friend's wife and a few of his relatives came down. I was in a small town hospital. They treated me well, but all I could think about was getting home."

"Yeah, when you're away from home, you just want to be around familiar people and with your own doctor."

"That's right. Anyway, the body wounds healed, but not the emotional wound of losing my friend. I had to find his killer. The local and county cops down there didn't have a clue, said there was no evidence to speak of and they did nothing more than take down information. That wasn't enough for me. I took a three-month leave from my job and went down there. I looked into every possible clue and talked to dozens of people. It was an ugly mess. I linked up with people looking into other crimes in a tri-state area and with us all working together we solved it; four young guys strung out on drugs, going on a crime spree trying to get money to keep their habit going. It turned out they killed three other people in the course of six months, all in robberies to get cash or valuable items for resale. So, that's where I got my first experience of solving murders. Then word got around and I got called on to help with a murder of a school board member in Newberry, in the Upper Peninsula, and was able to solve that one."

"You said you're retired?"

"Yeah, this is more challenging than my old day-to-day job. Before I retired it was a no-fun job, not a healthy way to live. So, I took my pension and decided I'd do investigative work and write books about the experiences."

"I've read one of your books, Lou," Gavin said, realizing after my description of my traumatic experience that he'd read my first mystery novel. "It was a gift from a former student. I used to be a teacher and principal down in the Ann Arbor area. I wasn't in special education, but I may as well have been; I had a lot of kids with disabilities in my school. A former student of mine likes your work and sent me, I think, *The Murder of a Lesson Plan* or something like that."

"*A Lesson Plan for Murder.*"

"Yeah, that was it. The woman that helps you, forgot her name."

"Maggie. Maggie McMillan."

"Yeah, is she for real or did you make her up?"

"Oh, believe me, she's for real. She's a great detective. I think we've been successful because of the combination of our skills."

"Tell me about her."

"She uses a wheelchair. She used to work for an insurance company as a claims investigator. She put the screws to a guy with a back injury claim, caught him lifting all kinds of stuff. Anyway, she turned him in and he went berserk, knifed her in the lower back, and she never walked again. She quit her job and became an independent claims consultant."

"How did you two meet?"

"We met at a special education conference. She was talking about adjusting to a disability and I was in the audience listening.

"It occurred to me with her investigative skills and my background and interest in solving crimes, we'd make a good team. I talked to her about it over coffee and we've been working together ever since. That reminds me, I've got to call her and brief her about these missing folks."

Gavin looked at his watch, "Not going to call her now, are you? It's the middle of the night."

"She tells me she sleeps with one hand on the phone. We call each other at all times of the day and night. I also need to call Carol. Finally, I need to ask the front desk of the Grand if any messages are waiting for me."

"The phone's out in the hall."

"I've got my cell phone. No sense having you get a bill for all my calls."

"I'll get some sheets and a blanket for you."

"Thanks, but don't bother. I'm only going to take a few hours nap. I'll be comfortable on this sofa, if you don't mind?"

"Fine with me, but a good bed is right in that guest room. Might as well be comfortable for a few hours."

"Thanks. By the way, do you know any of Jessica's relatives?"

"She's single. I know that. Her parents live in Traverse City. Her dad works at the local paper and her mother's a schoolteacher. I've met them. They came up a few years ago when Jessica was renting for a couple of weeks."

"Their name is Williams?"

"Yeah, Ed and Clara Williams. Going to call them?"

"I'm fairly certain that Officer Adams didn't contact any relatives from the Island. He wouldn't know who to call. I'll call the Traverse City Police in the morning and have a talk with a detective there. They can carry the news. I imagine Adams doesn't even have this as a missing person case at the moment. He seemed quite convinced that most missing people show up sooner or later. My fear is that she'll appear, but it will be on a shore somewhere."

"Think you're right, Lou. I'll get your towels and an extra blanket. The number of the Grand Hotel is in the front of that small directory under the phone."

I thanked Gavin and dialed the number. "Grand Hotel."

"This is Lou Searing. I'm calling to see if you've any messages for me. My room number is 245."

"One minute please."

About fifteen seconds later I heard, "You've got one message. It's in a sealed envelope. Do you want it opened and read?"

"Yes."

"There's no name, but it reads, 'Stay away from investigating the disappearance of Jessica and Mike. You are advised to leave the Island first thing in the morning. If you don't heed this warning, harm will come to your family.'"

"Is that message handwritten?"

"Yes, sir."

"On plain paper?"

"It's on our hotel stationery."

"You said it wasn't signed, correct?"

"Correct."

"OK, put the message and the envelope into a larger envelope and attach the following message. Ready?"

"Yes."

"I want this to go to Erin O'Brien who's a guest in your hotel. The message is, 'Erin, please keep this for me. Call me as soon as you get this message.'"

"Let me repeat it, sir." He did, and it was accurate.

"May I speak to the manager?" I asked.

"At this hour, I'm the only one at the desk. I'm the assistant manager."

"Okay, you heard the nature of the message for me. You can see that I've been threatened. If anyone inquires about me, my whereabouts, if I've checked out, or in any way is curious about me, please get their name, and get a good description."

"Will try."

"Please do more than try. Your work could be critical. What's your name?"

"Bob Brockington."

"Thank you, Mr. Brockington. If someone does seem curious about me, please let Erin know. Understand?"

"Yes, sir."

"I think I gave the clerk my credit card number when I checked in a couple of days ago."

"Yes, our computer shows that you did."

"Make up the bill through tonight and check me out. I want someone to awaken my wife Carol, let her know that I'm okay but could not return to the hotel because of the weather. First thing in the morning she should gather our belongings and go to the airport by carriage. She should be at the Island airstrip by 9 o'clock. Oh, and

Bob, I would like her escorted to the airport and I want someone with her till the plane is in the air. I'll pay for this."

"I'll take care of it, Mr. Searing."

"Thank you. When will your shift end?"

"I'll personally handle this. I'm always at this hotel. I'll inform the manager that I want to be consulted if anyone asks about you. Even if I need to be awakened, I'll handle it, sir. You can trust me."

"I sense that I can. Thank you very much."

"You're welcome."

Gavin came into the room with a towel, washcloth, and an extra blanket. "Jessica and Mike are in trouble. If I investigate their disappearance, my family may be harmed."

"Oh, my God. This is terrible."

"I'm safe on this island. No one knows I'm here. Erin O'Brien is to call me as soon as she gets my message. Do you know anyone who can go to the airstrip on Mackinac Island and bring my wife over here to Bob-Lo?"

"I'll call my friend Wags in the morning. He'll be glad to go."

"Thanks. "

"When I woke up this morning, I never dreamed my night would be so eventful," Gavin said, shaking his head. "I hope you'll be okay, Lou."

"Don't worry about me. This is my job. This isn't the first time my presence or work has been threatening to others. It is, however, the first time my family has been threatened, so I'm taking this much more seriously than past threats. I probably won't go back to the Island."

"You're welcome to stay here as long as you need to. You can stay in Jessica's A-frame. Our next guests arrive a week from Saturday."

"No, I don't think anyone should go in there. It should be treated like a crime scene till this thing gets settled."

"You can stay in our other A-frame then. We rent two. The other is on the east side of the house."

"If you don't mind, I'll take you up on that offer. I'll pay you whatever your rates are."

"We'll worry about that later. Let's just try and find Jessica. You can count on me, too, Lou. I'm no detective, but if you need a ride anywhere, or if you need to use our fax machine, phone, or anything, just let me know."

"Thanks, Gavin, I appreciate it."

"We'll have breakfast for you in the morning. As I said, my wife's name is Jenny if you happen to come out of your room and find her cooking breakfast."

"Thanks. You've been a big help."

"Sure. Can't get Jessica off my mind. Such a sweet woman. Just knowing that she might be in trouble bothers me. Why would anyone want to harm her?"

"Don't know, but it'll be solved and explained. I'll need some time, but these things are like puzzles. Slowly, but surely, Maggie and I will find information and clues that will help form a picture."

The rain was falling, lightning was flashing in the northern Michigan sky. "I'm turning in, Lou. See you in the morning."

"Me, too. Right after I call Maggie. Thanks again, my friend."

Gavin turned off the kitchen light and went to his bedroom. I went to the guest room, closed the door, sat on the bed and dialed Maggie McMillan's number in Battle Creek. After two rings she answered.

"Hello."

"Good morning, Maggie."

"Had to be you. What's happening, Lou?"

"I'm up on an Island called Bois Blanc or Bob-Lo. A woman and her date were taken in a boat from Mackinac Island and didn't come back. I came over to this island with Gavin McRae, the landlord of the lady who's missing. I thought I'd check out her cabin and if she wasn't there, look for evidence. The weather kicked up a bit and Gavin invited me to stay here. I got a phone message at the Grand Hotel saying to stay away from investigating this disappearance or my family would be harmed."

"Well, that explains in part what happened here tonight."

"What's that?"

"I got a call about twelve-thirty. A woman told me to stay away from investigating the disappearance of Jessica and Mike. I told her I didn't know what she was talking about. She said I would hear about it from you."

"Did she threaten you too?"

"Said I'd lose my two good limbs."

"These people are pretty good at trying to put fear into our minds, aren't they? They know where we're vulnerable."

"They sure do. I love solving these things with you, Lou, but going from a paraplegic to a quadriplegic isn't worth solving any crime."

"Don't worry, we won't allow these threats to be carried out. We've just been given our biggest challenge."

"What do you mean?"

"We're going to solve this from Bob-Lo. Our work will be behind the scenes and nobody but a few that we trust will know of our involvement."

"That'll be a challenge."

"Are you up to it?"

"Sure. But I've got to have these arms, Lou."

"I know, I've got to have my family. We'll be careful."

"Count me in as usual. Check back with me in the morning or whenever you learn anything."

"Will do, apologize to that wonderful husband of yours. Sorry to awaken him with this call."

"He's sleeping like a baby. He never heard it ring."

"Later, Maggie."

"Bye, Lou," Maggie said, as she set the cordless phone on her bedside table, pulled up the sheet and tried to get back to sleep. She knew this signaled her next adventure.

I looked up the number for the Mackinac Island Police. I found it and dialed. "Police Department, Adams speaking."

"Tony, this is Lou Searing."

"You still up, Lou?"

"Hey, once I get involved, I don't rest til the case is closed."

"I should've known that. What's on your mind?"

"Just checking in to see if you've learned anything about the missing couple?"

"Not a word. The Coast Guard called off their search around two this morning. Storms in the area. No bodies were found, but I don't expect to see one for a day or two. I'm still not convinced they're missing."

"Listen, Tony. I'm off the Island and don't expect to get back. I'm going to work on this case from a distance. Can I count on you to let me know what you folks learn?"

"Not a problem. How do I reach you?"

"I'm going to give you my phone number. Call at anytime of the day or night and leave a message. My number is area code 616 555-8763. One more thing, Tony. Some people may be coming to you in some capacity related to this case. Listen to their names. Whoever I send will always have a first name with an F and a last name with an N. This means fictitious name. So, the person might be Fred Nowland, for example, or a woman could be Fran Nichols. When you hear these names with the FN initials you will know it's someone from me. It's absolutely critical that no one know that we are involved and we ask you not to let on that we're involved. Understand?"

"You've got my word."

"Thanks, Tony."

"By the way, I forgot to tell you when we talked earlier that I questioned the owner of the ship in the marina that Betsy said carried Jessica and Mike out and back. He's the skipper of the boat called *Slinky* and he said he never heard of Jessica or Mike. Said he was coming back from seeing friends in Petoskey. I trust him, Lou. He's well-known up here. He's telling the truth."

"If you believe him, I believe him. Say, Tony, are the comings and goings monitored with video cameras or are boaters required to record their departures and arrivals?"

"No, that's not necessary. Some tell the harbormaster their plans, but that usually occurs only if the boat is going to another port. An out and back is rarely reported."

"So, *Slinky* left and returned last night?"

"No question about it."

"No one else in the marina noticed anything out of the ordinary. No one heard any screams or witnessed any struggles."

"I talked to several people and nobody heard or saw anything out of the ordinary."

"OK, Tony, thanks for the information."

"You better get some sleep, Lou. The case will be there for you tomorrow."

"Can I assume you didn't call any next of kin?"

"I didn't call anyone. I'm treating this as a missing person case at the moment. Besides, I wouldn't know who to call. We haven't gotten any information on them yet."

"OK, I'm going to get some sleep now. Thanks, Tony."

"Sure, Lou."

I set the alarm for seven. I could probably sleep until noon, but there was too much to do. A few solid hours of sleep would energize me and I'd be fine.

჻

While I was about to get some sleep, at the other end of Bob-Lo, about twelve miles to the southeast as the crow flies, Jessica Williams was bound and tied to a bed in a small hunting cabin on an isolated dirt road near Mud Lake. Her mouth was taped shut. Her wrists and feet were tied. She hurt badly but was still awake. The adrenaline flowing through her veins kept her alert and on edge. She knew she was lucky to be alive as she had overheard comments about killing her on the boat.

Jessica didn't know she was on Bob-Lo. She didn't hear where they were taking her and she was blindfolded the whole time. She knew that she couldn't be far from Mackinac Island, but whether the boat sped toward the Les Cheneaux Islands to the north, to St. Ignace to the west, to Mackinaw City or even to Bob-Lo to the immediate south, she couldn't be sure. She thought Cheboygan was a bit far given the time on the boat, but in her stressed condition, travelling that far was indeed possible.

Jessica had been taken from the boat to a car, forced to lie on the back seat, and then driven on bumpy roads to a cabin. Mary Chandler had looked for a desolate setting and she had found one. Once inside, and with lights turned on, Mike stretched and said, "So far, the plan is perfect." Mike was short, but had a compact and muscular body. His long blond hair was pulled back in a ponytail. He was a good-looking man. In fact, Mike and Jessica looked like a couple of soap opera stars.

"No, the perfect plan would have her dead in the Straits," Mary countered. "Let's get her dead and buried and get off this island." Mary was a 39-year-old self-employed consultant and advocate for people with blindness. To some she was a troublemaker, to others she was a saint. She was short, overweight, and wearing jeans designed for someone who was ten pounds lighter. She wore glasses that were anything but stylish and without makeup, she looked very plain.

"No killing tonight. Sound travels easily in the dead of night. We keep her bound and gagged and kill her later," Mike responded quickly.

Jessica was disturbed that she hadn't read the signals and been more careful. Now she was paying the price. The last thing she thought would happen, however, was to be betrayed by Mike. She was shocked to realize that Mike would be a party to her demise.

Jessica would like to feel that she was a victim, but she understood why she was in this predicament. Jessica knew that the chance of escaping death was somewhere between nil and impossible. Still, as long as she was alive, there was hope.

"We've pulled off the perfect crime," Mary said, assured they were alone in the desolate setting. There's no way she'll be found on this island. We could even put a grave marker over her dead body and it wouldn't be found for decades."

"'Gotta hand it to you, Mary. You covered every base. How did you know the comings and goings of the *Slinky*?"

"Well, as you know, I've been planning this night for a long time and it took a lot of connections. I left nothing to chance. I knew the *Slinky* would be out and it was. The skipper took her to Petoskey."

"I'd be more comfortable if I knew that Searing and McMillan will not be looking into her disappearance," Mike remarked.

"I put the fear of harm to Lou's family and Maggie losing her two good limbs into their minds. If they have any grey cells upstairs, they'll pass this one by," Mary responded. "Even if they do get involved, they won't find anything. I find some joy in knowing this will be the first case they can't solve. I'll enjoy watching them struggle a bit. Once we put a bullet in Jessica's head, bury her, and get back to Cheboygan, this job is over and we can get on with our lives. We'll do that tomorrow."

Jessica, in another room, could only hear muffled voices and couldn't string enough words together to get any sense of the conversation. Of one thing she was certain—the talk was about her death; how, where, and what to do with her body.

$$\backsim$$

Jessica had a lot of time to wonder how these two got together to plan her death. She would never know how it happened, but it had all started six months earlier, last February 14th, Valentine's Day. Mike and Mary were attending a national convention of Advocates for the Blind in Atlanta, Georgia. Because the two had been good friends over the past twenty-five years, they decided to spend the evening together.

The evening entertainment was a variety of music, dance, a comedian, and a magician. Before the acts began there was a *Newlywed Game* segment, based on the early TV show of the same name. Three couples were invited from the audience to participate. The wives went offstage and the husbands were asked three questions. They were to answer as they thought their wives would answer when they came back to the stage. The first question was, "If you could be a towel, other than your wife, who would you like to be wrapped around?" The audience offered whistles, chuckles, and a few shouted out possible answers.

The men's answers were recorded and the second question was asked, "Who will your wife say has revealed a secret that should never have been revealed?" Once again, oohs and aahs came from the audience, chuckling about the answers and the secrets that were never to have been revealed.

Mary turned to Mike and said, "If I were up there I'd have a quick answer, but I could never reveal the secret."

"Yeah, that would be an easy one for me, too."

"I told someone a secret once and I made it clear that if my secret ever got out, well, let's just say I made it clear that it had better not get out. She knew I meant business."

"Well, we're soul mates on this one, Mary, because I did the same thing. My problem is that it did get out and a price will have to be paid for her mistake in judgment."

"This is getting a little eerie. My secret also got out and I have to teach her a lesson. A lesson that will probably cost her her life."

"You're going to kill someone over a secret?" Mike asked.

"Well, let's put it this way, if you knew the secret, I think you'd understand."

"Same here, if you knew my secret, you'd understand why I need revenge. I'm not planning a murder, but a head has got to roll," Mike said, and then he added with a smile, "I don't want you to ever tell me a secret, because if I err and let it out, I don't want to pay for it with my life."

"If it was the secret this woman let out, you'd expect to die for letting it out."

"Is this woman in Michigan?" Mike asked.

"Yeah."

"Someone I know?"

"Yeah. Pretty sure you do."

"Better stop right here. Because if you do kill her and I've heard that she died, then I'll know who did it, and I sure don't want you thinking I'm telling the cops or lawyers about this conversation."

"You got a point there. Do I know the person who let out your secret?" Mary asked.

"Yeah, probably."

"She's in Michigan?"

"Yeah. She's an advocate?"

"Yeah. Whoa, I'm putting the brakes on. Let's get our attention back to the show."

"No, wait," Mike replied. "This could be the same person and if it is, we could settle this score together. You know, two heads are better than one."

"Might work."

"Well, I guess we've got to reveal who has been telling our secrets."

"Jessica Williams," Mary said.

"I don't believe it, Mary. We've been talking about the same person."

"Doesn't surprise me. She has a serious character flaw. She obviously can't keep secrets."

"Well, I don't want to know your secret and I won't tell you mine."

"Fair, but are we agreed that we'll work together to silence this woman?" Mary asked.

"Has to happen, Mary."

"It would work much more smoothly if I had someone helping that I could trust. You sure you can handle this? Killing a friend?"

"I'm not looking forward to it, but she knows something that nobody else in the world knows and now that it's out, my whole life is in jeopardy and I can't be certain she won't tell someone again. For me, it isn't so much killing Jessica as killing the secret."

"I'm the same way. We'll be in touch."

By now the wives had returned to the stage and were failing to answer the questions correctly, but their answers were humorous and drew many laughs and hand-clapping from the audience.

When Mike and Mary returned to Michigan they communicated regularly as plans were made for the perfect crime. The best plan for this to happen was to kidnap Jessica from Mackinac Island the night of the special education ball, kill her and dump her in the Straits. The back-up plan was to bring her to Bob-Lo. Once on that desolate island, there would be no way they would be seen or caught for snuffing out her life, the payment for talking, for sharing, for making the mistake of betrayal.

CHAPTER TWO

Sunday, June 2
Bois Blanc Island

The next thing I knew I was waking up to the smell of bacon and pancakes. The aroma of fresh coffee was mesmerizing. The sun was up and it took me a few seconds to register where I was. I quickly realized that I was in Gavin and Jenny's summer home on Bob-Lo. I looked at the digital clock on the bedstand and saw 7:19.

I got up, looked in a mirror and hardly recognized myself. I looked like death warmed over. I put on my tuxedo slacks and a wrinkled shirt and walked out in the hallway and into the living room of the McRae home. I followed the delightful aromas into the kitchen. "Good morning," I said.

"Short night, my friend," Gavin replied.

"Yes, it was."

"Lou, this is Jenny and her mother Myrtle. Ladies, meet Lou Searing, investigator and author." Both women smiled and nodded.

"Nice to meet you. Breakfast will be ready in a minute," Jenny said, flipping a light and slightly browned hotcake.

I smiled at Jenny. She was attractive, slim, medium height and she had a beautiful smile. She had obviously inherited those traits from her mother. "Smells great," I said. I wandered over to the large front window and looked out onto Lake Huron. I could see a freighter making its way toward the Mackinac Bridge. The sky was blue and the Straits were calm. "That freighter coming from the Soo Locks?"

"Yup. When a freighter passes by we know it's probably hauling Canadian grain to Chicago or it could be hauling taconite to the steel mills in Gary, Indiana. The freighters that are heading for the St. Lawrence Seaway or going to Chicago from Detroit always pass through the southern channel between Cheboygan and the southeastern part of this island."

"Interesting. That your dog running up and down the beach?"

"Yeah, that's Marph. He likes to get his morning exercise chasing anything that moves. His friends are other dogs, deer, seagulls, and whatever wildlife he can tempt to join him."

"Reminds me of our dog."

"What kind of dog have you got, Lou?"

"Golden retriever. Her name's Samm."

"A golden retriever is a beautiful and smart dog."

"Samm loves to run along the beach, too. Carol and I have a home on Lake Michigan, south of Grand Haven. We love the scenery and the setting. I was raised in Grand Haven. I lived on Grand Avenue south of town. A hospital parking lot now sits in the block where my boyhood home was, 419 Grand Ave. Back in the 50s, I used to go to the lake all the time, had a paper route that took me around the oval and up among all the cottages with nice views of the lake. So, when retirement came along, we headed for my boyhood home. We love it there."

"We've been to Grand Haven. Big musical fountain is there, right?"

"Yeah, that's a crowd-pleaser."

"Bet you never figured you'd be waking up on Bob-Lo did you, Lou?" Myrtle asked.

I shook my head. "No, I was going to a big party at the Grand Hotel and didn't expect to be doing anything other than celebrating with friends and going back to Grand Haven. Strange how life deals you its cards. Here I am, across from Mackinac Island, beginning to investigate a possible kidnapping, standing in a living room in a tuxedo and without even a toothbrush."

"We've got a care package for you," Jenny said with a smile. "We always keep a set of toiletries because our guests often forget an item or two. The Hawk's Landing General Store is a long way away. We've got some clothes for you, too. Why don't you clean up, put on these clothes and join us for a hearty breakfast."

"You folks are treating me like a king."

"You are, as far as we're concerned."

"Just trying to help find your friend."

"That means a lot to us. We'll do whatever we can to help you."

"I appreciate your hospitality. Guess I'll do as you suggest and clean up."

"The hotcakes, bacon, coffee and fruit will be here when you come out," Jenny said.

⌇⌇

Before sitting down to a wonderful breakfast, Gavin called Wags and explained my request. He handed me the phone. "Hi, Wags," I said. "She'll be at the Mackinac Island Airport at nine. Her name is Carol."

"Got it," Wags said. "Can you describe her so I can recognize her."

"She looks much younger than her sixty-two years. She's relatively short, dark hair with some grey, round face, cute nose, and she'll have a light brown leather suitcase."

"I'll have her at the Bob-Lo airstrip by nine-thirty."

"I'll ask Gavin to take me there or I'll borrow his Jeep. Thanks, Wags."

"Glad to help."

"I'll pay you whatever your expenses are, Wags. Oh, Carol is not a big fan of flying in small planes and flying over water doesn't make it any better."

"I'll make the crossing as smooth as possible and there will be no payment for the flight. Friends help friends."

"I'll make your effort worthwhile in some way. Thanks so much."

I immediately called Bob Brockington at the Grand and explained that a man named Wags was going to arrive shortly before nine and would bring Carol to Bois Blanc. Had I not called, Bob would probably not allow Carol to simply get on a plane with someone not known to him or her. Bob said he'd see that she safely got on the plane. He asked to be called when Carol arrived on Bois Blanc so he'd have a sense of mission accomplished.

᭟

I was eating my second stack of hotcakes when my cell phone rang. "Hello."

"Lou, this is Erin."

"Thanks for calling, Erin. I can't tell you where I am and I can't be working on the disappearance of Jessica and Mike. My family's been threatened if I get involved."

"Are you okay, Lou?"

"I'm fine. I'd like to talk with you, but I can't have anything to do with the case."

"So unlike you."

"I don't mind solving some crimes but not at the expense of harming my family."

"I understand."

"Are you calling from the Grand Hotel?" I asked.

"Yes. Calling from my room. I called when I got your message."

"I appreciate it. I wanted to tell you that there's no way I'll get involved."

"Can't say that I blame you. Are you on the Island now?" Erin asked.

"No."

"When will I see you?"

"Guess when you get back downstate. Would you do me a favor?"

"Sure, Lou."

"Bring some fudge back with you. I left so quickly that I didn't get a supply."

"What flavor do you want?"

"I like Murdock's White Chocolate Mousse with Walnuts and Cherries. If you can't find that, call me and I'll give you my second choice. Get me five pounds, please."

"Will do. Glad you're OK. See you downstate with five pounds of sugar."

"Thanks, Erin. By the way, Maggie won't be getting involved either. Threats were made against her and she's wanting to be cautious. So, this case will not be looked into by Searing and McMillan. No amount of money or pressure could convince us to get involved."

"I don't blame you. Talk to you downstate. Bye, Lou."

"Thanks for picking up the fudge, Erin. Safe trip to you. Oh, you did a great job putting on that dance last night. It was one of Erin O'Brien's finest parties, wouldn't you say?"

"It was a lot of fun. Too bad it might have a tragic ending."

Gavin and Jenny couldn't help but overhear the conversation. "That didn't sound like you. I thought you'd be ready and anxious to get going on the case," Gavin said.

"That was all phony. I said that because the people or the person behind this may have been listening in on the conversation since the call was made from the Hotel. I made up that fudge name so she'll have to call me as I asked, but she'll do it from a pay phone in the downtown area. They won't have the capability of bugging a pay phone so I can talk once Erin calls back. Now, if Murdock's has a fudge choice like the one I described, she won't call and I'll have a setback. My bet is that Erin will call because she must have sensed a need to carry on with our conversation. We'll see."

"More coffee, Lou?"

"Please. Delicious breakfast, Jenny. Best maple syrup I've ever had."

"It's made right here on Bob-Lo. Wags and his wife Jacquilyne make it. It's sold as a fund raiser on the island. The Volunteer Fire Department has their annual maple syrup sale each summer. All the residents look forward to it and most of us buy quite a few containers to get us through the season."

"I can see why. Great tasting stuff."

"Glad you like it."

"By the way, why do you folks call this island, Bob-Lo? The map says Bois Blanc."

"I'm not one-hundred percent sure, but the story I've heard is that it comes from the Indians' pronunciation of the French words, Bois Blanc, which by the way mean, white wood," Gavin replied. "The translation came out sounding something similar to Bob-Lo, and over time, folks simply called it Bob-Lo."

"Humm, interesting. Can either of you tell me more of Jessica's life?"

Jenny began, "She's in her late-thirties. She's been a teacher and a principal. Most recently she has been an advocate for children with disabilities in Traverse City. She works for a statewide advocacy organization. I don't know the name of the outfit."

"CAUSE," I said.

"Yeah, that's it. She's got a few horror stories to tell. People can be mean to one another, Lou."

"Listen, I understand people being mean. When I was state director, they gravitated to me like flies to garbage."

"Did she mention one of these horror stories since she arrived up here?"

"Yeah, now that you mention it, something was obviously bothering her," Gavin said.

"Tell me about it."

"Well, as best I can recall, she was advocating for a family somewhere in the thumb area. Seems that the family felt the child should be getting some subsidy or service or something and they couldn't get it."

"Sounds pretty common. Don't know why that would be so troubling to her, those kinds of conflicts are very routine for an advocacy organization to deal with."

"You two better think about meeting Lou's wife and Wags," Myrtle reminded us.

~3~

Gavin and I walked toward his truck to go to the airport. "Let me show you my pole barn. We've got a minute or two."

"Almost as big as your house," I said, quite impressed with the size of the building.

"You might refer to this as 'Home Depot Two'. I've almost the same inventory, but my stock doesn't rise in value. You see, up here, we try to help one another. I let folks know that these tools, supplies, hardware and all kinds of stuff are here for them to use."

"Mighty nice of you, Gavin."

"Well, the doc gives his services, others have talents and things to share. Bob-Lo's a community that needs to have people caring and sharing for it to work."

"So, they just borrow or use stuff when they need it?"

"Yup, simple system. The only thing I ask is that things be put back where they belong and if a piece of hardware, you know, a screw or some nails are used, they be replaced when folks get back from the mainland."

"Great system."

"It works and people seem to appreciate it."

"Hey, is that your Harley over there?" I said pointing to a motorcycle.

"Yeah, it's about ten years old. I tinker with it from time to time. It's great for getting around as long as you don't have to move a grand piano!"

"Looks a lot like mine. Mind if I take it for a spin later today?"

"Not at all. You may need to do a little work on it, but we can work on it together."

"I love to feel the wind on my face. I used to say wind going through my hair, but age and a lack of the stuff caused me to change my line." Gavin laughed along with me.

"Yeah, we'll fire it up later. You'll get a good ride from this baby, Lou."

After being impressed with the barn looking like a good sized hardware store, we got in Gavin's truck for the ten minute ride to the airstrip.

❧

"I notice you wear a couple of hearing aids," Gavin said, while pulling out of the driveway.

"Yeah, had the measles as a little boy. They think that caused it."

"My dad needs hearing aids but he won't get 'em. Stubborn old guy."

"I have to wear 'em, I'd miss a lot if I didn't, and having a sense of humor helps a lot, believe me."

"I'll bet Carol appreciates your wearing them."

"Yes, she sure does."

"Is there a support group for folks with a hearing problem?"

"An excellent one. The group is called SHHH."

"Kind of a strange name for a group that can't hear very well."

I chuckled, "Yeah, but it stands for Self-Help for Hard of Hearing People. Great publications, national meetings, local chapters. It's really good to meet with others who have the same problems you have. The folks in my chapter are great. We understand each other and support each other. We also have members who are spouses and we try to help them understand hearing loss. It is a great group, believe me."

"Wish we could get Dad to accept his loss, but I don't think he'll hear of it, pun intended," Gavin said with a smile.

"Well, I hope he and the family have a sense of humor. They and you'll need it. Not hearing well gives you a lot of reasons to laugh."

"For example?"

"Carol and I were driving to a Christmas tree farm to cut a fresh tree for our home. I didn't have my aids on, or if I did, the car noise got in the way of understanding what Carol said. She said, 'We don't need a huge tree this year, do we?' I thought she said, 'We don't need a USED tree this year, do we?' So I said, 'Why would we want a used

tree?' Carol said with a smile, 'I said a HUGE tree not a used tree!'
We laughed about it, happens all the time."

⟋⟍

Wags and Carol scattered a group of seagulls as the light plane
sped down the east-west runway on Mackinac Island. The plane lifted
off the runway and banked to the south. The view of the Island, the
Mackinac Bridge and the Straits was spectacular. About five minutes
later, as they approached Bois Blanc Island, Carol asked loudly over
the drone of the engine, "Is that a lighthouse down there to the left?"

"Yeah, that's the Bois Blanc Island Lighthouse. It served quite a
purpose before all the new fangled technology came into the shipping
industry. This island is the first big hunk of land ships come upon as
they head north and before they swing under the Bridge to Chicago."

"Who owns the lighthouse?"

"Some folks bought it a few years ago. It's a private home. It's
kind of hard to get to and the folks don't give tours. You can't expect
them to, it's their home, but you know, some folks have a hobby of
lighthouse stuff, taking pictures, touring. This one's off limits."

"Looks neat from up here."

"Look over there to the right and you can see a small bay area."

"Yeah, I see it."

"That's Sand Bay. At one time a huge lumbering company
operated out of there. A railroad line went across the island east to
west. Lumberjacks would cut and pile lumber on a train. The train
would take it to Sand Bay for processing. At one time there were
hundreds of people living there. It was quite an operation. They even
had a school in Sand Bay. Much of the island was devoted to the
lumber industry. Folks lived a rugged life, that's for sure."

"Interesting. Lou would love to fly around this island."

"We'll get him up soon. Time to get you down on the ground."

"Thanks for the information. Very interesting."

"Sure." Wags used his radio communications system to let planes
in the area know of his plan to circle and land. It wasn't required but

was a safety precaution and a courtesy.

At the same time, Gavin and I were at the airport looking upward for Wags and Carol. The plane circled the airport to make sure there were no deer in the vicinity and then softly landed on the grass strip. The Cessna taxied up to us and Wags shut it down. Carol emerged. We hugged and her first words were, "Well, this is sure a different morning!"

I replied, "I never said being married to an investigator would lack surprises. Carol, this is Gavin McRae. Gavin, meet the most beautiful woman in the world, Carol Searing."

"Pleased to meet you, Carol. I feel like I know you from reading about you in Lou's book."

"Nice of you to take care of Lou. He meets the most wonderful people in his work."

"Well, he's trying to find Jessica and we'll help him anyway we can," Gavin said.

Wags finished his required tasks after the flight. "Thank you very much for bringing Carol over," I said, hoping the time would come when he would take me up for a scenic flight around this beautiful island.

"You're welcome. Glad it was a smooth crossing."

"Wags gave me the smoothest flight I've ever had," Carol said with a smile. "Beautiful scenery all about us. I didn't realize this island was as large as it is. You certainly get a different perspective from the air."

"I imagine so. Well, welcome to Bob-Lo," I said, giving Carol another hug. "I'm glad you're here safely and that you've got our luggage with medications, toiletries, and clothes. I'm anxious to get out of this penguin outfit and into something comfortable." I called Bob at the Grand and announced Carol's safe arrival and thanked him once again for his work.

Gavin drove us back to his home where I introduced Carol to Jenny and Myrtle. All of us were getting acquainted when my cell phone rang and interrupted our discussion.

"Hello."

"Lou, this is Erin. Murdock's doesn't have chocolate mousse with walnuts and cherries."

"Good. You're at a pay phone I hope."

"Yeah."

"I didn't want to talk to you when you called from the hotel because the phone could have been bugged. This was my best way to get you to call back away from the hotel."

"I thought something wasn't right, but I didn't think of the bugging angle."

"Thanks again for calling. I'm going to need your help. You may, if you choose, become more involved in this investigation than you've ever dreamed of."

"Not a problem. If I can help, I'd be glad to."

"The first thing I need you to do is talk with the assistant manager on duty, Bob Brockington, and have him get for you a list of all registered guests at the hotel for the past few days. I'll call him and tell him you'll be talking with him."

"That's all. Just get a guest list?"

"No, then we may need anything a guest writes on, any handwriting will do, registration cards, credit card bills. I don't want you to collect all of this, but we may need to seek it for certain people. Tell Bob not to destroy anything a guest could have written on."

"OK. Anything else?"

"Yes, see what you can find out about Mike Miles. He was staying at the Henderson Bed and Breakfast."

"OK, will do. Anything else?"

"Does it look like you're being followed or watched?"

"I'm looking around and there's a guy looking over at me. I don't know if that's because he's curious about this call or captivated by my beauty. I draw admiring stares all the time. What can I say?"

"Ah, that old Irish sense of vanity. Glad to hear it's alive and well!"

"He just signaled to a woman about fifty feet down the street. This could be more than I want to get involved with, Lou."

"You'll be fine. Just don't get yourself alone in some deserted place. Always have people around you."

"OK, anything else?"

"Yes, keep that envelope and message that Bob gave you. We may need it later. Please don't lose that, Erin. It may be our ace in the hole."

"Guard it with my life, Lou."

"Good. Now go into Murdock's and get five pounds of chocolate walnut. I know they have that, I've eaten about fifty pounds in my lifetime."

"Chocolate walnut it is. I'll be in touch, Lou."

"Thanks, Erin. Call me from a pay phone every four hours or more frequently if needed. I can't reach you but I need a lifeline." I hung up and felt that while solving a crime in absentia would be a challenge, it could be done. I felt that Maggie and I only needed extensions of ourselves.

Jenny had been listening. "Do you think that Erin is up to this risky challenge?"

"I think so. She's a feisty, Irish gal. She's the curious type, likes people, organizes things well. I've known her for quite awhile. She used to work in the Department of Education when I was there. She was a problem solver, analytical thinker. This is right up her alley. She has also earned a black belt in karate. Erin's about five foot two, can't weigh more than a hundred pounds, but she could deck a Detroit Lions lineman in a minute if she had to."

"Irish women are a rare breed. My aunt was Irish; assertive, challenged by new opportunities, and fun to be with."

"That's Erin O'Brien. You'll meet her when we gather to celebrate solving this thing. You'll like her."

My pager went off. I looked at it and saw Maggie's car phone number. "Hi, Maggie, Lou here. Don't tell me. My guess is that you're somewhere between Clare and Grayling."

"Not bad. I'm coming up to the Grayling exit at the moment. I think I can get to Gaylord before needing gas. I was getting restless in Battle Creek. Thought I'd get on up to Bob-Lo."

"Great."

"Am I going to have a place to stay?"

"Yeah, I think there's room in the McRae house. I'll ask. They're wonderful folks. They'll find or make room."

"Good. I appreciate it. Anything you need before I come over?" Maggie asked.

"I'll ask Jenny."

"Anything you folks need from the mainland? Maggie's coming over."

"I never pass up an opportunity to get some supplies. Ask her to call when she gets to Cheboygan. I'll have a list. With three more people on the island, we'll need a few bags of groceries. The ferry leaves at two-thirty so she needs to be at the dock by two. Tell her to allow enough time for shopping and getting to the ferry dock."

"Jenny says she can use some supplies. The ferry to Bob-Lo leaves at two-thirty and you need to be at the dock by two so leave yourself plenty of time for shopping and checking in."

"I already looked into the ferry situation. I have a reservation on Plaunt's two-thirty crossing."

"Good. We'll await your call when you get to Cheboygan. Glad you're on your way. Solving a case from an island will be a new adventure."

"Sounds like fun. At least we don't have to worry about being shot or knocked around."

"That's true. At least I hope it's true."

"Talk to you from Cheboygan." That was the Maggie I knew. She simply had to get to where the action was. I was surprised she didn't go right to Mackinac Island and begin to investigate this thing. I know she values her two good limbs just as I value my family, so I guess I wasn't surprised that she used caution and made plans to join me on Bob-Lo.

⌁

Jessica got a couple hours of sleep in the middle of the night. Her body felt like it had shut down. Her arms and legs were tied to the bedposts and her mouth was covered with electrical tape.

"Those moans are driving me crazy. Can we make her a bit more comfortable?"

"Leave her as is. She hasn't much longer to live. Give her the moans, Mike."

Jessica continued to groan. She had only taken in some milk with a straw in an opening of the tape across her mouth. She thought back to the trauma that started this threat to her life. She knew the boat was moving and the length of time the boat was on the open waters was about twenty to thirty minutes.

At 4:30 in the morning, according to their devised back-up plan, Mary left to go to her yacht at the main dock and take it back to Cheboygan. She would return the next afternoon on the 2:30 crossing to prepare for Jessica's execution. Mike's job was to stay in the cabin and make sure Jessica was held captive and no one disturbed the tranquility of their hideaway.

Since they were in a back-up plan, Mike knew that once home, he would have to explain to the authorities his absence as well as Jessica's disappearance. The plan was to say that they did return to the Mackinac Island Marina. The boat docked at a different slip, far from where they boarded the *Slinky*. He'd simply tell the authorities that he kissed Jessica good-bye and never saw her again. He'd explain that he was slow to get home because he wanted an extended vacation and stopped in to visit friends in upper Michigan. And, of course, he would show great concern for Jessica, perhaps even feigning significant grief.

While at the boat and before crossing to Cheboygan, Mary put Jessica's purse and other items no longer needed into a white plastic trash bag. She took the bag to the main gate of the transfer station which was a short walk from the main dock. She wanted the trash off her boat and decided to set it by the gate and the worker would simply pick it up and toss it into one of the many large bins inside the compound. As with her arrival a few hours ago, not a soul could be seen anywhere in the darkness. The perfect murder continued to be assured.

Mary pulled away from the dock and headed south to Cheboygan, pointing the *Stinky* to her slip in the Cheboygan Marina. She'd tie up, get a good long nap, eat breakfast in downtown Cheboygan, gather a few food items and wait for the Plaunt Ferry at two-thirty.

Erin O'Brien got on a rented bike and rode to the Henderson Bed and Breakfast. She went to the front door and rang the bell. The door opened and a woman greeted her. "Welcome to Henderson Bed and Breakfast."

"Thanks. My name's Erin O'Brien and I'm working with a private investigator and we're trying to locate a missing couple. I'm looking for some information about one of your guests. His name is Mike Miles."

"Mike's missing?"

"Yeah, got on a yacht last night and hasn't been seen since."

"Humm. He only spent one night with us. That was Friday night."

"What can you tell me about him?"

"Let me look at my register."

"Here he is. He's from Lapeer, Michigan. He was personable and good looking. That's about all I know."

"Do you recall anything about his stay Friday night?"

"He seemed to get a lot of visitors. Popular guy."

"More visitors than usual?"

"Oh yeah, most people check in and rarely does anyone come to call. But Mike had visitors through the night."

"Do you know who they were?"

"No. I didn't get a good look at them. I'm a light sleeper, plus I feel responsible for all of my guests. I want to maintain a quiet atmosphere here."

"I understand."

"I'm sensitive to noise and activity around my place. You have to allow people freedom of movement and activity, but you want to maintain peace and quiet."

"Sure."

"Anyway, it wasn't bad, but yeah, Mike had visits throughout the night."

"Can you describe who came to see him?" Erin asked.

"I looked out of my curtains only once and saw two men, probably in their forties. They looked like tourists; T-shirts, shorts, sandals. They weren't obnoxious. They came in, went to his room and I'd say they were there for about a half hour. They left and then I heard others come to his room later, but I didn't see who that was. Could have been the same guys or maybe different people. Then a third time he went outside and I could hear him talking to someone for about five minutes. He also made a phone call in the early hours of the morning."

"A lot of activity."

"Yeah. I didn't get much sleep. I got up to make breakfast. He appeared with the other guests and didn't say anything out of the ordinary. He told folks about a big party that he was attending last night."

"But he didn't have a room for last night?" Erin asked.

"No, not with me. Maybe he found a cheaper place."

"He left you Saturday morning after breakfast?"

"Well, not really. He said he didn't get much sleep which made sense with all of his visitors and he asked if he could go back to bed. I said that would be okay, but I'd need him to be gone by one o'clock at the latest."

"And he did?"

"Yes, he left around noon."

"Left with his luggage?"

"Right. Said he was going down to the marina."

"I may be back to ask a few more questions. I appreciate your information. Thanks, Mrs. Henderson."

Erin got back on her bike and headed for the closest phone and called me. "Lou this is Erin on the Island. I talked to Mrs. Henderson."

"Good. What'd you learn?"

"She says Mike had visitors throughout the night last Friday."

"Men? Women?"

"She only looked out once in the middle of the night and there were two men, in their forties, who looked like tourists. She heard more commotion later but didn't get up to look to see who was there."

"Strange, but we'll note it. Anything else?"

"Mrs. Henderson said he had no reservation for last night. When he left, he took his luggage and said he was going to the marina."

"So, he didn't have a place to stay after the ball?"

"I don't know that. He just didn't plan to stay at the Henderson B and B. Seems strange that he wouldn't stay at the same place."

"Maybe he wasn't going to need a place to stay Saturday night after the ball?" I asked.

"Maybe he knew he was leaving on the *Slinky* and wouldn't be coming back to Mackinac Island?"

"Maybe he's a part of the problem and not a victim?" I wondered aloud.

"Could be, Lou. Anything else for me to do?"

"Did you talk to Bob Brockington at the hotel yet?"

"No, going to do that as soon as I finish talking with you."

"Good. How much longer are you going to be there?"

"I'm leaving late this afternoon. I have to take care of some paper work with the hotel concerning our party last night and I thought as long as I'm here I might as well enjoy it. But, if you need me to stay longer, let me know."

"We may need you longer, if you don't mind helping out. A call every few hours would keep us in touch with you and whatever you learn. In the meantime, no assignment. I feel quite certain that whoever is involved in Jessica's disappearance was staying in the Grand Hotel last night. So, if I'm right, we can narrow the suspect pool down to several hundred people."

"OK, I'll stay put."

"Oh, when you talk to the police. Ask to see Officer Adams and from now on, as far as he is concerned, you are Fran Newby. Got that? If you don't like that fictitious name, you must come up with a first name that begins with F and a last name that starts with N. I told Adams that anyone coming to him that was working with us would have initials that were FN for fictitious name."

"Fran Newby is OK. Just gets me in the door with Adams, right? It's not a name I've got to have on my gravestone."

"That's right."

"OK, I'll call every four hours. Brockington at the Grand knows we're working together, so he is to be trusted."

"Good."

"This detective stuff might get into my blood, Lou. I may follow some leads of my own. Who knows?"

"Hey, as long as you don't get yourself killed, go for it."

"Nothing could make me happier than to solve a crime before the famous Searing and McMillan!" Erin exclaimed with a chuckle.

༄

In Traverse City, a police car pulled up in front of the Williams residence. Clara, short, pure white hair and showing the beginnings of some osteoporosis, peeked through the curtains and was surprised to see the police in front of her house. Perhaps a robbery had occurred in the neighborhood? She waited for the knock on the door, opened it and greeted the two officers.

"Are you Mrs. Williams, Jessica William's mother?"

"Yes, is something wrong?" Clara asked as Ed Williams, tall and distinguished looking, also with white hair and a well-trimmed moustache, walked to her side.

"We've been notified by a private investigator that she's missing."

"Missing?" Clara replied, looking distraught and turning to Ed for comfort.

"She was seen on Mackinac Island last evening. The police there have her as a missing person. They tell us that people often appear and it was simply a miscommunication problem, but we wanted you to know. If we have any more information, we'll give you a call."

"What happened?" Ed asked.

"All we know is that she got on a yacht with her escort for the evening for a cruise in the Straits and didn't come back. The Coast Guard and all law enforcement units are looking for her. We're sorry to give you this news, folks. Just thought you'd want to know what we know."

"Yes, thank you. You'll call as soon as you hear anything?" Clara asked.

"Yes, ma'am. We will. Here's my card, you can call me anytime. OK?"

Clara shut the door and the two gave each other a hug and began to talk about how to deal with a potentially frightening future.

CHAPTER THREE

June 2, Sunday
Bois Blanc Island

When lunch was about finished I said to Gavin, "Seems to me a special education colleague has a place on this island. Do you know Jackee Miller?"

"Oh, sure. Jackee loves Bob-Lo. She's been coming up here for years. She and her husband John are building a retirement home on Twin Lakes."

"Yeah, I think I heard about that. I think they've got beehives on the island now."

"Yes. They're doing quite well as I understand it. They're selling their honey at Hawk's Landing. It's good stuff."

"Seems like this island would be a good place for beehives. From what I can tell, you've got a lot of milkweed and wildflowers."

"I agree. We've got some of the Miller honey. I suggest you put some on a piece of toast in the morning or on some of Jenny's oatmeal. Mmmm, good."

"OK, I'll do it."

"So, Jackee knows you, huh?"

"Yeah, from special education. We go way back. She graduated from Eastern Michigan University. The last time I saw her she reminded me that I guest lectured in one of her classes when she was there. That seems like a lifetime ago, Gavin."

"I don't know her well, but if she's like most of the folks who love this island, I'll bet she'd like to be here year round."

"I imagine so. Jackee's a fan of my mysteries, and a good special education administrator, I might add. Where do they live now?"

"They're on the east end, down by Walker's Point, about a mile past the old Coast Guard station. They've a beautiful view of the Lower Peninsula and of the south channel. You're welcome to give her a call. Number's in the book. There is only one John Miller."

I picked up the phone book, found her number and gave her a call.

"Hi, Jackee. Lou Searing here. You'll never guess where I am at the moment?"

"Hopefully you are in your car heading for our home?"

"Almost. I'm at Gavin and Jenny McRae's out on the west end."

"You're kidding. What brings you to our little slice of Heaven?"

"Believe it or not, I'm involved in another case. My next book might feature your heavenly isle, Jackee."

"Murder here on the 'Rock'?"

"Well, could be. I don't have a body, a motive, or a witness. All I've got is a couple of missing persons."

"Anybody I know?"

"Jessica Williams for one and... "

"Jessica Williams from Traverse City?" Jackee interrupted.

"Guess so. She's a CAUSE advocate and yeah, she lives in Traverse City."

"Oh, my God! Jess is a great person and a marvelous advocate. There must be some mistake."

"Well, she was at the special education banquet at the Grand last night. She and an escort went out for a cruise on a yacht called *Slinky* and they haven't been seen since."

"I sure hope she's okay."

"Doesn't look good. A friend named Betsy Bowers reported them missing.

"Who was her escort?"

"A guy named Mike Miles. Know him?"

"Suspect number one, Lou."

"What do you mean?"

"He's bad news. You've heard the phrase 'opposites attract'? Well, Jess and Mike are about as opposite as you can get. Keep an eye on this Mike and you just might solve your case."

"Humm, interesting. Any chance we can meet in the next day or two?"

"Oh, sure. You can come over for a visit or we can meet at Barb's Tavern."

I plan to meet Maggie when the ferry arrives shortly after three. How about if we have lunch at the Tavern about one o'clock tomorrow?"

"See you then, Lou. Thanks for the call."

The Williams called and talked to Gavin who assured them all was being done to try and find Jessica. He invited them to come over to the island if they wished to do so. Gavin knew Mr. Williams was a pilot and said, "If you fly over, give us a ring and we'll pick you up at the airstrip."

✦

Maggie was at the Plaunt Transportation dock at two o'clock. The owner, Curt Plaunt, greeted her. Maggie had called ahead and explained that she was a wheelchair user. She drove a van that had been accommodated for her. Curt explained that she would be able to back the van onto the ferry and that he would ask her to be one of the first vehicles on the boat. Curt told her that she would have to stay in her van for the five-mile crossing as the vehicles would be parked close together and her exiting would be impossible. Maggie understood.

As expected, Curt guided Maggie's skillful backing of her van onto the ferry and had her park the van on the far left side. Once she was in position, she spent the rest of the time watching people come aboard as well as all the other activity that goes into preparing a ferry for a crossing.

At precisely two-thirty the *Kristen D* pulled away from the dock, turned in the harbor while the State Street bridge began to lift, then slowly headed north to Bob-Lo Island.

Unaware of each other, two women on the ferry were headed toward events that would draw them together in a drama in the hours and days ahead. Of all the people Maggie watched, Mary was one that drew the most attention. Maggie had no idea that Mary was a player in the investigation that she was undertaking with Lou. But, private detectives have a habit of watching people, analyzing situations, and being observant.

As the *Kristen D* slowly made its way north out of the Cheboygan harbor, careful not to create a wake, Maggie looked out of her van to marvel at the yachts lined up along the western side of the harbor. She wondered where people get the money to enjoy such lavish homes on water. She couldn't help but smile at the many names given to the boats. She saw *My Mate's Best Friend*, *Paradise on Water*, *Instead of Alimony*, *Stinky*, and *Floating A. Loan*. Of these she wondered about *Stinky*. *That's a strange name for a yacht*, she thought.

⁓᷒

While Maggie was approaching Bob-Lo, Erin was able to locate Bob Brockington at the Grand Hotel. "I'm working with Mr. Searing, Bob. We need your help."

"Sure. What do you need?"

"We need a list of the guests who were staying at the Grand last night and I think I'd like to see the list for the night before as well. Then, Lou wants you to identify anything that a guest would write on; if possible, he'd like you to collect that from last night's guests."

"The lists are very easy. I can print that off of our database. Let's see, guests would sign in and we would have all of the registrations. They would also sign credit card slips upon leaving. That would be all the writing we would see. Of course, they might leave a message or two and they may drop off mail for us to send to the post office."

"I don't need the copies of everything signed, but it would help if you would note where it would be, so if we do need it, it'll be available."

"OK. You do know that we only need one signature when a family or couple registers. Many more could be assigned to a room, a suite, or several rooms with only one signature."

"I understand. Mr. Searing and I appreciate any help you can give us."

"I like him. I'm going to be there for him."

Erin left to go to downtown. She thought she'd ask a few questions of the harbormaster.

While Erin was riding her bike to the marina, Bob Brockington was calling Lou. "Mr. Searing. I just talked with Erin O'Brien about the information you requested. I'm believing I can share anything with her?"

"Yes. She'll be my eyes and ears on the island."

"Well, I didn't tell her what I'm about to tell you. I was about to call you when Erin appeared."

"What have you got?"

"Well, somebody came up to the desk. Actually, there were three people, two men and a woman. One of the men asked if you had checked out. I told him you had. He looked at the woman and smiled. He then asked if your room had been cleaned. I told him it had. He said, 'Well he wasn't on the first boat for the mainland this morning and we haven't seen him or his wife get on a Shepler's, the Star, or an Arnold's boat. So unless they are awesome swimmers with a couple of suitcases, they're still on this island.'"

"Humm. What else did he say?" I asked.

"First, I said something like, 'We don't monitor the comings and goings of our guests. Our records show that the Searings have checked out. They could be at some other resort or a bed and breakfast. It's not uncommon for a guest to spend a night with us and then go someplace else. Mr. Searing could have gone to some other accommodation or perhaps he left on a boat from the marina?'

"Then the man said, 'The marina has been monitored as well.' I simply told him that our records had shown that you had checked out. Then I tried to get something from him. So I said, 'He's a friend. Is that why you're looking for him?'

"'No, he's not a friend," he said. 'We are acquaintances and we were at the special education banquet last night. We're just curious where he could have gone, that's all.'"

"Is that it?" I asked. "Then they left?"

"Yeah. I asked them for their names in case you should happen to come in. They said that wouldn't be necessary. The man said he'd contact you when you got home."

"What did they look like?"

"The guys looked like typical tourists. They were in their forties, wearing slacks, T-shirts and sandals. The woman was not very attractive. Her hair was shoulder-length and uncombed or brushed. Looked like she just got up."

"Were they guests in the hotel?"

"I don't know."

"You did well, Bob."

"One thing will make you very proud of me, Mr. Searing"

"What's that?"

"I have their picture."

"You do?" I said, pleasantly surprised.

"Yeah, I signaled the hotel photographer to get a photo of them and he did. They didn't know it."

"Great work."

"Thanks. I talked with him and said that I may need a photo or two of some people thinking that if someone asked about you, I'd want a photo taken. Sure enough, I gave him a signal we had agreed upon and he got the photo. I had it developed and am looking at it now."

"You're fantastic, Bob. I'd give you a promotion if I could. Please give that photo to Erin and ask her to call me."

"She told me she was heading to the marina. I'll see that she gets it. Hope it helps."

"I know it will, Bob. Please continue to be vigilant. Others may be asking. Those three weren't satisfied with your answer, either.

You may wish to alert hotel security as they may attempt to enter my room, thinking I'm there or my belongings are."

"I'll handle that."

"Good work, Bob. Very good work!"

ᴣ

At exactly three-ten the *Kristen D* arrived at the main dock on Bob-Lo Island. There were approximately twenty people at the dock waiting for family or friends to arrive. Several people were waving and smiling at loved ones. It only took a few seconds for the *Kristen D* to be secured to the moorings. This procedure is done several times a day every day so it goes like clockwork. The gates were removed and one at a time, each vehicle pulled onto land and headed to a cabin or home throughout the thirty-eight-square-mile Island. All vehicles either went west or east on the main road.

Mary turned to the east and drove for about five miles before pulling onto what the islanders call Mud Lake Trail. She followed the rough road until she came to another trail to the right. About four hundred feet later was a cabin. It was a small deer hunting cabin. It had two small bedrooms, a small kitchen with a dining table and four chairs. The cabin had a fireplace and hearth. It was the nicest part of the cabin. A television was on a stand in the corner, but it only got a couple of channels and they were fuzzy. There was a worn out sofa and an easy chair, lamp, and an end table near the hearth. There were some windows on all sides with cheap and discolored shades offering some privacy.

The place was simply a deer hunting cabin. It was not clean and served only to bunk deer hunters. But, it did have lights, hot water and screens on the door and windows so it was livable and served the purpose as a hideout to commit a murder in a private setting.

Mary shut off the car engine and looked around. Everything seemed quiet. Mike looked through the curtains and she waved. She got out of the car, grabbing the groceries she'd purchased, went into the cabin. She greeted Mike who asked her if she wanted a beer.

"No thanks; I take it Jessica is cooperating."

"She's got no choice."

Maggie had twice as far to drive in the opposite direction, and so about fifteen minutes later Maggie pulled into the McRae's driveway and turned toward the A-frame. Gavin was putting the finishing touches on a make-shift ramp up to their front door. "You must be Maggie McMillan."

"Yes, I am. I got all the groceries Jenny asked for in the back of my van. Probably ought to get the milk and eggs in the refrigerator."

"Thanks for picking up some supplies. Saves us a day trip to the mainland. There is no such thing as driving to the corner grocery up here."

"I'm glad I could help. Is Lou here?"

"Yes, he's in the barn getting a tool I need to put your ramp together. I'll tell him you're here." As soon as Gavin said that, I appeared.

"Found us, huh, Maggie?"

"If I challenged you to find a more out of the way spot in Michigan, I don't think you could do it!" Maggie said.

"Yeah, I agree. It's so peaceful here. In its own way, it's a perfect place to be. Wait till you see the stars tonight. You may even get lucky and see the aurora borealis."

"Anything new on the case?" Maggie asked, as her automatic lift descended and allowed her to leave the van for the first time in a few hours.

"I'll tell you all I know once you meet the McRaes and settle in. But, in a nutshell, no, I have nothing of any significance." Maggie thanked Gavin for putting a make do ramp to the door. It did the trick and she appreciated Gavin's kindness. She guided her power wheelchair up to the porch and into the McRae home.

I introduced Maggie to Jenny and her mother Myrtle. There was an instant rapport as the three women appeared to hit it off immediately. Maggie, of course, knew Carol and gave her a friendly hug. Within a few minutes, one would have thought four lost sisters had been reunited.

I took advantage of this break in activity to go to the pole barn to see if I could get the Harley going. Gavin came into the area.

"This looks like a 1990 Fat Boy."

"You got it, Lou. You really know your Harleys!"

"I'm not a walking encyclopedia but I do have a fairly good working knowledge of the Harley. I've got a small library of books on the company."

"Yeah, this is a FLSTF Fat Boy. It's got the trademark sixteen-inch front and rear wheels."

"I like this model. Great style and the silver paint scheme is stylish."

"Yeah, I got this bike when it came out in 1990. Actually I was lucky to get one as they were quite popular. A dealer friend of mine had one for sale and gave me a call."

"I've never ridden one. Mine is a 1993 Cow Glide. They only made a few thousand that year and like you, I had a connection that gave me the opportunity to purchase one, so I did. Can't believe Carol gave me the blessing, but I guess she thought it less of a vice than some others I might have chosen."

"Well, once we get this purring, you can take this out around the island whenever you want. It would be good for it to get in some good rides. I really don't take it out much anymore."

Gavin and I wiped it clean. Gavin got on and attempted to start it. He couldn't get anymore than a spark plug to fire a couple of times. The fuel didn't seem to flow into the carburetor.

In the house, Carol asked, "Did I just hear a motorcycle?"

"I think Gavin is showing Lou his Harley," Jenny replied.

"Well, we've just lost Lou. Maggie, you'll have to solve this thing all by yourself. When Lou gets his hands on a Harley, he becomes obsessed. Please, Jenny, ask Gavin not to offer to sell this bike to Lou. Tell him to tell Lou that it's a family keepsake," Carol said with a smile. "He seems to gravitate to those bikes. At least he isn't gravitating to wine, women, and song." The three women nodded and agreed that a motorcycle here and there could easily be endured.

Like a couple of kids in auto mechanics class, Gavin and I got some rags and set about checking this and that and getting our hands and fingernails covered with grease, oil, and any other fluid that was involved in getting a motorcycle to purr.

"Not enough gas is getting to the carburetor," I said.

"Well, the problem's either with the gas line or the fuel filter."

"We're getting some gas into the carburetor after each attempt to start it. If the gas line were plugged, we probably wouldn't get any fuel in the carburetor."

"Guess we'll need to replace the fuel filter."

"Will that take a trip to Cheboygan?"

"Naw, got one here. There isn't one of something that I don't have in this barn, Lou."

Gavin and I worked on the Harley for about an hour and then we joined the women and began to focus our attention on the investigation into the disappearance of Jessica and Mike.

 ༀ

Erin parked her bike at the entrance to the Mackinac Island Marina. Walking along the docks, she admired the yachts that were moored there. She couldn't afford one of the inflatable dinghies tied to the back of a yacht let alone the down payment on one of these incredible watercraft.

She walked up to the harbormaster's office. "Good afternoon. Who's in charge here?"

"At the moment, I am," said a young college teenager wearing cutoffs, sandals and a T-shirt with the logo of the marina on it. His sunglasses hung in front of him, connected to a colorful cord.

"At the moment, because the manager isn't here or are you really in charge of the marina?" Erin asked.

"Well, whenever my Dad, Leo needs a break, which is often, he puts me in charge."

"Well, then, I need a little information."

"OK. Like what? Places to eat? Bike rentals? Cheapest carriage ride? Distance around the island? Best fudge? I've had 'em all. Bet there isn't a question you've got that I can't answer. Try me."

"Do you know anything about a couple disappearing around here last night?" Erin asked a surprised young lad.

"Disappearing? What are you talkin' about?"

"Last night around ten, a woman and her guest were invited onto a yacht based here in your marina. The ship's name was *Slinky*. The yacht went out into the Straits and didn't return them. So, do you know anything about that?"

"I sure don't. I don't know what to say. People aren't kidnapped up here on the Island. They'll show up in time."

"Could be. Hope you're right."

"We've got a boat registered called the *Slinky*. It belongs to Bert and Norma Richards. I can assure you they didn't have anything to do with their disappearance."

"You think that or you know that?" Erin asked.

"I don't know for certain because I wasn't here, but I'd bet everything I own that the *Slinky* is not involved in any foul play,"

"But it could've been, right?"

"I guess so."

"Who was working the marina last night?"

"Well, we shut down at ten o'clock. People know they need to get gas before ten. We have a night security guy who walks through every hour or so. He's also contracted by a number of stores downtown and property owners who are off the island. My brother Les worked till ten."

"He'll be back this evening?" Erin asked.

"Yeah, he'll be here about five o'clock."

"I'll stop back to see him. Thanks. Your name is?"

"Larry Little. My dad, as I said, manages this marina."

"Thanks, Larry. My name is Erin O'Brien." Erin had a hunch that Larry was right, the *Slinky* didn't kidnap Jessica and Mike. But, it all had to be checked out. She walked over to the *Slinky*, trying to be discreet in looking around hoping someone would come out.

As luck would have it, an older man did. "Hi, there. Beautiful day!" Erin said.

"Typical northern Michigan June day; perfect, simply perfect,"

Bert Richards said, stretching and enjoying the bright sun.

"Nice yacht you got here."

"Thanks. It's our summer home away from home."

"Where might home be?" Erin asked.

"Chicago. Can't take a big city like that for more than eight months a year. We come up here to take a deep breath. Do you know what I mean?"

"Sure do. I understand there was some commotion around here last night?"

"Commotion? What kind of commotion?"

"Lady and her date apparently took a boat ride and didn't come back."

"Yeah, Officer Adams talked to me about that. Couldn't help him. We took our boat to Petoskey last night to visit Chicago friends."

"Her friend says she and her date took a ride out into the Straits in a boat named the *Slinky*."

"Her friend's got a vision problem. My boat is the only boat named *Slinky* and nobody got on this boat last night. Nobody."

"How do you know that your boat is the only one with that name? Is there some registration procedure or some rule of the sea that there can only be one name per registered boat?"

"No. Anybody can name their boat anything they want. There could be hundreds of boats named *Sea Goddess* for example. I take a lot of pride in the name of my craft. I'm a distant relative of the inventor of the Slinky toy. I'd be very surprised if anyone would want to name their boat *Slinky*."

"I see. I had a Slinky as a kid. Tell the inventor when you see him that I liked it."

"Thank you, I will. Like a lot of things, it was a simple idea but it is often the simple ideas that turn out to be popular with people."

"Well, I'll be on my way, Mr. Richards. Thanks for talking to me."

"Sure. Hope you find out whatever happened to that couple. I can assure you that neither this boat nor anyone in my family had anything to do with the disappearance of those folks last night."

"I trust you, Mr. Richards. Have a good day."

⤳

Mary took over watching Jessica while Mike took a well-deserved nap. When he awoke, the conversation turned to the next phase of the perfect crime.

"None of my business, Mary, as I simply agreed to kill her with you, but what's your conflict with Jessica?"

"I don't mind going over it for the last time."

"If it's too personal, I understand," Mike replied.

"No, I can tell you. If I trust you to kill someone, I guess I can trust you to keep to yourself the motive behind the killing."

"Since I know how you operate, you can be assured that I'll keep this to myself. I, the hunter, need not become the hunted," Mike said, wondering if he'd just made a mistake in asking for the reason for the about-to-be-committed murder.

"Jessica and I were roommates at Eastern Michigan University, majoring in special education. We wanted to become teachers of blind children. I come from a very strict Catholic family and I mean very strict. My father was preVatican II and lived his life hanging on every word of the Pope. My mother was a devout Catholic and while not as married to the doctrine, she certainly was committed to following all the laws and most doctrines of the church. My sister and I were expected to follow suit.

"My sister had enough, rebelled and left the church and the family. My parents would have disowned her if she hadn't beaten them to the front door so to speak. They eventually got back on speaking terms, and they sort of tolerate each other now. My mom died a few years ago and I was glad they made some peace. My father sat me down and told me once again about honoring thy father and mother and that to do so would mean that their inheritance was mine. The condition of course was not to stray from the teachings of the church. My sister had been written out of the will.

"But to go back to my college days, I met a stud at EMU who promised to teach me what ecstacy really meant. I was naive about effective contraception, and the next thing I knew I had missed a period. When I told Jessica, she thought I should go to the health clinic and find out if I was pregnant. I did and I was.

"I either had to admit to being with child or have an abortion. I chose the abortion and made an agreement with Jessica. I told her that this must never become known to anyone. If my father found out, not only would I be disowned but I'd lose an inheritance worth millions of dollars.

"She promised never to say a word. I told her at the time that if she didn't keep her word, since I had already taken one life, I wouldn't hesitate to take another. Well, she's about to pay the price for poor judgment."

"I take it she didn't keep the secret."

"She didn't. It got back to me that she told someone and believe me, Jessica is the only person on this earth who knew about the abortion. She knows why she's here and about to die. This isn't some kind of surprise.

"What's your motivation, Mike? You said you wanted her dead, but I never learned why."

"Same problem. I told her a secret and she couldn't keep it."

"Willing to share?"

"Sure, you shared your secret. Gerald Zimmer, a friend from home, and I rented a cabin to go deer hunting right here on Bob-Lo. Gerald wanted company while he hunted. I'm not a hunter, but I always wanted to go to a deer camp and grabbed the chance when he asked me to go along. The second night up here we did some heavy drinking. We got into a silly argument. We began to scuffle and traded some punches reminiscent of when we were in high school. I landed a punch that sent Gerald backwards. He lost his balance and struck his head on the hearth. It was a foot high brick shelf. I guess the angle his head hit the brick caused his neck to snap and just like that he was dead.

"I was afraid to report it because I thought everyone would think it was murder. The autopsy would clearly show the body blows and since I was winning, there were no marks on my body to give me a self-defense alibi. It seemed easier to simply bury him and then report him missing and leave it at that. So, the next morning I reported to the sheriff's department that he had gone hunting in the morning and hadn't come back. They searched for him but of course never found him. I was very careful where and how I buried him.

"Gerald was a loner; no wife or children. He had an elderly father out in California or Oregon. I got the impression that he wasn't close to him. He was closest to the people where he worked and they would accept the fact that hunting accidents happen and he didn't come back.

"So, Gerald died. It was an accident, but I killed him nonetheless. In a very weak moment, I told Jessica. Like you, I said it absolutely couldn't get told and I later learned that she had let it out. I'm certain she told a mutual friend. If the cops get wind of this in any way, I'm in Southern Michigan Prison for life and I just can't have that. Jessica knows this was very important to me. She isn't in that bedroom wondering why her life is going to be cut short."

"We both erred in telling her something very critical in our lives."

"Yeah, but it was based on trust and she broke that trust."

"Our plan's perfect so far and I really don't see how it can miss now that we're safely on this island."

"The next phase of our plan is to wait a bit to kill her?" Mike asked.

"That's right. We need to be assured of a couple of things. First we need to know that Searing and McMillan are not getting involved. They're good, and as tight as we've planned this murder, I do believe they can find some minor error that will spoil the best plans."

"You threatened them out of the picture, didn't you?"

"Well, that was my first activity. Lou is a devoted husband and dearly loves his wife. Any threat to her safety should be enough to scare him off this case. Maggie is still adjusting to not having the use of her legs and the thought of not having the use of her arms should be enough to scare her away as well."

"I took care of making sure they were watched and not getting involved on the island. My colleagues did a good job," Mike said, sure that the planning last Friday night paid off. "But if these scares don't work?"

"Well, we may not carry out the threats, but they will be significantly harmed which as you know is our back-up plan."

"Yes. What's the second thing?" Mike asked.

"The second thing is to be assured that we are not suspects. Once I'm convinced that Searing and McMillan are not on the case, we'll kill Jessica, bury her, and then we'll go back to Cheboygan, get on my yacht and sail away, content in having executed the perfect crime."

"So far, the plan is on track. And, I see no reason to suspect it won't continue to be perfect."

The two continued to talk about their past. "I know Jessica went on to become a teacher of blind children. And, so did you," Mike said, encouraging Mary to keep talking.

"Yeah, I did. We sure went our separate ways. We took the same courses, had the same professors and experiences, and then after graduation Jessica became a strong advocate for blind kids staying in their neighborhood schools and using technology to communicate. I became a strong advocate for self-contained programs for kids who are blind and for using Braille. We see different sides of the issues. I respect her as an advocate. I liked her as a roommate, but it was when the secret got out that I lost my respect for her as a person, and knew I had to take some desperate action."

❧

Bob Brockington saw Erin riding her bike along Mackinac Island's main street dodging the carriages and all the "Fudgies." He waved to her and let her know he needed to see her. Riding her bike up to him, Erin asked, "Looking for me?"

"Yeah. I talked to Mr. Searing and I told him that I had a photo taken of some people who were asking for him. He said to give the photo to you and ask that you call him. Here's the picture," Bob said, handing Erin a business-size envelope.

"OK, thanks. Anything else?"

"No. Sure would like to be able to help Mr. Searing and solve this thing for him."

"So would I."

Bob explained the photo. "These people were asking if Mr. Searing had checked out. When I told them he had, they said that he hadn't left the Island because they had been monitoring the ferries and the marina. They're convinced he's still on the Island."

Erin opened the envelope and said, "Well, let's take a look at who we have here." She glanced at the photo. "Humm, that's interesting."

"What's interesting?"

"These are folks from a new organization called The Blind Advocating for the Blind or TBATB. The woman is Claudia Hosen. She's an advocate on their staff. The taller of the two..."

Bob interrupted, "He's the one who talked to me. He smiled at the woman when I told him the Searings had checked out."

"This tall man is Brent Phillips. He's a parent of twins who are blind. The shorter man is Richard Walls. I'm not sure what his role is with the TBATB. I think he has something to do with governmental affairs, or maybe he's their lobbyist."

"Why would they care if the Searings had checked out?" Bob asked.

"The only thing that would make sense is that they don't want him to investigate Jessica and Mike's disappearance."

"Let me write down their names. I'll check the guest list and see if I can find any writing from them. Mr. Searing wanted writing samples."

"Good idea. I'll call Lou like he asked me to. Thanks, Bob. I've got a feeling that we'll be a good team. Let me know if these three are registered at the Grand for tonight. We may want to monitor their activities."

"Will do."

Before Erin called Lou she took the photo to the Henderson Bed and Breakfast. She parked her bike out by the front fence, walked up to the door, knocked and waited for Mrs. Henderson. "Oh, hi, thought you were my first guest for tonight."

"No, would you look at a photo and see if you can identify the people in it?"

"I'll try. Sure."

"You said that a couple of people visited Mike in the middle of the night last Friday. Were these the two guys?" Erin asked, as she handed the photo to the innkeeper.

"I think so. It was dark and I didn't get a good look, but yes, one was tall and one was short. They had on clothes like these men and they looked about the same age. I can't be absolutely certain, but I think they were the visitors."

"Thanks."

෫ᴏ

Once Maggie had unpacked and settled into the McRae home, she was ready to get down to business. She turned to Lou, "Well, what do you make of this Jessica Williams and her date's disappearance?"

"I have to presume that they're in danger. We know they were on Mackinac Island last night, and that they went for a boat ride and didn't come back. If Jessica was okay, she would have been at the marina at twelve-thirty to be picked up by Gavin or left word for him. So, I'm fairly certain that they're not on the Island."

As Maggie gazed out the window, she asked me for more information. "Tell me about this boat called the *Slinky*."

"Her friend Betsy said she saw her get on a yacht named *Slinky*."

"*Slinky*?" Maggie asked. "You mean like that toy, a rolled up piece of wire?"

"That's what she said."

"Kind of a rare name for a boat. It doesn't even fit a nautical theme."

"There's a boat in the marina named the *Slinky,* but according to officer Adams and Erin, the owner swears his innocence, says he was in Petoskey visiting friends. I called the Petoskey marina and they verified that a boat called the *Slinky* was in their marina until at least eight o'clock."

"Great. Now we have boats impersonating boats. Who is Erin?" Maggie asked.

"Erin is the person who put on the special education gala ball last night at the Grand Hotel. I know her quite well and she's helping us on the Island. She's our liaison to the police and the hotel. In a sense, she's an extension of us on Mackinac Island."

Maggie lowered her head as if in deep thought. She raised her head and said, "Lou, if a boat took Jessica and Mike from the Mackinac Island Marina and did not return them, it could have gone to a thousand places along the shores and inlets of Lake Michigan and Lake Huron. Has the Coast Guard been alerted to be on the lookout for a boat that fits the description of the *Slinky*?"

"Not by me. The police on the Island contacted the Coast Guard. Officer Adams really doesn't think they've been kidnapped. He says most people show up, so he expects Jessica and Mike to show."

Maggie called to Jenny who was working in the kitchen. "Jenny, does anyone on this island work for the Coast Guard?"

"Yes. Well, no. I was thinking about Buck Ramsey, but he retired from the Coast Guard. He was stationed in St. Ignace for years and when it came time to retire, he bought a place on Bob-Lo. He's kind of a hermit. He has a place back in the woods. He feeds the deer, the raccoons and other critters year round. He told me once, 'People are a pain in the backside, but animals mind their own business and leave me to mine.'"

"Do you know him?"

"Yeah, we know all the residents over here. Some we know better than others."

"You know him such that you could call him and he would know who you are?"

"Yeah. Like I said, most permanent residents know each other. Those living here year round need each other's knowledge and skill to make it. I won't say we all love each other, but we know who everyone is and will help each other if need be."

"We may need to talk to Buck," I said. "Could you arrange that?"

"Sure. Do you want to drive to his place?"

"We can do that. Could Maggie get into his home with her wheelchair?"

"Nope. It is a log cabin home with about four or five steps leading up to it."

Maggie said, "You go, Lou. We both don't need to go."

"OK, I'll make notes so I don't forget to tell you what we learn."

⌘

Late that afternoon I was sitting along with Gavin in the living room of Captain Buck Ramsey. "Thanks for agreeing to see me, Captain."

"If you want to know anything related to the Coast Guard, I'm afraid I can't help. I've been out quite a long time," Buck said, seated in a very comfortable chair. He looked like a retired miliary officer. His full head of hair was neatly combed and his shirt pressed and creased. His shoes shined as if he were about to face a boot camp inspection. The inside of his log cabin looked like a natural history museum. The walls were adorned with stuffed wildlife that he'd killed on the Island and on hunting trips. There were also many mounted fish which gave evidence of his angling skill.

"What do you need?" Buck asked.

"Just need some procedures. I doubt they have changed over the years. I'm looking into the disappearance of a couple. They were last seen leaving the Mackinac Island Marina aboard a yacht named *Slinky*."

"Must have been Bert Richards' boat."

"Right. We know about his boat, and we're convinced that Mr. Richards is not involved."

"Somebody's trying to frame the boat then. The boat that took the couple out no doubt looked like the *Slinky*. Are you absolutely sure the name of the boat was *Slinky*?"

"That's what the invitation said and a friend of the missing couple said they got on the boat."

"Yeah, so what do you want from me?" Buck asked.

"I want to learn what procedures the Coast Guard would use in trying to find this boat?"

"When I was in the Coast Guard a couple of things might have happened. We might have conducted a harbor check which means the Chief might dispatch a vehicle and we'd physically go through the different marinas or we might call the harbormasters and ask them if they've seen a boat that matches the description."

"Would you ask for help from other boats in the area?" I asked.

"Yes, we might put out a pon pon message on the radio that would go something like, PON PON, PON PON. This is United States Coast Guard, St. Ignace, all vessels in the area of the Straits of Mackinac be on the lookout for a 46 foot white Tiara. If spotted, call the nearest Coast Guard Station, PON PON, PON PON, Coast Guard Station, St. Ignace, OUT."

"You said someone may be trying to frame Bert's boat. How's that done?" I asked.

"Letters can be put on, painted on, or changed."

"I thought those were all painted on by professional painters."

"Used to be. Now you can buy letters and put them on yourself. So, if someone wanted to frame Bert's boat, they would simply put the letters SLINKY on their boat."

"But why would someone want to frame Bert's boat?" Gavin asked.

"Then Bert would be the suspect in the disappearance of the couple," I said to Gavin. "Whoever did this would have to hope that the real *Slinky* would go out into the Straits often or that the owner wouldn't have an alibi for his presence when the two were taken."

I turned to Buck, "So, if letters were put on, they could be taken off and the name on the back of the boat wouldn't help us at all."

"That's right. They could have put on those letters to confuse the harbormaster or others in the area."

"Who is the harbormaster?" I asked.

"Leo Little."

"Are boats registered, Buck?"

"Yeah, they are. You get a number. That's what you see on every boat."

"Do you have to put the name of the boat on the registration form?"

"No, you need the name of the owner. But, you don't need to put the boat's name. That can change. Some guy could name his boat *Anne's Dream* , for example. Anne takes off with some other guy and the owner now wants to name his boat *Anne's Alimony*. Naw, you need the legal name of the owner, but that's all."

"This is helpful, Buck. Thanks."

"Like to keep talking to you guys, but I've got animals to feed. Got to get out the corn for the deer and fudge for the raccoons."

"Fudge for the raccoons?" I said in amazement.

"Yeah, old fudge from the Mackinac Island. My son has one of the Island fudge shops. You can't recycle old fudge, so he brings it over here and I put it out for the raccoons."

"You mean 'Fudgies' on that Island pay big bucks for that sugar and these critters get it free for showing up each evening?"

"That's right. You men are welcome to stay around and watch the picnic."

"I think this is something Carol and Maggie would like to see," I said, shaking my head in disbelief. "Could we maybe come back tomorrow and watch? I assume you feed them everyday."

"That'd be fine. Yeah, everyday of the year at this time."

Gavin and I thanked Buck for the information and we left explaining that Carol, Maggie and I might be back tomorrow. I felt like he deserved a salute, but shook his hand firmly and headed for the car.

As soon as we got back to the McRae home I briefed Maggie on what I had learned. I referred to my notes several times to be sure I hadn't left anything out.

"Asking the Coast Guard to be on the lookout for a boat like the *Slinky* probably wouldn't yield much information," Maggie concluded. "Those Tiara's are popular. And, most boats are white. I don't think we could narrow the description down to be of any help."

"I agree. Oh, well, I met a fascinating gentleman and learned Coast Guard procedures for finding a missing craft, so all was not lost."

That evening after dinner, Gavin suggested we continue our conversation on the shore of the Straits. He had gathered up several pieces of wood and placed them by the rock circled fire pit. We all moved to the shore as the fire began to blaze.

The shore was fairly rocky but Maggie didn't have any problem powering her wheelchair out to the fire's edge.

The crackle of the fire, the soft yellow and orange glow of the embers against the moon's reflection on the water brought back memories of summer camps.

"Carol and I enjoy a few fires each summer on the beach behind our home in Grand Haven."

"Stop right there," Jenny said. "I'm a psychic and I know what you're going to say next."

"No way," I said.

"You were going to tell us how Carol whips out the Hershey bars, marshmallows and graham crackers, right?"

"You got it. Love those S'mores!"

"Well, we don't disappoint here on Bob-Lo," Jenny said, as she reached around for a paper sack holding marshmallow roasting sticks and all the items necessary for the scrumptious evening treat by the fire.

When it came time to snuff out the fire and head to bed, Maggie went to the McRae home. Carol and I went to the east A-frame.

$\backsim$

Shortly before 2 a.m. while Jessica slept, and most of the Island was peaceful, the living room of the small cottage on Mud Lake Trail was anything but calm and serene. Mary and Mike were almost coming to blows.

"What is your problem, Mike? We kill her now and get off this Island. Am I making myself clear?"

"I know what you want, Mary, but this isn't the right time."

"There is never a right time, Mike. We committed to killing this woman and all I've gotten since we got her on board is some excuse to keep waiting, but this is insane. Our mission was to kill her and now is a good time to kill her. What's to talk about!"

"What's to talk about is strategy. We can't afford any slip up."

"How can we slip up. The whole Island is asleep. We kill her, put her in the ground and take the boat to Cheboygan in the morning. End of discussion."

"Not the end of discussion. Listen to me. We're missing people; Jessica and me. No one cares about me, but Jessica is another thing. People are looking for her. They know she left the Island on a boat. The deputy on this island knows your dad's boat was tied up at the main dock. He may be hitting you up for the docking fee as soon as he sees you. Yours is not a boat often docked there. He may have been in touch with the police and the Coast Guard."

"I guess I should kill you, too, bury both of you and get on with my life."

"Well, maybe you better because this is not the time to kill Jessica and she'll only be killed over my dead body. You understand?"

"If that's the terms, I'll see if I can arrange it."

"Don't be ridiculous."

"I'm serious. I've been planning this murder for months and weeks and days. Everything was all set, every detail clearly outlined and we were on course for the perfect murder, but you convinced me to foil it and come here and now when the time is right to finish the job you come up with more excuses."

"Too risky, Mary. Not the right time."

"Mike Miles. There's never going to be a right time! You know what I think? I think you don't want Jessica murdered and you're not man enough to say so."

"Don't start those games, Mary. She'll die soon and we'll be safely off this island. We lay low for now. We lay low, understand?"

Mary shook her head and walked away, swearing under her breath. She'd lost control. At some point, probably shortly after the *Slinky* had moved into the Straits, the control shifted to Mike and this did not please Mary Chandler in the least. There would have to be a change of attitude because the killing of Jessica Williams was

Mary's idea, Mary's goal, and Mary's mission. She was now convinced that it was a mistake to allow Mike to get involved and now for him to control the murder was more than Mary could accept. She vowed to change things.

CHAPTER FOUR

Monday, June 3
Bois Blanc Island

Jessica awoke in pain. She was hurting from the burn of the rope around her ankles and wrists. In fact, the tightness of the ropes and her movement caused some raw areas on her wrists to bleed. She remained confused in not knowing what would happen to her or when. She was hungry, having gone for more than a day with nothing more than some milk. She knew that Betsy and Gavin would realize that she was missing and contact authorities. People had to be looking for her.

Every four hours she was let into the bathroom. She looked into the mirror and was shocked at seeing her image. She was still wearing the outfit she wore to the special education banquet.

The last time in the bathroom she had looked out the window and could see nothing but trees. She knew she was no longer on Mackinac Island. The clue that let her know for sure was the name on the power box outside of the house which read, "Presque Isle Electric." It was the same sign as one outside her A-frame on Bob-Lo.

"OK, come on out. You've had enough time in there!" Mike shouted.

Jessica came out, was guided to the bed and after a sip of milk, was tied once again to the bedposts.

⤳

Following breakfast, I decided to call the director of the CAUSE organization, Dr. Susan Pratley. CAUSE is a parent training and advocacy organization in Michigan. Sue was a friend of mine and would be able to tell me if Jessica was working on a difficult case. I used my cell phone to give her a call. "Good morning, Susan. Lou Searing calling."

"Good to hear from you, Lou. Don't tell me CAUSE is a suspect in one of your murder investigations?"

"Sorry to disappoint you, but you're clean on this one. However, one of your advocates may be in trouble."

"Oh, really. Who might that be?"

"You haven't heard?"

"Heard what, Lou?"

"Jessica Williams and Mike Miles were at the special education banquet at the Grand Hotel Saturday night. They went out in the Straits for a cruise and they've been missing ever since."

"Oh, my God. Not Jessica."

"She may be okay. The Island police only have her listed as a missing person now, but in a worst case scenario, she may be buried in the Straits."

"This is terrible. You couldn't find a nicer woman and very competent, too. I sure hope she's all right."

"So do I, Susan. I'm calling to find out if she was working on a highly controversial case for CAUSE. Do you know?"

"Everything we touch is controversial. We generally don't get involved unless efforts to resolve the conflict at the local level have been unsuccessful. By that time you often have a couple of people at each other's throats."

"Was she in the middle of a substantial conflict, Susan?"

"I've got our records here, let me see if it will refresh my memory." A few seconds later she said, "Oh yes, Jessica got involved in a placement issue over in the Bad Axe area."

"What's that about?"

"The Blind community was pushing for the youngster being placed at a school for the blind. The flip side to this is the local school district who thinks that the youngster can best be served in their community."

"I can see where that would be pretty controversial. So Jessica finds herself in the middle of a big controversy and she takes one side which leaves her open for a major conflict with opposing thinkers."

"That's right. But not murder, Lou. We have disagreements, different viewpoints in special education all the time. You know that. Our entire profession is laced with groups advocating one point of view or the other; inclusion vs. separate center programs, manual vs. oral education, Braille vs. large print and technology, whole language vs. phonics, the list goes on and on. But, murder? No issue is worth taking a human life. I sure hope this little controversy isn't the cause of Jessica's disappearance."

"Don't know. But, thanks for the information. If you hear of any other conflict that Jessica might have been involved with or somebody in her past that would want her harmed, give me a call, will you?"

"Sure. By the way, Lou, who was her date?"

"Mike Miles. Know him?"

"Yes, he's the leader of the group that opposed Jessica in this issue. He's with The Blind Advocating for The Blind organization."

"They date once in a while so the relationship must have been able to set differences aside."

"I don't know what Jessica ever saw in Mike. I'm no detective, but if I were looking into the disappearance of Jessica, I'd start with Mike and wouldn't be surprised if you ended your investigation with Mike."

"Has he got a record?"

"I don't know about a police record, but he's not respected, admired, or seen as anything but an adversarial person, Lou."

"Do you know where he lives?"

"Yeah, he's from the Lapeer area. He's a loner, no family. No one will miss him. If you want to know how much this guy is loved, call the Lakeside Director of Special Education. Get ready for an earful."

"OK. Thanks for your help."

"Do I call you at home if I get any info?"

"Yeah, call my home number and leave a message on my voice mail. I check it several times a day."

"OK, will do. Good luck, Lou. Oh, while you're on the line. When you solve this one, I'll treat you to 18 holes of golf. You game?"

"Sure. Let's hope Jessica is able to play with us."

"That's my wish, too."

⟋⟍

Erin and Bob Brockington were at the Grand Hotel. Bob was going over the guest list trying to find the people from The Blind Advocating for The Blind organization and any writing from the three. The phone rang. Bob picked it up. He knew it was hotel staff because it was not coming in from an outside line. "Bob Brockington."

"Mr. Brockington, we've got a break-in in room 245."

"What happened?"

"Looks like someone kicked the door in."

"Don't touch anything. I'll be right up."

Bob said to Erin, "The room assigned to the Searings has been broken into. Gotta go up and secure it. I'll tell the officer to come to the employee entrance in the back and you come up with the officer when he or she gets here. OK?"

"Will do."

Bob called the Island police and headed up to room 245 while Erin calmly walked to the back door of the Grand Hotel to wait for the officer.

When Bob arrived, he found the cleaning crew waiting for him out in the hall. He looked at the damaged door, saw that it had been kicked in and the door-facing was ripped apart. He looked in and saw that the room hadn't been cleaned but it was empty of any of the Searings' items. There was nothing for the intruder to discover other than a room ready to be made up for the next guest.

When Erin and the officer arrived, Bob briefed them on what little he knew. The police officer called the station and reported what he had found. He asked for someone to come to the hotel to take fingerprints of the door handle and in the room.

The traditional yellow tape was put across the entrance to the room and the officer stayed on the scene to assure that no one would touch the hardware or go into the room.

Erin and Bob went downstairs to his office. "They didn't believe me when I told them that he had checked out," Bob said.

"Referring to The Blind Advocating for The Blind folks?"

"Yeah. My guess is that they were hoping to find him hiding there or at least his belongings."

"They got a big disappointment. Have they left the Island yet?"

"Yeah. I asked one of our carriage drivers to let me know what happened to them. He told me they went out on the first Arnold's line this morning."

Erin asked, "Why do you think whoever broke into this room would want to do that? What's to be gained from finding Lou or Carol in their room?"

"If they killed Jessica, they know that Lou'll solve it. They want him taken out of the picture, too, I guess."

"Yes, but if they killed Jessica they would know that Lou was on this Island and would eventually be involved in the investigation. Why wouldn't they take him out at the same time they took out Jessica?"

"Maybe they had planned to?"

The two went back to look over the guest list.

"Here it is. The two men had a room and the woman had a room. They arrived two evenings ago and they were due to stay tonight and check out tomorrow. The woman signed her own registration and Brent Phillips signed for the room shared by the two men."

"Good work, Bob. I'll report all of this to Lou."

"OK, I'll keep my eye on the three and let you know if anything suspicious happens."

Meanwhile on Bob-Lo, Gavin and I spent some time getting the Harley to purr. Gavin invited me to take it to the other end of the island. I jumped at the chance and thoroughly enjoyed my ride.

I met Jackee at Barb's Tavern for lunch as we had planned. The tavern faces the Straits and is a few miles east of the main dock. Patrons can sit at the bar and have a drink, or if planning to have a meal with others, can sit at one of several tables. A pool table is off to the side and there's room for dancing or for a performer. We ordered sandwiches and drinks. "I've been wanting you to see my island for years, Lou. I didn't expect you to finally get here working on a crime."

"I love this place!" I exclaimed. "There's so much beauty, quiet, and I feel so isolated from the world. Too bad I ended up here on an investigation. I'd like to kick back and just enjoy the island."

"I told you you'd like it here. You're right. You can't beat it for an escape from the world. The lifestyle is just what we land owners want. That's why we're here."

"I understand this place has a unique history, too."

"The folks who've been here for decades could tell you fascinating stories. If you'd like to hear a few, I can arrange it."

"Yeah, that'd be great."

"How about you and Carol coming over tomorrow evening and we'll have a hollow log fire. I'll invite our friend Jim Vosper over for dessert and you'll get an earful of history."

"Great."

Jackee and I ate our meal and chatted about people in common, the investigation, and the importance of my being anonymous. Before I picked up the bill and made my way back to the west end I said, "I'd like to do a little fishing, could you tell me where fish may be biting?"

"You may want to go with John. He's the fisherman. But if he can't make it, I suggest you go to the Lake Mary dock, go east as far as you can go on the main road and then turn off the road to the right a hundred feet or so before the lakeshore. Go about a quarter mile and you come to an "L" shaped dock and you can fish there."

"Thanks. Tomorrow I may try my luck."

Upon my return to the McRae home, there were no messages and nothing to do with the investigation. It was one of those slices of time when you simply seem to be on hold waiting for something to happen. I was missing my daily run. So I announced, "Think I'll go for a jog. I need to get my mind off all of this. What's the best route?"

"How far are you expecting to jog?" Gavin asked.

"Oh, ten miles max. I'll walk some of it, but about ten miles, I guess."

"Well, you've got two options," said Gavin, thinking of good scenic routes. "You could go right to the Hawk's Landing General Store. It's about ten miles away. You know the route you took when you met Jackee for lunch. Sheila will let you use her phone. Call me when you get there and I'll come to pick you up. You'll get a lot of scenery that way and all you have to do is follow the main road."

"OK; my second option?" I asked.

"Out and back, I guess? You could go five miles toward town and then turn around and come back. The road's flat. If you want to do some trail running, you can leave the main road and venture into the woods."

"I think I'll head for Hawk's Landing and call you when I get there."

"Fine."

"This should take me a couple of hours. If I don't call, come looking for me."

"OK, it's 4 o'clock now. I'll expect a call around 6."

"Sounds fine." I made sure I had my Medic Alert chain around my neck and after stretching, I started out for some long overdue exercise.

It was wonderful to be outside in nature. There were some deer grazing in an open field and an occasional doe could be seen monitoring my progress along the road. The road was dirt and other than a passing car kicking up a cloud of dust, the ground was soft for the jog. The trees were all colors of green and in places they formed an arch over the roadway and provided a cool and shaded path for my jog. Oaks, maples, pines, and spruce trees dominated the island. On occasion, the sun would break through the trees and the bright light seemed to highlight the beauty that was around me. The jog was good for my body and the views were good for my soul. I took the time to think about Jessica's disappearance. I've found that jogging is a good time to clear my mind and to do creative thinking. Often I can put my mind in line with the criminal and this helps me get clues as to how the crime may have been carried out. The only thing that struck me during the run was the reoccurring thought that Mike may be the kidnapper and not an innocent victim.

I was making good time with my jog and I liked being out in nature. The clean air and the exercise were invigorating. There was only one car that kicked up dust and the quiet was refreshing.

I was making good time and averaging around 11 to 12 minutes a mile with stretches of jogging and walking. The signs that I was approaching the Pointe Aux Pins area appeared earlier than I had expected. I noted the cemetery on my left, the post office and volunteer fire department pole barns on my right. The small red schoolhouse was on my left and about a block ahead was the Hoover Community Building, built with a nice log cabin motif.

The waters of Lake Huron were ahead as I moved into an area of cottages and homes. I had learned that this used to be an active place early in the twentieth century. People from Detroit would come up here for vacation. Their settlement was called 'The Wilderness Club'. It only lasted till the depression, then with no money, it faded into oblivion. Many of the cottages and homes remain and are being restored.

Passing the Library/Historical Society building, I made a mental note to stop in on another occasion. I'm interested in history and would enjoy seeing photographs and relics of this unique island. To my right could be seen the Lower Peninsula five miles across the channel. A freighter was making its way toward the Mackinac Bridge. Pleasure craft were intent on plying through the choppy waters, each with a destination in mind.

I saw Hawk's Landing up ahead and decided to go in and see if I could have some diet pop on credit. When I entered I noticed, on my right and left, a set of tables and benches where folks could be seen eating a meal or relaxing over a cup of coffee or an ice cream cone. I passed through a second door and saw a variety of general store items. On a couple of racks were Bois Blanc T-shirts, sweatshirts, or caps. Coolers with milk, pop, and cold beer were along the back wall. A limited selection of household items were on a few shelves. The cash register is located to the left as you enter the store and if you're lucky, Mackinac Island Fudge Ice Cream and other flavors will be in supply and a *Detroit Free Press* will be for sale.

"You look like you just finished a marathon," co-owner, Sheila Godbold said, taking a break from serving ice cream cones to a family of four. We get a lot of bikers and hikers passing through, but runners, you folks are rare."

"Believe it or not, only one car passed me on my way from the west end."

"This isn't exactly I-96 in Detroit, so it doesn't surprise me. What can I get you?" Sheila asked.

"Well, first of all I need to see if my credit is good."

"Do you know anybody on this island?" Sheila said with a smile.

"Yeah, I'm staying with Gavin and Jenny McRae. I also know Jackee Miller."

"Your credit is good. What do you want?"

"Diet Coke or Pepsi. Just jogged from the McRae's A-frame and I need something to drink."

"Quite a jog."

"Yeah, but it felt good."

"Going to be with us long?"

"Depends. Hope to be gone by the weekend."

"Up here for a restful vacation?"

I paused. I didn't want to let on that I was investigating the disappearance of Mike and Jessica as I wanted my anonymity. So, I simply went along with the expected response, "Yeah, I am."

"Here's your drink. I'll put this on the McRae tab or you can pay me the next time you're in." I thanked Sheila and walked out to wait for Gavin to appear and return me to the west end.

༄

Mary Chandler pulled up to Hawk's Landing. She walked into the store and looked around. She was looking for something to read. The cabin was bare of books or magazines and Mary was an avid reader, she needed some mental stimulation. She couldn't find a display of books, magazines, or newspapers so she asked, "Have you folks got any reading material for sale?"

"There's a box of used books back in the corner there by the housewares stuff. But, we don't have any books for sale. Sorry," Sheila said.

"Hungry for a good book and thought you might have a mystery or something."

"Well, had a mystery writer in here a few minutes ago. He could probably spin you a good yarn, but I can't help you with a new book."

"Who's the writer?" Mary asked.

"Lou Searing. Ever hear of him?"

"Can't say that I have. What does he write?" Mary asked, with her heart beating faster.

"He's an investigator, specializes in education mysteries. He solves 'em and then writes the book. Seems like a nice guy."

"You sure it was him?"

"It was him. I recognized him from seeing his picture on the back of his books. Jackee Miller knows him and has shown me some photos of the two of them. I'm sure it was him."

"I guess investigators and writers need a vacation like the rest of us," Mary said, not at all happy to hear that I was on Bob-Lo.

"I love mysteries and especially Michigan-based stories," Sheila said. "Lou is relatively new. I like his style."

"You think he's here on vacation?" Mary asked hoping for a 'Yes' answer.

"I don't know. He stopped in for a Diet Coke. He'd been jogging. My guess would be that he's up here looking into the disappearance of that couple on Mackinac Island."

"Yeah, heard about that. Well, I'll see if one of the used books is to my liking."

"Just take what you want. I don't sell 'em, just act as a broker for old books."

"Thanks."

Mary looked over the selection and found something to keep her mind occupied. She then walked out to her car, alarmed and disturbed that I was on the Island.

$$\backsim$$

Mary returned to the cabin and got Mike's attention, "Listen, we've got complications."

"What's the problem?"

"Searing and probably McMillan are on this island."

"Not good news."

"No, it isn't," Mary said, shaking her head. "We must kill Jessica now and get off the island before Searing comes snooping around."

"Absolutely not, this is the worst time to kill her," Mike countered loudly.

"Mike, I've had about all I can take of this control trip you're on. She's to die and to die before midnight. End of discussion."

"Mary, listen, you're letting your emotions cloud your common sense."

"I won't listen to your excuses any longer, Mike. She's to be dead by midnight and buried out back. I want the woman and our secrets, yours and mine, buried on Bob-Lo."

"Mary, at least hear me out. If Searing is on this island, it means he's asking questions, talking to people, and talking to authorities. It means he could possibly have his eye on us as we talk. A dead Jessica puts us in the slammer for life. I mean, who else on this island could have killed her. On the other hand, there's no reason why we can't stay quiet. Jessica is going nowhere and as far as we know, nobody knows we're here. Doesn't it make more sense to have an alive Jessica with us if we are caught than a dead Jessica?"

"I guess you do have a point there," Mary said, calming down a bit.

"Then when this Searing guy leaves and the coast clears, we can easily kill her and get off the island."

"I may not be able to wait for Searing to get off this island. I might just have to put him in a grave."

"That's another judgment call we'll make..."

"I'll make, Mike. I'm calling the shots from here on out," Mary said, with a loud voice. Her anger was spewing forth as her emotions had been held in check too long. "You've been taking control and I'll even admit that you made sense from time to time, but this was my murder and from now on, I'll call every shot. If you want to walk away, walk now, but if you walk and squeal, your secret will not be buried on Bob-Lo, just remember that."

"Now you turn to blackmail? Is that your first decision in taking control?"

"Now I turn to handling this murder as it should've been handled Saturday night in the Straits. Now it will be handled before midnight." Mike Miles got up from his chair, walked outside, and seriously thought about his options. He came inside and said, "Tell me this, is Searing about to die?"

"He's got to pay the price of not listening to my warning."

"You said a while ago that we weren't going to follow through on the threats."

"I said we may not follow through and besides, that was a while ago. Now is now and if I want Searing dead, I'll kill him!"

"Killing anyone other than Jessica was never part of the plan I agreed to."

"Well, it's part of the plan now. Are you in or walking away?"

"Where's Searing staying?"

"Don't know. That's my next mission. Once I find that out, it's lights out. Too bad, I liked Lou and his stories, but he didn't take the advice to protect his family and himself."

꘎

Jessica had plenty of time to put together what was happening. Another four hours had elapsed and they allowed her into the bathroom where she was given her privacy.

The bathroom was traditional; sink, toilet, bathtub with shower curtain, and a medicine cabinet over the sink. She opened the cabinet under the sink and found a small tool box. She found a glass cutter and immediately looked to the bathroom window. If she could cut the glass evenly and then place the shower curtain over the bottom edge and sides of the window, she thought she could get her slim body through the window. She would attempt an escape the next time she was allowed to go to the bathroom. While she didn't know the time, she knew it would be after dark judging by the long shadows and the beginning of dusk.

Back from the bathroom, she lay on the bed, and in her mind, replayed the reasons for her life now being threatened.

She had a flashback to being at a pro-life rally in Traverse City. She was approached by a woman who remembered her from her days at Eastern Michigan University. They were not pursuing the same major in college, but they knew of each other from Traverse City High School.

Jessica had some strong beliefs about life. While it wasn't something she was willing to take up a placard and join a picket line for, she did believe strongly in the pro-life movement and had taken this opportunity to show her support. She thankfully never had to make this choice in her life and she hesitated to judge women who did make the difficult choice, but she felt that life began at conception and that taking life was wrong. That belief put her in the pro-life camp.

In fact, while she recognized her old high school classmate, she couldn't come up with a name. Rather than admit to it and ask, she simply made reference to having gone to Traverse City High School and sharing a school play, the band or some school activity. When the subject of abortion came up, Jessica stated her belief which obviously was met with warm feelings by everyone around her including the old high school classmate.

Jessica said that an abortion decision for her would be an easy one and that would be for the baby to live. She went on to tell people including this woman that her college classmate had had an abortion and it had been a traumatic experience not only for her roommate, but for Jessica as well. But, Jessica told people that she respected her friend's right to choose to have an abortion, and trusted that she made the right decision.

While Jessica remembered that she was letting out a secret that must never be shared lest grave consequences follow, she felt safe because she didn't use a name and this high school acquaintance had no idea with whom she had roomed.

The high school friend's name was Shirley Anderson and she did more than listen. Shirley was strongly anti-abortion. She was also associated with a radical group whose purpose was to harass women who've had or were considering an abortion. Doctors and clinics supporting abortion were also subject to her harassment practices. With Jessica's statement, Shirley found a mission.

Putting two and two together, the next morning Shirley contacted the housing office at EMU and requested the name of Jessica Williams' roommate in 1979. She said she was doing some reunion work and the information was very important to her research.

The office clerk came back on the phone after a minute and gave her the name of Mary Chandler. The clerk told Shirley that Miss Chandler lived in Ludington at the time of enrollment at EMU. Armed with this information, Shirley went to Ludington and looked up addresses for the name Chandler. She noted the information, asked for directions and drove to where she thought Mary might live. She sat in her car and watched the house. A woman pulled up and parked in the driveway. Shirley believed her to be a sister or a relative and so she approached and said with anger, "Mary Chandler killed a baby and will go to hell for her sins!"

The woman was taken aback by the words and emotions of this stranger. "What are you talking about?"

"Mary Chandler had an abortion at EMU! She'll pay the price of hell for her murder!" Shirley said, with much anger and almost uncontrollable rage.

The woman was Joy, Mary's sister. She didn't know what to make of this emotional outburst. While not particularly close to her sister, there was a family bond that caused her to come to Mary's defense and demand that the stranger immediately leave and never return. Shaking in anger, Shirley turned and walked swiftly to her car and drove off feeling that her actions were justified.

Joy knew the episode couldn't be shared with her father. His health was such that his heart couldn't take this news. Plus, for all Joy knew, the information was false and there had been some terrible mistake. Joy did feel a need to tell Mary what she had learned. She wrote her a note. It read,

Dear Mary,
Something happened this afternoon that was very disturbing. A woman approached me and perhaps she thought I was you. She said that you had had an abortion and would go to hell for murdering an innocent baby. I told her to immediately leave and never to come back.

I do not even know if this is true. If it is, I wish you would have felt comfortable sharing it with me as I would have been a supportive sister. Your decision not to share it is also respected. I'm sorry that we have not been closer over the years. I thought you would want to know of this upsetting incident.

Love, Joy

When Mary received the note, she knew that Jessica had told someone. It was the only way the word would have gotten out. She didn't need to know who she told, Mary only needed to know that the word was out. In addition, Joy knew and she would surely tell their father who would predictably disown Mary and immediately rewrite his multimillion dollar will and estate.

Mary immediately contacted Jessica and let her know that the word was out and that if she recalled correctly, the price to pay for sharing this secret would be disastrous. Jessica didn't try to defend herself, because it was true, she did say her roommate had had an abortion and she couldn't deny that. The consequence would be forthcoming and this very moment was the manifestation of Mary's promise.

CHAPTER FIVE

Monday Evening, June 3
Bois Blanc Island

Jessica's parents, Ed and Clara Williams decided to go to Bob-Lo. Before taking off, Ed had called Gavin and told him that he and Clara were coming over and asked him to meet them at the Bob-Lo airfield.

The Williams touched down and taxied up to the small cabin by the airstrip. Ed shut off the engines and they both exited the single-engine Cessna. Gavin was waiting for them. He gave each a hug and expressed his sincere hope that Jessica would soon be found. The Williams appreciated Gavin's kind remarks, and taking their small suitcase, walked to his Jeep.

As they drove to the McRae home, Gavin briefed them about what he knew. "All I can tell you is that Lou Searing and Maggie McMillan are working on finding Jessica. We've heard nothing from the Coast Guard, the Island Police, or the Mackinac County Sheriff's Office."

"We sure do appreciate all that you're doing," Clara Williams said sincerely.

"Well, we're not doing much. We're housing Mr. Searing and Mrs. McMillan and trying to be helpful while staying out of the way.

They don't have anything to go on, either. They're good, so I'm sure Jessica will be found."

Maggie and I were in the McRae home when the three entered. Introductions were made and once people were comfortably seated, Maggie and I began our questioning of Mr. and Mrs. Williams, hoping to hear something that would give us a clue to Jessica's disappearance. I told them what they feared the most. "I don't mean to alarm you further, but the fact that we've not heard from Jessica and there has been no word from any abductor like a ransom note or a threat, lead Maggie and me to think the worst. As you know, she may be okay, but from what I've learned about your daughter, she's very conscientious and mature, and if safe, would have informed you or Gavin of her whereabouts."

"Yes, Jessica would certainly tell someone where she would be," Ed responded.

It was at this time that Clara gave us an important clue. "Jessica simply couldn't keep a secret. I was always afraid it might get her into trouble someday."

"What do you mean?" I asked.

"It seemed that if you told Jessie, 'Now this is just between you and me,' it was a reason for her to go and tell someone."

"And you think this weakness relates to her being missing?"

"Oh, I'm sure of it. Jessica probably found herself in possession of someone's deep, dark secret, and as I told you, she couldn't keep things to herself, so she undoubtedly told someone else. As much as I hate to think of her being in trouble, that may be the reason for her disappearance."

"Who would confide in Jessica?" Maggie asked.

"Jessie was a good listener and lots of people confided in her. She seemed to delight in sharing what nobody else knew. I cautioned her many times to keep the secrets to herself because that's what a good friend would expect."

"I understand, Mrs. Williams, but do you know someone who may have shared something with Jessica that would be so sensitive that the person would want to harm her?" I asked.

"In the last few years, I haven't known her friends, but there is an older man that she sees on occasion. I don't know his last name, but Mike is his first name. Very nice-looking man."

"Mike Miles of Lapeer," I said.

"Yes, that's him. She often tells us about him and that she enjoys being with him. They share an interest in helping people who are blind."

"Did she ever tell you any secret that Mike asked her not to share?" Maggie asked.

"Only one that I recall. She was visiting us a few months ago and she said that Mike had told her that he had seen a man die several years ago. He had been able to keep this from the police and as far as he knew, no one suspected the death had a witness. She said that if the authorities were to find out that Mike was a witness he would have to defend himself and he was certain that he'd be charged with murder."

"Is that all she told you?" Maggie asked.

"Yes. He must have known he took a big risk in telling her, but he couldn't have chosen a worse person to tell a secret to."

"Have you told anyone else about this, Mrs. Williams?"

"No, unlike Jessica, I can keep things to myself. This is the first I've said a word. I never even mentioned it to Ed. Right, dear?" Ed nodded while looking down at the floor. "I'm only telling you to help find my daughter."

"Did Jessica tell you that she had, or was going to tell anyone else?" I asked.

"No. I mean, I don't know. She didn't tell me she was going to tell anyone else."

"Did she say anything more about this death involving Mike?" Maggie asked.

"I can still see her standing in the kitchen saying, 'Mom, you can't tell another soul about this. I know I shouldn't have even told you, but I can't help it. The authorities on Bob-Lo must never learn of this.'"

"Bob-Lo? This island, Bois Blanc?" Maggie asked.

"Yes."

"The murder happened on this island?" I asked, not certain I understood her response.

"That's what I remember her saying. Also, she never said he murdered anyone. He witnessed a death."

I turned to Gavin. "There's been a murder up here?"

"Not that I know about, Lou. Remember we're gone all winter, but I think the rumor mill is healthy enough that Jenny or I would have heard about it."

"Can you link me up with someone who would know for sure?" I asked.

"Oh, sure, that would be Gerry White, the Mackinac County deputy sheriff. He lives on the Island."

"Well, we need to talk with him and soon."

"Not a problem. I'll get him on the line."

Gavin called and asked to speak to Deputy White.

"He's not here, Gavin. He went down to Detroit. He'll be gone all week," Mrs. White explained.

"OK. I assume we contact the sheriff's office in St. Ignace if we need anything?"

"Right. Gerry calls each day to keep in touch, but he won't be here until next Saturday."

∿

Jenny McRae knew Curt who had published the *Bob-Lo Bugle* in the mid-nineties. Curt VanVorhees kept every copy of the paper. The name of the paper was changed to the *Bob-Lo Tattler* in 1997 when Bunker Clark became the editor. "Bunker is the current editor, but if you want some information from the past, you need to talk to Curt. If something happened on Bob-Lo several years ago, and it was in the *Bugle*, Curt will know about it."

"Maybe first thing in the morning, we could talk with Curt?" I asked.

"Why wait 'til morning?" Gavin questioned. "We can see him tonight if he's home. He won't mind."

"Fine with me," I replied.

Suddenly Jenny McRae realized that she now had five guests in her home. Jenny called Jacquilyne, Wag's wife, and asked if Ed and Clara Williams could stay with them since Maggie occupied their guest room. Jacquilyne said that would be no problem and since the two men were pilots, they would have much in common.

Jenny had a freezer full of food so feeding people wasn't a problem. Everyone volunteered to help and the kitchen became quite a busy place. My specialty was setting the table. Carol assured everyone that my skills in food preparation were limited to a bowl of All-Bran, a glass of juice, and a piece of buttered toast.

Jenny set about making spaghetti which seemed an easy meal for a crowd. Carol gathered ingredients for a tossed salad and Clara spread garlic butter on French bread to be broiled to a golden brown. So that Wags and Jacquilyne could meet and get to know the Williams a bit before housing them for the night, they were invited to dinner. Jacquilyne brought a chocolate cake that satisfied everyone's taste for a sweet treat.

The dinner conversation centered around Gavin's stories about the island. This took the crisis off the minds of Ed and Clara and gave others an entertaining half hour or so.

Praise was offered to the cooks and the dinner dishes were rinsed and put in the dishwasher. The men set about cleaning up which accounted for their contribution to the group meal. As it was approaching seven-thirty, we decided to head to Curt's. He had a ramp to the front door so Maggie went along.

I opened the conversation. "Curt, we're curious. Have there been any murders on this island in the last several years?"

Curt lowered his head as he thought. Several seconds later he raised his head and said, "Well, there was the guy from Ann Arbor who was shot deer hunting ten years ago but I think everybody concluded that it was an accident. Then there was the plane crash twelve years ago. Remember, Gavin? The plane didn't clear the pines at the south end of the runway. There was a lot of talk that someone may have done something to that plane so it wouldn't lift. The pilot was not liked up here. But, I don't think that was murder. Nobody ever claimed he was murdered and the family never demanded an investigation. Those are the only two deaths that come to mind that involved people dying in some tragic way."

"This death would have involved a guy about five years ago," I added.

"Oh, there was a young man up here with a friend. The friend was missing, but I don't think there was a murder. There was an article about that. Remember, Jenny? Front page."

"Well, now that you bring it up, I guess I recall something, but details elude me," Jenny said, trying to recall the news item.

Curt was going through a stack of papers, "Here it is. Lower right corner of the front page. Headline, 'Hunter Missing.' The article goes on to report that a man by the name of Gerald Zimmer was visiting the island with a friend, Mike Miles, of Lapeer, when Mike reported that his friend went out hunting and never returned. There was never a trace of him. This is crazy because as all of us know if you walk a straight line you have to come to a road, a beach, or a power line. Don't get me wrong, people get lost on the island but we all joke about it thinking he'll show up when his gin runs out or we'll make some smart aleck comment about 'we'd get lost if we was married to his wife'- you know, things like that. In reality, anybody who gets lost on this island owes some rent on the upstairs. Know what I mean?"

"Nobody saw hide nor hair of this guy?" I asked.

"Guess not; Curt Plaunt didn't recall taking him back to the mainland. No body was ever found."

"Strange," Maggie said.

"I don't know what may have been investigated down in the Lapeer area, but no one ever came up here looking into the disappearance, or I would've known about it," Curt noted.

"There are disappearances that don't get solved for decades," I said. "Some folks up and leave whether they commit a crime or not. They simply drop off the earth. My great-grandfather Searing was like that or so the story goes. Apparently he simply packed his grip and was gone. Nobody ever heard of him again and once he left, very little was ever said about him or at least that's what I was told."

"Does it say where Mike and this Gerald were staying at the time?" Maggie asked.

"Nope. I guess they rented a cabin somewhere."

I asked Curt if he had a copier and would be willing to make me a copy of the news article.

When he handed it to me, I noticed that the article was written in the fall of 1995.

⤳

It was 10 o'clock and time for Mike to let Jessica go to the bathroom. He untied her hands and feet from the bed. Almost sympathetically he helped her to her feet. She slowly walked into the bathroom and closed the door behind her. In the tool box was a small glass cutter. She cut the glass out of the window and snapped the pane in two. Whenever she thought she'd make some noise, she'd flush the toilet to mask out the noise. She then lined the window with the shower curtain so as not to cut herself with the glass.

She wrote a note and passed it under the door. It read, "Need more time, got the runs." She then lifted the tank top and lifted the ball so the sound of running water would be continuous and once more mask any sound of her escape.

She heard, "OK, but hurry it up." She then pulled herself up and headfirst tried to put her body through the window, but she simply couldn't get there. She needed another inch or two for her shoulders and hips to clear.

Mike's verbal command, "Come on, get a move on," fell on deaf ears. A few seconds later he knocked on the door and shouted, "I said, let's get going!!" Mike put his ear up to the door and he could hear running water. A third time he shouted, "Get out here!" Again, no response.

Mike opened the door and saw that Jessica was about to escape. Grabbing her around the waist, he pulled her to him. He shook her by the shoulders and forcefully returned her to the bed where he once again tied her hands and feet to the bedposts. He went into the living room to report this sudden change of events. "Jessica almost escaped out of the bathroom window!"

"How could that happen?"

"She knocked out the window and used the shower curtain to keep from getting cut."

"That's the last straw. We can't take any more chances. Mike, you take this knife and kill her and we'll bury her out back and leave this Island in the morning."

"Mary, I don't think it...."

"Stop right there, Mike. No excuses, go in and kill her. Right now!" Mary shouted like a mother angry with her son for not obeying some directive.

Mike took the knife and walked into the bedroom. Jessica was lying on the bed. She looked up at Mike and in her face could be seen both panic and pleading. Mike stood there and realized that he couldn't attack and kill Jessica. He returned to Mary.

"I know you want her dead, but having this cabin bedroom spattered with blood isn't wise. It's obvious that you are renting this cabin. Not me, mind you, but you. A missing woman's blood all over the floor and bedding is your one-way ticket to prison for life. I'll kill her if that's really what you want me to do, but once again, emotions are clouding your common sense. Even killing her outside is still going to leave evidence of her death and any prosecuting attorney will easily convince a jury of your guilt. Think about it."

Mary thought for a few seconds. "This time, you're right, Mike. We'll hold off till tomorrow."

Jessica knew that she had been given a gift. When she saw Mike standing there in her room, his right hand wrapped around a kitchen knife, she was sure her time was up. When he didn't go through with it, hope once again flickered in her mind. Jessica had a flashback as to why Mike was working with Mary to plot her death. Mike applied for a job and used Jessica as a reference. She had known Mike as an advocate for people who are blind for about ten years. She knew he was sincere in his advocacy, had leadership skills, and quite frankly would be an excellent candidate for the job. She wrote a wonderful letter and sent a copy to Mike. Mike was appreciative and even sent a bouquet of flowers to Jessica as a thank you. The letter ended with 'If you wish to discuss my letter in greater detail, please do not hesitate to contact me.'

At a conference where Mike and Jessica were both present, Mike saw Jessica talking with the potential employer. From across the room he noted the two in serious discussion. The prospective employer said, "Jessica. You know Mike pretty well. Are there any skeletons in the closet with this guy? I don't need to hire him and then find he has a drug problem, a drinking problem, or has some problem that will be embarrassing to us. In confidence, is there anything in this guy's past that I need to know?"

"Well, there's one thing. I don't think it would interfere with his leadership, but at some point I suppose it could be an embarrassment to your agency. Mike was involved in a strange death on Bois Blanc Island up in the Straits. There were no charges and I don't think he murdered anybody, but if the body is ever found, he'd probably get accused of murder and he wouldn't be able to convince a jury that he was innocent."

When the prospective employer heard this, he shook his head, looked up and raised his arms and said, "That does it. I can't hire anybody with that albatross hanging around his neck."

"I know, and I feel terrible for telling you, but you said 'in confidence' and since you're a good friend, I felt I had to tell you."

"I appreciate it, Jessica. Yes, no one will know that you told me, but I won't offer him the job."

Mike didn't get the job when he was clearly the best candidate. He recalled the scene between Jessica and the potential employer and immediately concluded that Jessica had told his secret.

After receiving the call that the job had gone to another candidate far less qualified than he, Mike called Jessica and told her of his observation. Jessica vividly recalled the conversation. "I didn't get that job I had my heart set on."

"Oh, I'm sorry, Mike. You'd have been perfect for that job."

"I saw you talking to that guy, Jessica. You said something and then he put his arms up, shook his head and well, I think you told him my secret."

"Mike, I answered his questions, but I wouldn't do anything to keep you from getting that job. I care too much for you, you know that."

"I don't believe you, Jess. I didn't get the job because you told him I might be suspected of murder down the road."

"Mike, I ..." The phone went dead. The two eventually seemed to put this behind them and began seeing each other again, but Jessica knew that Mike would never forget her betrayal.

Jessica knew that the two people who asked her to keep a secret were in control of her life now. They were about to kill her and bury their secrets on Bob-Lo.

CHAPTER SIX

Tuesday Morning, June 4
Bois Blanc Island

W e were finishing a scrambled eggs and bacon breakfast when my cell phone rang. It was Tony Adams. "Good morning, Tony."

"I just got off the phone with a deputy sheriff in St. Ignace. He gave me some information I thought you should have."

"Thanks. What have you got?"

"Well, they got a call from Tom Wilson at the transfer station on Bob-Lo. Seems Tom saw the outline of a purse in one of the bags of trash. He opened the purse and saw that it belonged to a Jessica Williams. Her address was in Traverse City. The deputy was going to send it over to me, but I told him you'd stop by to get it. There may be a clue for you."

"Very interesting, Tony. Guess that places Jessica on this island or at least someone who's been with her since late last Saturday night."

"While you're on the line, Tony, what can you tell me about the disappearance of a hunter five years ago? Did you folks get involved in any way?"

"I don't know anything about a disappearance. I'm long off this island by deer hunting season, Lou. You'd have to ask Deputy White about that."

"OK, will do. Listen, did you check with the Lapeer Police and the Traverse City Police to see if either Jessica or Mike have appeared at their residences?"

"Yeah, we did and there's been no activity around their homes or apartments. I would have contacted you otherwise, Lou."

"I know, just a thought and I wanted to ask you about it."

"I'll tell you anything I learn, Lou."

"Thanks. We'll be in touch, Tony. Are you planning any activity concerning Jessica?"

"No, I guess not. We've still got her as missing. We haven't heard anything that would cause us to go any further with the investigation. From this point on it is with the county sheriff and the Coast Guard."

"Thanks for the heads up, Tony."

"OK, Lou. Let me know if I can help."

I hung up and called everyone together in the McRae living room. "That was Tony Adams from Mackinac Island. Jessica's purse was found in a bag of trash down at the Transfer Station. The worker there, Tom Wilson, saw the outline of a purse in a garbage bag. I've got to get to the transfer station to pick it up."

Maggie spoke up. "Great tip. She's on this island. And, her kidnappers are on the island as well."

"I agree, Maggie."

Carol said, "They may not be on the island now, but they sure were on this island some time between late Saturday night and now."

"I think we can only assume that Jessica, Mike, and their captors are on this island as we speak," Maggie said emphatically. "It won't be easy, but we need to flush 'em out."

"I agree, but we need to be very cautious. If Jessica is still alive, we don't need to give them reason to panic and kill her."

"Yes, and I think we need to be in touch with the county sheriff," Maggie suggested. "They have jurisdiction for this island. With Deputy White gone all week, we need to be coordinating our work with someone in law enforcement."

"That's right. We may need search warrants and we may need an arrest. We can do the investigating but at some point we're not empowered to take the case to its final stages," I added.

Ed Williams offered to fly me to St. Ignace so I could talk with whomever would be assigned to the case. I called the sheriff's office and asked to speak to the sheriff or to a deputy who would be responsible for Bob-Lo Island in Deputy White's absence. The sheriff told me that Deputy Lyn Largent would be handling any investigation on Bob-Lo. I asked to speak to him. A minute later he came on the line.

"Deputy Largent. This is Lou Searing."

"Yes, Lou. The sheriff took a few seconds to brief me. What can I do to help you?"

"My partner and I are looking into the disappearance of Jessica Williams and Mike Miles."

"Missing from Mackinac Island, correct?"

"You know about Jessica's purse being found over here, right?" I asked.

"Yes, the sheriff has alerted me to that."

"We think they may be here on Bob-Lo."

"I would agree since the purse was found there."

"My purpose in contacting you is to touch base, let you know we are looking into their disappearance and are willing to share what we know about the case. We may need some help that only you can provide."

"The sheriff assigned the case to me until Deputy White returns. If there is a lead over on the island, I'll be glad to look into it and your help is welcome."

"Thank you. If you need any land transportation when you get here, we can help with that."

"My parents have a place on Bob-Lo so I am quite familiar with the island. I'll contact you if I need any help."

"Let me give you my phone number so you can contact me if you need to. It is area code 616 and the number is 555-8763."

"Got it, Lou. We'll be in touch, I'm sure."

"Yes, we will. Thank you, Deputy."

I put my phone in my pocket and told Maggie about the contact. I let Maggie know that I liked him and thought we'd make a good team.

Gavin offered me the use of his Harley for the trip to the transfer station. With some adjustments here and there, the bike was purring like a kitten; actually, it made enough noise to drown out a rock concert. I thoroughly enjoyed the ride to the transfer station which is located by the main dock, about a dozen miles from the McRae's.

I met Tom and said, "I understand you've got a purse for me."

"Yeah, the deputy said you could use it. You must be a detective or something?"

"I dabble in solving crimes," I said as I put a pair of latex gloves on. I didn't want to add any fingerprints to the purse.

"I recognized the name in the purse as the same name as the lady missing a couple days ago in the Straits."

"Well, I'm glad you found this."

"Sure, hope it helps. I called the number in the purse but only got a message to leave a message. I said I had her purse. That's before I realized the name was the same as the lady who was missing."

"Did you keep the trash bag where this was found?"

"Naw, sent it on over to Cheboygan. It was just trash."

"I'm curious where it came from."

"Somebody left it outside of the fence. Those folks are polluters. We go through their trash looking for an ID and if we find any, the deputy fines 'em. That's how I found that lady's purse. I didn't find anything else. It could have come from one of the boats docked not far from here, but I can't be sure."

"Thanks. I appreciate your help. You may have discovered a major clue and you certainly may have helped us in finding Jessica." I carefully placed the purse in a plastic container.

I decided to stop in at Hawk's Landing for a cup of coffee. While there, I saw Gavin talking to someone. Gavin said, "Professor Heckstall, meet Lou Searing. Lou's spending the week with us. Professor Heckstall teaches at MSU."

Doc Heckstall was a tall, distinguished-looking gentleman.

"I know Lou. I saw his name on a faculty mailbox a semester or two ago."

I quickly tried to recognize his name, but nothing came to mind. I taught a class or two for MSU after retiring, but thought I was clearly an unknown. "I'm sorry, I didn't recognize you, Professor."

"Oh, I wouldn't expect you to, Lou. Too many of us for everyone to know each other."

"So, you come up here every summer?" I asked.

"My wife, Annie and I have been doing that for about twenty years now. For us, it's a sanctuary from the stresses and strains of the work-a-day world."

"This is sure a good place for that."

"Well, I've got to get the *Free Press* home to my wife. Nice seeing you, Gavin, and good to meet you, Lou."

"The pleasure's mine."

Just as we were about to head to the west end, out of the blue, Gavin said, "Did I hear Maggie say you had an interest in magic?"

"Yeah, that's right. I've always been fascinated by the sleight of hand."

"I agree, it's fun to watch."

"I taught a doctoral course at Michigan State a year ago and one of my students was a magician. He did private gigs and worked a sports bar in DeWitt. Carol and I went to see him perform and he was terrific. He was a natural with kids. He did some tricks that evening that I didn't get. I mean I didn't have a clue as to how he could do it."

"What's his name?"

"Grayson, Gary Grayson. Yeah, he'd always have a trick of some sort with him."

"You're not going to believe what I'm about to tell you."

"I've believed you so far. What have you got?"

"Well, Gary Grayson performs at Barb's Tavern here on the island. I mean it could be a different Grayson, but I doubt it. He is a friend of Doc Heckstall. He's up here this summer to get away from it all and to use this isolated place to pour all of his attention into his dissertation."

"Let's go find him," I said enthusiastically. "It'd be great seeing Gary again. He's an interesting guy.

As we headed out to the parking lot, Gavin said, "Gary's staying with Doc Heckstall, not too far from here. Gary entertains when he feels like it and the tip money goes to Doc and Annie for room and board. Gary is getting quite a reputation on the island. In fact, he's about the only live entertainment we've got. Gary's show is fun and folks are almost needing to get there a half-hour before show time to get a seat. Kids love the guy."

"Yeah, I can imagine. As I said, he's good with kids and he puts on a great show."

"I'll drive and save you some dirt in your hair," Gavin said. I accepted and within a minute or two Gavin pulled in the drive. Doc Heckstall was surprised to see us at his door. Gavin told him about my knowing Gary and asked if he was in. Doc said that Gary was in his room, probably studying or maybe napping. He said he'd get him. A few minutes later Gary appeared, wide awake and wearing an MSU T-shirt and shorts. I shook his hand and he was as surprised to see me as I was to see him.

"Well, Doctor Searing. Good to see you. You up here writing a mystery or investigating one?" Gary asked with a smile.

"Of those choices, investigating one."

"Murder on Bob-Lo? That's rare."

"Well, I don't know if there was a murder. I don't know if it happened on this Island, but a series of events has Maggie and me looking into a disappearance of a woman and her escort. They were attending a party in the Grand Hotel last Saturday night."

"Are you two close to putting on the handcuffs?"

"The pieces are coming together, but no, we haven't a clue at this moment as to who did it, or if in fact, a murder was committed."

"You'll get to the bottom of it. Is Carol with you?"

"Yes, and oh, I apologize, this is Gavin McRae. Gavin, Gary Grayson." Both men greeted one another with firm handshakes. "To answer your question, Yes, Carol is with me and so is Maggie. I was on Mackinac Island for the big special education ball Saturday evening and heard that a couple was missing. So, I began looking into it. The missing woman, Jessica Williams, was renting one of Gavin's A-frames here on the island. He brought me over here to look around. Maggie will probably hit on the clue that will get it solved. She usually figures it out or comes pretty close, as you know."

"Yeah, you two make a good team."

"Thanks. So, Gavin tells me you are the Island's summer hit."

"I'm having fun. It's basically the same show you and Carol saw in DeWitt, but since folks keep coming back with their kids or visitors from the mainland, I try to add a different trick now and then."

"I'll bring Carol and Maggie and we'll cheer you on, if we can get in. I hear you're quite popular."

"I'll see that you get a seat. I might have to hide you in the box with the rabbit, but I'll see that you get a good seat."

"Do me a favor, Gary. When we're there, do that trick where you read the minds of the people and put their answers in the three squares on your board. I'm amazed at that one."

"Not a problem. That one's in every show."

"Great. Even the great Maggie McMillan won't figure that one out."

"Before you go, Lou, tell me a little more about this case."

"Not much to tell, Gary. Jessica and Mike accepted an invitation to go for a late-night cruise on a yacht named the *Slinky*. They went out, didn't come back. My family was threatened if I got involved, which only served to encourage me to solve this thing. But, whoever is involved, threatened harm to Carol and threatened Maggie, so we're being very cautious, but we're challenged and we'll figure it out."

"I'm sure you will," Gary said confidently. "Doc and Annie have been kind to me. I can peacefully work on my dissertation and I'm not tempted by the outside world like I would be down in East Lansing. But, I miss playing golf!"

"Yeah, I haven't seen any signs to a golf course on this island."

"No, and you won't, either."

"Sounds like a perfect arrangement for you, Gary. We'll be on our way. When's your next show?"

"Tonight around nine o'clock. It doesn't start at a specific time. I appear, talk to some folks and then the show evolves. It'll be great having you, Carol, and Maggie at the show. I'll try to come up with a trick you haven't seen."

I shook Gary's hand and told him I hoped we'd be at his show and the only reason we wouldn't be there would be if something popped on the case. Gavin drove me back to the Harley in the parking lot of Hawk's Landing and I returned to the west end. I led the way so I wouldn't have to eat dust for about ten miles.

⤳

After lunch, Maggie and I sat on the porch and I began to brief her on what I'd learned in town. Our attention was drawn to Carol standing on the shore practicing Tai Chi, a traditional Chinese martial art distinguished by graceful, flowing movements. Carol has been taking lessons and enjoying this activity for six years. She seemed to be one with nature. Her graceful movements seemed to mimic the wind moving through the trees, the slow moving waves coming to shore, and the rhythmic flapping of seagull wings over the Straits. I took in the magnificence of the moment. I recognized "white crane spreads its wings" and "wave hands like clouds", two movements in the short form. It may have been exercise for her, but the scene was peaceful. It will be difficult from now on to look out toward the Straits and not imagine Carol gracefully moving with wind, waves, clouds, and birds. When she finished, Maggie and I gave Carol an unexpected round of applause.

My attention went from Carol's graceful movements to the case. "I can't seem to make sense of all of this, Maggie."

"Information is all over the place, Lou. It isn't focused on a person, a place, or a situation. You often compare our investigations to puzzles and putting the pieces together until we see the whole picture and it makes sense and is as clear as a bell. Well, we have lots of pieces here and there, but we can't get any pieces that bridge the sections together."

"Yeah, it's frustrating, Maggie. I want this thing finished. I want to get back to Grand Haven. What are your thoughts at this point?"

"I think Jessica and Mike are dead, murdered. We have no bodies and we've no evidence to expect that they're alive or dead for that matter. But, I think they're dead. Who did it? We don't have anything that points to anyone. A kidnapper would kill soon after capturing the victim or victims. No murderer would want to take their time waiting to kill. It's been a few days. So, what do I think? I think they were taken against their will and killed."

"So you think Mike is a victim?" I asked.

"I think so. What do you think, Lou?"

"I don't think Mike is a victim. He very well could be involved in kidnapping Jessica. I agree, it makes no sense to wait to kill, so I agree that Jessica is dead, but Mike could be the killer. Only a hunch, but I feel it."

"Yeah, I can agree with that."

"We'll get a break. We always do. How about a magic show tonight, Maggie?"

"A magic show? On this island?"

"Yeah, this morning I met an MSU doctoral student I had in class a year ago. He's a great magician. He's up here staying with a professor and his wife. He earns his room and board from tips following his magic shows at the tavern. He's really good. How about if we get out of this house for a few hours and see a good show?"

"Is it accessible?" Maggie asked.

"Oh, I doubt it. But, we'll get you in there. What do you say?"

"Sure, I'm game. I like magic. Are the McRaes going with us?"

"I'll suggest it."

I did, and the Williams wanted to go as well. We all decided to head to the tavern about eight so we would beat the crowd.

$\backsim$

Erin called me to report that she was heading home. "I think I'll leave the island, Lou. The people in the organization for the blind have left, and I've done all I can do to help you."

"Thanks a lot, Erin. You've been a big help and we appreciate it."

"Lou, a strange thing happened. You need to know about it because it might help you and Maggie solve this case."

"What happened?"

"As I was walking to Shepler's dock to catch the four o'clock boat to Mackinaw City, a man approached me, stepped in front of me and said something like, 'Are you the one looking into the disappearance of that beautiful lady the other night?'

"I was taken aback mainly because I was startled. I stepped back, looked at the stranger and said, 'Yes, I've been curious and asking around. Why?'

"He said, 'Cause I know where she's at.'

"'Really?' I said. 'Where is she?'

"'She's on Bob-Lo, over there,' he said, pointing to the land mass to the south of Mackinac Island.

"I didn't recognize the guy so I said, 'Who are you?'"

"'That's not important.'

"'Is she alive or dead?' I asked.

"'She's dead.'

"'You know who killed her?'" I asked.

"'No, but there is magic in solving the murder.'

"'You mean she got sawed in half or stabbed by swords?' I asked.

"'No, I don't mean she was killed in a magic trick, I mean there's magic in solving the murder.'

"I asked him the logical question, is the murderer a magician?

"'No,' he said. "'There's magic in solving the murder.'

"'Who are you and why are you telling me this?'" I asked.

"'I knew you were working on her disappearance and I wanted you to know that my clue to solving it is the magic.'

"Then the guy turned and walked away. I cried out, 'Hey, wait, who are you? How can I contact you if I need to talk with you?'

"The man continued to move quickly and didn't look back. I followed for a few blocks, but I lost him in the Fudgies on Main Street.

"I had a ticket on the Shepler crossing at 4:00 and I wanted to get home, so I got on the boat and crossed to Mackinaw City."

I thanked Erin for the information which made no sense to me, either. Before hanging up, I told her how much I appreciated her help. She threw one great party and was a gem of an assistant on the Island.

༄

It was now about seven-thirty and time to get everyone loaded into Maggie's customized, accessible van for the twelve-mile ride to Barb's Tavern for Gary's show. Maggie inserted the key into her van which activated the lift to lower it to the driveway. She got on for the short, upward ride. When the lift device stopped, she wheeled herself up to the steering wheel, strapped herself in, retracted the lift, and then we all got in for the ride.

"Tell the McRaes about this vehicle, Maggie," I suggested, knowing folks would be curious.

"I needed to be an independent traveller. I learned that Clock Conversions, a company in Grand Rapids, were experts analyzing situations and then converting vans to a person's special needs. And, for me, they did just that."

"That lift picked you right up," Clara said.

"Yes, it's very efficient. I've got a Ricon remote to open the door. The lift is steel, has a non-skid platform and a hydraulic pump that takes me right up and into the vehicle. I love it."

"How do you use the brakes and give it gas?" Gavin asked.

"They installed hand controls. I steer with my left hand and use my right hand to control the brakes and the gas. I don't know if you can see this, but I push forward to brake and I pull back to accelerate. It's very simple, actually. What you do with your right foot, I do with my right hand."

"This technology sure gives you mobility!"

"Yes, it does, but you can see why I need that little extra room at the parking slots for people with disabilities. I couldn't lower the lift and get in and out of this vehicle without that extra few feet."

"Look to the right! See the deer?" I said, interrupting. It was such a beautiful scene of nature that I didn't want folks to miss it.

"They are early evening roamers. Some years they are plentiful.

Other years, you don't see many," Gavin responded.

We arrived at Barb's Tavern and Maggie found they had one handicap accessible slot by the front door. Lucky for us, it was open. We got out and stretched our legs while Maggie lowered herself to the ground. We were all pleasantly surprised to find an accessible ramp leading up to the front door of the tavern. Once inside, we found good seats off to the side but near the front where Gary would perform. Maggie stayed in the back. We often split up in public settings when investigating a case. It's easier to cover for each other.

People began to come in and take their seats. It reminded me of folks out West coming in for a travelling show or the circus. There were no advance tickets, no advertising blitz. It was simply a man in town with an entertaining show. Those who were interested showed up.

The kids were going up to the front of the make-shift stage and sitting cross-legged waiting for Gary to arrive and begin his show. A favorite of the children was Gary's bunny, Buster, who appeared in one of the tricks. The kids loved to pet Buster at the end of the show. He was a big hit.

The kids had plenty to do on the island: hiking, fishing, boating, but having a show to entertain them on evenings was a special treat for all concerned. Sheila, who co-owned Hawk's Landing General Store, and sold Mooney's Ice Cream, was especially indebted to Gary for bringing folks together as she easily sold fifty to sixty cones after every one of Gary's shows.

I got up and got a few baskets of popcorn while Ed ordered a round of drinks. Ed and Clara had come with Wags and Jacquilyne. I looked around and saw that the place was full and this wasn't even a weekend. This was Tuesday night.

"This is a good opportunity for me to use my stand-up wheelchair," Maggie said to Jacquilyne in the back of the tavern and anxious to demonstrate another device to give people with disabilities their independence.

"Your what?" Jacquilyne asked.

"I got a new device to help me stand up when I need to be in that position."

"Really?"

"Yeah, I often take it with me when we do these investigations. I never know when I'm going to need to be able to look in a window, see over a bush, reach up to open a cupboard. Tonight it will give me a good view of the performance and the people attending this show. I also like to see kids having a good time."

"Where did you get it?" Jacquilyne asked.

"A place called the Standing Company in Saginaw. They were as helpful as the folks at Clock Conversions and worked with me. This chair really comes in handy, plus, it is great to look at the world as I once did, from a standing position."

It was time for the show to begin. Barb, the owner of the tavern, walked over to the front of the crowd and looked around for something to get the crowd's attention. She saw a tall glass with a fork beside it. Barb tapped the glass. "Listen up, folks. Listen up!" She had to repeat herself since many of the people were taking this opportunity to talk about everyone and everything.

Finally Barb was able to get everyone's attention. "Once again tonight, on Michigan's Bob-Lo Island, it is my pleasure to welcome you to the magic show of soon-to-be <u>Doctor</u> Gary Grayson." Everyone applauded. "Gary's show has gained quite a reputation on our island. We're happy to host his show and to provide a place for you to grab a bite to eat and enjoy his magic. So, ladies and gentlemen, I'd like you to give a Bob-Lo welcome to the amazing Gary Grayson!" The audience cheered as if a movie star had happened by.

Gary came out and thrilled the audience with a variety of tricks. He didn't have major props with him for the summer, so he didn't do the ever popular guillotine or saw the lady in half trick, traditional with many magicians. But, he did a variety of tricks that were amazing and brought many comments of 'How did he do that?' from the young and old alike.

After a short intermission, something happened that turned the case around. Gary took out his magic board, 3 three-by-five-inch squares, and a piece of chalk. He told everyone, "Now I'm going to attempt to read the mind of someone in the audience. I need a volunteer. Anyone willing to be my assistant for a few minutes?" No one quickly volunteered so Gary looked at Mary. "How about you?"

Mary had strong reservations about being singled out in front of all these people, but with everyone looking at her, she felt refusing to play along would be more suspicious than joining Gary.

Mary stood up and said she'd volunteer. No one in the place recognized her. Usually Gary chose, with Doc Heckstall's help, a prominent island personality so that the audience would chuckle at this person's antics. "What's your name?" Gary asked.

"Mary."

"Mary what?"

"Mary Chandler."

"Nice to meet you, Mary, and thanks for helping me out." Mary smiled and nodded.

"Well, Mary, I'm going to attempt to read your mind, if you don't mind—little play on words folks, could I have a chuckle or two? Come on audience, the humor is weak tonight, but at least give me a few laughs." The children giggled which caused some of the parents behind them to giggle a little too.

"Mary, I'm going to ask you three questions, one at a time. Here are three small envelopes and three pieces of paper and a pen. When you think of your answer, write it down on a piece of paper, put it in one of the envelopes and seal it. Don't blurt out your answer until I have time to concentrate. I'll read your mind, and write down what you're thinking in this square on this board I'm holding. Then I'll clip on this three by five inch cover so no one can see what I wrote and then you'll tell the audience and I'll put your answer directly below mine. Got it?"

"I think so.

"If I say, 'think of a toy,' and, you think of a ball, you write it on a piece of paper and seal it in the envelope and then give me a few seconds to read your mind. If I get something, I'll write down 'ball' and cover it up. You then tell the audience what you were thinking and I'll write it under what I thought you thought."

"I think I got it."

"Well, it might sound a bit complicated, but you'll get the hang of it once we start," Gary said.

"OK, my first question," Gary said, before turning back to the audience. "Let me also explain that I'll use categories where there are a lot of possible answers so you don't think I'm picking some category with a few choices, like think of one of the current living presidents of the United States, for example."

"That'd be Lincoln, right, Magic Man?" Mary replied, to which the audience let out a spontaneous laugh.

"Oh, now you're turning the tables on me, huh, is that it? I invite you up here as an assistant and you're trying to steal the show, get all the laughs, is that it?" Gary asked, once again in total control of his show and garnering hearty laughs.

Jenny McRae took out her camera and took a few photos of the children in the audience. She knew many of them and wanted to give the pictures to their parents as gifts. She also took a photo of our group enjoying Gary's show.

"OK, let's begin. Think of the name of a woman. Now everyone will have to admit that you've got hundreds of choices with this one. Any woman's name and you can choose a name that can be a man's name, too, if you want, like Jan, but don't use that one. OK, got a name?" Mary nodded. "OK, now write it down and seal it in one of the envelopes and then concentrate on that name while I try to pick up what you're thinking."

Gary put the envelope up to his head and closed his eyes as if in deep thought. "OK, I'm getting something and I think I've got it, but I'm not a hundred percent sure. I'll write down in my square what you were thinking." Gary did so and kept his choice hidden from the audience. "OK, Mary, tell the folks what you were thinking and I'll write it down in your square."

"Mary."

"Mary is what I'll write down. You sure went for the obvious. Most folks come up with Camille or Willetta or something to challenge my skills, but using your own name is fine. OK, it's written down in your square."

"The second one is a fun one for Michigan summer folks. You

know how you go into marinas on Mackinac Island, for example, or anywhere along the coast of Michigan and you see the names of boats in big letters on the backs of the boats. There are some real creative names, aren't there?" The audience nodded and smiled. I saw one last week named *Instead of Alimony;* the audience laughed. Or how about *Floating Paradise.* Neat names, huh? Well, Mary, my second category is boat names. So, think of a boat name, write it down, seal it in the envelope, and hold it in your mind. Ready?" Mary nodded.

"OK, hold that thought for a minute while I try and get it." Once again, Gary held the envelope up to his forehead, concentrated and then said, "OK, I've got it, and I'll write my choice down on my square out of view of the audience and cover it up with my second square, like this. Now, tell the audience the name you were thinking of and I'll jot it down."

"Stinky."

"Did you say *Stinky* or Slinky, that toy kids play with?" Gary asked. The kids in the front giggled as did the adults behind them.

"I said *Stinky*. That's the name of my boat."

"OK, got it." Gary wrote her response on the square below his covered answer. "Now it's time for the third question. Since most of magic is a mystery and since most people like to read mysteries, I'm going to ask you to think of a way for a murderer to dispose of a body. You know, like they supposedly threw Jimmy Hoffa's body into concrete. Again, Mary, don't use that one, but think of a way to dispose of the body for my mystery question." Mary closed her eyes as if thinking hard.

"I'm ready," Mary said, while jotting down her choice and sealing it in the third envelope.

"I picked that up easily, Mary; I think I'm going to get this one right. OK, I'll write down what I think you were thinking and cover it up with my last card."

Gary turned back to Mary and said, "OK, now tell the audience what you were thinking."

"I was thinking, bury it."

"OK, I'll write 'bury it' on your square."

Gary held up his six square board to the audience and said, "Now let's see how I did. I want to say at the outset that I usually get all three. I don't mean to be a smart aleck, but I can read the minds of most people. We'll see. OK, the first category was the name of a woman. You said, 'Mary, and I thought you were thinking Jessica,'" Gary lifted the card covering his answer.

The audience booed and shook their heads. Someone shouted, "You're way off!!" I looked at Maggie and our eyes met and locked.

"You sure you weren't thinking of Jessica?" Gary asked. Mary looked shaken and everyone could see that she was surprised.

"No, I was thinking of Mary."

"Humm, I sure got Jessica. Oh, well, the audience is right. I blew it and you win that one. You sure you didn't think of a Jessica for a second when I was trying to read your mind? That's all it takes, is for the word to creep into your mind, and I'll see it."

"Nope. I know a Jessica, but she wasn't who I was thinking about."

"Well, OK, I didn't get that one. The second category was names of boats. You told the audience you were thinking of a boat named *Stinky*, and you said that you were thinking of your boat, right?" Mary nodded.

"OK, let's reveal what I thought you were thinking." Gary took off the cover and he had written, *Slinky*. The audience howled and sustained their laughter for a few seconds.

"Now Mary, you sure you weren't thinking *Slinky* instead of *Stinky*?"

"Nope, I was thinkin' *Stinky*."

"Well, come on folks, one letter here, I didn't see the cross on the 'L'. Give me credit for coming close. Let me have this one, okay?" Half the audience clapped approval and the other half booed.

"OK, I hear you, a tie. Mary gets a half point and I get a half point."

Once again I looked at Maggie. We were obviously reading each other's minds thinking this was all getting too close to reality here.

Gary continued. "Well, this is the worst I've ever done; I'll always have at least one of the first two!!"

"You picked me," Mary said. "It's not my fault you're no good at this." Again the audience laughed. Mary was beginning to enjoy his showmanship and the audience was loving her being on stage.

"Well, let's see if I can salvage this trick, er, mind reading skill that I have," Gary said with a smile. "The third category was a mystery question, what to do with a dead body. Granted there are limited choices I suppose, but let's see if I get this one. Mary said, 'Bury it.' Pretty obvious guess. I'll lift my card and you'll see what I saw in Mary's mind: I saw 'Bury it.' Hey, how about that, I got one!" The audience cheered.

"Now open each envelope and show the audience your three choices." She did so and handed all of the trash to Gary, who said, "Let's have a big hand for Mary. Thank you. Oh, by the way, where you from, Mary? You're not a land owner up here, are you?"

"I'm from Ludington. I'll be leaving soon to go home."

"For helping me, Mary, I'll buy you a cup of coffee for the boat ride off Bob-Lo. Thanks for being a good helper." The audience again clapped for Mary as audiences tend to do for unsuspecting participants who find themselves in front of people.

"You know, sometimes we magicians can read minds and get messages when you string the answers together," Gary said to the audience while Mary took her seat. "I used this trick in a show in Gaylord a few months back and I got all three that time and it was quite emotional. A lady was on stage with me. The three words she was thinking were, Anna, *Sea Lover*, and Overboard. She broke down at the end because she said her grandmother's name was Anna, and she was on a boat named the *Sea Lover* and drowned when she fell overboard out in Lake Michigan. So, with Mary here, she could have been thinking that Mary was on the *Slinky* and was later buried, or what I thought she was thinking, 'Jessica was on the *Stinky* and then buried.' Are we getting close to reality with this, Mary?"

"No way, Magic Man!"

Maggie nodded to me as if to say, "I think she needs to be watched." Others in our party were glancing at each other as they ate popcorn and enjoyed their drinks. I sensed most people in our group would have agreed with me.

I got up from our table and walked to the back of the tavern. I went over to Barb and said, "Great show you've got here. This guy's great. You're lucky he's visiting Bob-Lo."

"Yeah, a couple of loyal customers told me about him and I asked him to perform some magic tricks and well, the rest is history."

"He's fun to watch. You've got a great crowd pleaser with him, that's for sure."

"Thanks."

"Who was that woman up there doing the mind reading trick with your magician?"

"Never saw her before. She doesn't live here. Must be a visitor."

While I was talking to Barb, Gary was winding up his show with his rabbit out of a hat trick. As the show ended, the kids were petting Buster and their parents came up to the front to get their kids and to tell Gary they enjoyed the show. Most would drop a dollar or two into his "Tips for Buster" canister.

I went back to the table and told Gavin to keep an eye on Mary who continued to sit at the table and finish her meal.

As I sat down with a puzzled Maggie, she said, "I don't know what you're thinking, Lou, but Gary was obviously planting stuff for us to pick up on during his show. Mary may be involved in Jessica's disappearance. Now that I see her, I recognize her as someone who came over on the ferry when I did. She had two bags of groceries and seemed nervous. She walked off the ferry, got into a Ford, and went east."

I added, "You know, if Jessica was killed on this island she'd have to be taken somewhere to be murdered and as Mary just told us, 'buried.' To do that, they would need to use a car and if they did use Mary's car, there could be some evidence that Jessica was in the car."

"Absolutely."

While the crowd was breaking up, I wandered up to the area where Gary performed the illusions. I looked around trying to figure out how he did some of his tricks. I glanced down at the table, saw the written choices and opened envelopes from his mind reading act. I picked up a couple and put them in my back pocket. In the meantime, Jenny wandered over to Mary's table.

"You said your boat is the *Stinky*?"

"Yeah, it really belongs to my dad, but I use it most of the summer. It's docked in Cheboygan."

"I see your yacht when we go to Cheboygan. Nice craft."

"Thanks."

Vanessa Redhawk, a long-time island resident, was taking a host of photos on Bob-Lo. She was collecting her best for a pictorial book about the island. She enjoyed taking photos and giving them to people. Vanessa interrupted the conversation between Mary and Jenny and said, "Do you mind if I take a picture of you and the magician as a memento of your visit to our island?"

"Oh, no, I'm not a good person for pictures."

"Oh, please. We need some material for our newsletter and you gave all of us an entertaining evening with Gary."

Mary felt she should go along with the request and reluctantly agreed. "OK, I guess. How do I look?"

"Oh, you look fine. I'll call Gary over!"

Vanessa took a couple of photos of Mary and Gary. She thanked each and went about taking more photos of family groups.

⨯⟶

While Vanessa had been taking photos, I kept an eye on Mary and talked with Gary.

"What was that about?" I asked.

"Well, you were telling me earlier today about Jessica and the boat names and that you were investigating a disappearance or murder, so I thought I'd try a little magic and maybe you'd get a clue to solving this thing."

"So, you chose Mary?"

"I looked throughout the place and recognized many of the people in the audience from other shows. I didn't think Mary was from around here; I checked that out with Doc and Anne who seem to know everyone on this island. I thought if anyone in the tavern might offer a clue, it would be her. I simply tried to draw out of her a few words that may give you some help. If I was wrong, it's still a show and no loss. If she is, by some chance, a part of the drama, then all the better."

"Masterful job, Gary."

"Well, being a magician is being an entertainer. You've got to be good with words and different situations. We're all actors by trade."

"You may have been very helpful."

"You think so?"

"Not sure yet, but Mary said some things that clicked with our investigation."

"I thought she did too."

"Is Buster adjusting to life on Bob-Lo?"

"He adjusts wherever he finds carrots, lettuce or cabbage. If his daily food is available, he can adjust to the moon if need be. Yeah, he's doing fine. And, I'm doing great too. The quiet here is helping me concentrate on this dissertation. MSU should have a retreat center on Bob-Lo. It would be good for students' mental health."

"I think the doctoral degree rat race is part of the test. If you can survive the rat race, the stress, the bombardment of responsibility, the pressure to pass courses, get something published, keep up-to-date with research, work on the dissertation, supervise student teachers, then you can survive, and you win. You get the three letters after your name and the chance to spend the rest of your life trying to realize how unimportant it all is. If you don't make it, you only have to live with the unfortunate feeling of failure or the inability to follow through on goals. You're smothered either way you look at it. Well, forgive this old graduate student for getting on his soapbox."

"Hey, no problem, Dr. Searing. It's good to know someone who survived."

"Gary, it might look like I survived, but it's an illusion. If I could do it over, I might have remained a teacher in the classroom and stayed where I could've made a difference in children's lives. Don't ever forget, education is about children and helping them in a variety of ways."

"I don't think I will."

"I agree, Gary. I have a feeling that you'll keep your perspective, and, even if you get out of the classroom, you'll stay in touch with children. You're so good with them. I can tell by the way you work your magic shows. My guess is that if I saw you in the classroom, you'd be a natural."

"Thanks, Lou. I appreciate your comments."

During this rather serious discussion with Gary, I almost forgot to keep my eye on Mary. I glanced in her direction and saw that she was still in the tavern. I knew that I had a good opportunity to try and find out where she was staying.

ॐ

I knew that we couldn't follow Mary, but I did want to get her car identified, have someone follow her out of the tavern parking lot, and get as close to her destination as possible.

As it happened, Jackee and John Miller were at the magic show too. We talked for a few minutes and I said to Jackee, "Can you help me with the investigation?"

"Will it get me in your next book?"

"Sure will. I can't assure that you'll get the part when Hollywood picks it up, but you'll get in the book," I said with a chuckle.

"What do you need?"

"I need you to follow a woman when she leaves. I want you to track her to the point where continuing to follow her would be suspicious."

"What does that mean?"

"That means don't go down any driveway. Stay a safe distance behind on the main road and simply note which road she takes off the main road."

"That's all?"

"That's all. We need to know where she's staying, but I don't want her to think that someone is suspicious of her."

"For this I get in your next book—following a woman down a road?"

"Yes, indeed. See that woman over there by the bar, the one who was in the magic show? That's who I want you to follow."

"Will do. I assume I call you at the McRae's when we get home?"

"Please. For your sake, I hope she doesn't stay here till closing."

"Looks like she is asking for her bill," Jackee said. "She should be leaving soon."

"Thanks, Jackee. Don't make your departure obvious, just act like you're leaving and stay a reasonable distance behind her."

I stepped outside where a few of the folks were smoking cigarettes. When I got into Maggie's van, I called the Mackinac Island Police Department hoping to find Tony on duty.

"Mackinac Island Police, Adams speaking."

"Hi, Tony, Lou Searing here."

"Hi, Lou. What's up?"

"I need a favor. First of all, does your office have jurisdiction in this Jessica and Mike case?"

"Ah, not clear. She was last seen on our Island and we've no indication that she has turned up elsewhere. Why do you ask?"

"Well, I need an immediate analysis done by the State Police Forensic Lab in Grayling or in East Lansing. Can you request it for me?"

"Just call Jeff Horner and tell him what you need. Tell him you talked to me and he'll stop on a dime to help you. That's the kind of guy he is."

"OK, will do. Thanks. I recognize Jeff's name from a previous case I worked on. Any new information?"

"Nothing since the guy found her purse."

"Thanks, Tony. I'll be in touch."

I hung up, got out of the van and walked over to Ed Williams who was about to leave with Wags and Jacquilyne. "I'd like you to fly some material downstate in the morning."

"Not a problem. What do you need?"

"I need you to put down in Grayling. A man named Jeff Horner will be there to take an envelope from you. He'll be from the State Police Forensic Lab. I want you to give him Jessica's purse and some paper and envelopes that are central to this case."

"Sure. Let him know that my plane is a Cessna, NA6263. My guess is I'll be there about ten o'clock."

"Good. I'll see that you get the purse and papers yet tonight. Thanks, Ed."

"Anything to help you find our Jessica."

⌁

As Mary was about to leave the tavern, she was puzzled over the events of the evening. *Was it coincidence that she was singled out to work with the magician? Why did the magician know the name, Jessica? Why did he know the name Slinky? Why did the woman want her picture taken?* These thoughts went through her mind. She knew she had taken a chance in even going to the bar. When the place suddenly filled up and the show began she had gotten caught up in the evening's fun. But, she was beginning to feel sure something was up. If it was—Searing and McMillan were probably the ones involved.

The time for hesitation was over. She needed to kill Jessica and she needed to be even more careful from now on. She would need to be suspicious of everyone and she'd start now. She paid her bill, walked out, got into her Ford and looked around. There were some people talking and some people heading to their cars. In case somebody decided to follow her, she would head toward the main dock. Once there, she'd turn around, and if nobody was following her, she would go directly to the cabin.

Jackee told John about their mission. Mary decided to go right toward the main dock instead of left to Mud Lake Trail. The Millers watched Mary turn right out of the tavern parking lot. They waited a few seconds and followed in their red Ford pickup. Jackee took down the license plate number even though she knew Lou or Maggie would have noted it as well.

Mary's car kicked up a lot of dust, but Jackee and John stayed far enough back to keep her in their sight while not giving rise to suspicion.

Several cars were leaving the tavern and headed for Hawk's Landing for an ice cream cone. When Mary came to the main dock, she turned in, circled and waited for the cars to pass. John turned in as well and when Mary turned right so did John, after waiting several seconds.

Mary began to be suspicious as she continued down the road. She decided to go back to the tavern with the excuse that she had left something. If the red pickup followed her back onto the main road, she'd have to do something to shake it.

She pulled into the tavern parking lot. She went in for a few seconds and pretended to be looking for something. When she came out she saw the pickup again. Getting back in her car, she turned left in the direction of the cabin while keeping an eye on the rearview mirror.

"I think she's on to our following her," Jackee said. "I don't know what to do. I want to do what Lou asked and find out where she's going, but I don't want to create problems for him by letting Mary know we're on her tail."

"I say we just follow this road to our home," John said. "If we see her turn in, we'll note the road and keep on going home. If she hasn't turned in by the time we get to our driveway, we'll turn off and explain our decision to Lou."

"Sounds good." The Millers turned onto the gravel road and followed Mary from a distance at a steady twenty-five miles per hour.

Mary reached her road but didn't turn in because she was certain the red pickup was following her. She kept on going and soon saw the vehicle behind her turn off. She continued on a ways, turned around and headed back to Mud Lake Trail. As she parked and turned off the engine she had a sick feeling in the pit of her stomach. For the first time, she felt like the perfect crime may have a crack in its armor.

Mary came into the cabin and found Mike watching a ballgame on the small TV set.

"I think we're in trouble, Mike."

"Why's that?" Mike said as he turned off the TV with the Tigers beating the Yankees in Comerica Park, 6 to 4 in the 8th inning.

"I was having a beer and a hamburg down at the tavern and I was asked to help a magician and stuff came out that doesn't make any sense."

"Help a magician? We're supposed to keep a low profile and you're up entertaining folks?"

"Oh, shut up! What's done is done. We have to kill Jessica and get out of here!"

"Are you kidding? This is the worst time to kill her. If anything, this is the time to really lay low and hold our cards."

"I want Searing and McMillan off my back, Mike. They could have been in the tavern for all I know."

"Was there a woman in a wheelchair? She'd be about forty-five or so, attractive, brown hair, nice smile?" Mike asked.

"Yeah."

"Was she with a man in his late fifties, bald, fairly slim, two hearing aids?"

"I think so. I didn't memorize everyone in there, but it seems that I saw a man like that talking to the woman in the wheelchair."

"Then you were in the same building with Searing and McMillan."

"Well, then they heard the name Jessica and *Slinky* and *Stinky* and burying as a way to get rid of the victim of a murder."

"Oh, for cryin' out loud, Mary. You've got to be kiddin'!"

"But, Mike, they would have no way of knowing that Jessica is on this island, absolutely no way to know that. These people don't know me. I've never seen them, nor they, me. They couldn't possibly recognize me or know who I was. Also, we came here under cover of darkness and she's been in this cabin every minute. There's no way for them to think she's on this island."

"This I know, as long as they are involved, the pressure gets turned up and the screws get tighter and tighter," Mike said shaking his head.

"We can still pull this off," Mary said with confidence.

"I agree we can plan to find Searing and McMillan and threaten them again, but killing Jessica is not going to happen till things settle."

"OK, now we've got to find out where Searing and McMillan are staying. I recall a woman in the tavern taking pictures and she mentioned the name of a woman who was in that group. She said the name, 'Jenny.' I think I'll call the tavern and say I'm looking for a woman named Jenny and see what the owner of the tavern says. She called and Barb answered. After listening to her question, Barb said, "Jenny? Well, was she attractive?"

"Yes, I'd say so."

"Well, then it had to be Jenny McRae. They live out on the west end."

"She said she'd give me some information and I misplaced her phone number. Can you be more specific about where she lives or maybe give me a phone number so I can call her?"

"Sure. Let me get the book here a minute. " A few seconds later Barb came back on the line. "Here it is, 555-8974. Her husband's name is Gavin. Very nice people."

"Thanks."

"Well, we've got the number, now you call and ask to speak to Searing," Mary said. "If you get him, tell him you are a fan of his writing and heard he was on the island. All writers have egos and his must be pretty pumped up about now. Say you've got a couple books that you'd like signed and could you drop by."

꒰ꜝ

"Hello. McRae residence," Gavin said.

"Sorry to bother you this late, but is Mr. Searing there?"

"He's staying in our east A-frame next door. Is it an emergency or can you call again in the morning?"

"Oh, don't bother him. I'll call tomorrow."

"Can I tell him who's calling?"

"I'm a fan of his mysteries and was hoping to chat with him."

"OK, I'll tell him you called."

"Thank you."

Mike said to Mary, "He's staying in the east A-frame next to the McRae home."

"First thing in the morning, I need to go exploring. Hopefully there will be a sign out by the road."

⌁

Jackee called and let Lou know that she and John were not able to pinpoint the road where Mary turned, and that she suspected that Mary knew she was being followed.

"I got her license number. Will that help?" Jackee asked.

"Thanks. We noted it too. We know who she is, we need to learn where she's staying."

"So much for my short career as a detective, right, Lou?"

"You did what I asked. We may be dealing with a pretty sharp lady and she may have good reason to be extra cautious. You and John did the right thing. Thanks."

Wags, Jacquilyne, and the Williams had also come back to the McRae's after the magic show for coffee, to polish off the chocolate cake, and to get the material to take to Grayling in the morning. I reported to the group what Jackee had said and had just finished when Clara Williams, usually a quiet and demure person, bolted upright and said, "I've got an idea!"

Everybody in the room was taken aback by this burst of enthusiasm. All eyes turned to Clara as Maggie said, "Wonderful. We're all ears."

"I think Lou and Maggie should have a book signing on the island tomorrow evening at the Community Building. We'd have a day to put posters up, call friends, spread the word. Then we hope that Mary comes to this with or without Mike. Then, when she leaves, my husband and Wags, using radios, communicate with us on the ground and follow her car. That way we'll know exactly where Mary is staying and if Jessica is with her, we'll find her. My guess is that Mary won't be looking up and even if she does, she may not suspect that the plane is tracking her."

"Great idea. Only problem is, I don't have any books for sale on this island."

Carol said, "I'll bet your distributor could FedEx a couple of boxes in a day. They could be brought over on the five-thirty ferry and perhaps Jackee and John could pick them up on their way to the book signing."

I thought for a minute and said, "Very nice of you, Clara, but I really don't think I'm a draw."

"Of course you are. How often does this island have a mystery writer on its shores and get to meet an author and have a book signed? There is no bookstore on this island so my guess is that authors rarely set foot on Bob-Lo. I think you'd be a big hit. You'd do more than sign books, we'd bill it as 'The Mystery of Writing a Mystery, or 'The Life of a Bob-Lo Sleuth.'"

Maggie added, "I think Mary will come because she gave us those threats and as far as we know, she doesn't know who we are. We expose ourselves but also learn where she is, and that should be enough for us to monitor her and stay one step ahead. If we're going to find Jessica, we've got to find Mary."

"Well, what do you think of my idea?" Clara asked.

I thought for a second and said, "I'm uncomfortable with it. Once Mary can positively identify us we simply put ourselves out there for who knows what kind of danger. I mean she may come to the book signing and start shooting. If she feels she's backed into a corner, she's likely to act in some irrational way."

"I don't like it either," Maggie said. "Once she hears about this appearance she'll have time to plot. If Jessica is with her, Mary may see this as the perfect time to take Jessica off the island if she's still alive. After all, we'll all be at the Community Building."

"I guess it isn't such a good idea after all," Clara said, a bit disappointed. "I was simply trying to come up with a way to get her out in public so Wags and Ed could follow her to our Jessica. We have to start from some public place and work back to wherever she's staying."

"Well, we don't have to decide tonight," I said. "Let's sleep on it and talk about it over a bowl of cereal in the morning." Even though

I'd said we didn't need to decide now—I wanted some action and soon. I knew that the longer we waited to get to Mary, the less our chances were of finding Jessica alive or finding her at all

CHAPTER SEVEN

Wednesday, June 5
Bois Blanc Island

Maggie, Myrtle, Jenny, Gavin, Carol and I were enjoying a breakfast of cereal, toast, and orange juice. A steady morning rain was coming down. The sun was promised by noon. As Gavin passed the Cheerios, Maggie said, "Having thought about Clara's idea on and off all night, I think we should go with it. We can't take anymore time. We can monitor the marina and we can be at strategic points while being on the lookout for Mary's car."

"I think I agree with you, Maggie," I said. "But, we've got to do more than follow her back to her cabin or cottage or wherever she's living. We've got to finish the job or we simply subject ourselves to being the ones backed into a corner."

"Yes, but again, we must be very cautious lest we provoke Mary and anyone else who might be in on this with her, if she is the one who has taken Jessica and Mike. We still don't know that for a fact," Maggie added.

"I can fly to the airport closest to your distributor and bring back a couple boxes of books," Ed offered.

"That's in Holt, down in the Lansing area," I said.

"Not a problem. You already asked me to fly to Grayling. I'm practically halfway there. It's only a couple of hours down and a couple of hours back."

"OK. Let's do it. Book signing at the Community Building tonight at eight. We'll need a flyer developed, copied and placed in every mailbox and posted throughout the island."

"I can do the flyer," Carol said.

"I'll distribute it on the west end and I'll bet Jackee will distribute on the east end."

"Maggie, would you plan a strategy for apprehending Mary and Mike once we follow her back to where she's staying? That is, if we conclude she has kidnapped Jessica."

"Sure."

"We'll know by this evening if Mary and Mike kidnapped Jessica," I said with confidence.

The phone rang. It was Erin.

"Hi, Lou, Erin here."

"Good to hear from you. Where are you?"

"I'm over in Cheboygan. I got here last evening and stayed at a Best Western."

"Ready to go back to work?"

"Anything to help, Lou."

"I'd like you to drive down to Grayling to the State Police Forensic Lab. It is on the main drag right by the Au Sable River, in a light brown building. Give the envelope that Bob Brockington gave you, you know the one that contained the threatening message to me."

"Yeah, I've got it with me. I also have the handwriting from two of the people from the Blind Leading The Blind Organization."

"Good. Give all of that to Jeff Horner at the Lab. He'll know you are coming and will be expecting it."

"Will do. Can I then come over to Bob-Lo and watch you wrap this up?"

"You've paid your dues, Erin. If you leave now, you can get to Grayling, give it to Jeff and then he'll take you to the airport and you can fly on down to Lansing and then back to Bob-Lo with Jessica's father, Ed Williams. He's going to Lansing to get some books for a book signing here this evening."

"I thought you were solving a murder, Lou. Didn't think you had time for marketing and selling?"

"It's a ploy to try and bring the suspect out in the open so we can trace her back to where Jessica may be."

"I should've figured there was something behind it. Ok, I'm off to Grayling. Bye."

⌇

As soon as I hung up, I immediately called Jeff in Grayling to ask his help. Luckily he was at the Forensic Lab. I told him of Erin's expected arrival and of Ed Williams' plan to bring him some material by plane. I then told him what I needed and that I needed it by eight tonight.

"I don't know, Lou. That's stretching our capabilities."

"If my hunch is right and you tell me what I expect to hear, I can solve a mystery up here."

"For you and for Tony, I'll do whatever I can. Actually, I might need Mr. Williams to take me to East Lansing so we can use the technology at Headquarters."

"That's possible. Your call. If you need to be taken to East Lansing, just get in the plane when Ed gets there. Otherwise, if you can give me your answer by eight, a lot of folks would be indebted to you, my friend."

"I'll do my best."

Before Ed and Clara left to stay overnight with Wags and Jacquilyne, I gave Ed an envelope addressed to Jeff Horner. The contents included Jessica's purse, the invitation and envelope I found in the wastebasket the night Gavin brought me to Bob-Lo, and the envelopes I had picked up following the magician's stint with Mary. I wrote a note to Jeff and it simply said, "Erin O'Brien will give you an envelope with a few items. Enclosed are two other envelopes. My question is, does an analysis of the DNA contained in the licked envelopes provide any evidence that the Chicago postmark envelope and the magic show envelope were licked by the same person? Also, please see if any fingerprints are on the purse that might be helpful to us."

I also told Ed that he'd be picking up Erin and that it was possible that Jeff would be going along to East Lansing as well.

Carol created a nice flyer announcing the book signing. Gavin made a hundred copies on his printer. Jenny called to reserve the Hoover Community Building for tonight from eight to nine. Armed with flyers and a distribution plan, all vehicles and workers were off to stuff mailboxes and to post the notice in the post office and on a variety of community boards, in the Hawk's Landing General Store, at the Bob-Lo Tavern, and where the ferry arrives. Finally, a readable cardboard sign was created and strategically placed so vehicles going in either direction on the main road wouldn't miss the announcement.

♫

While everyone was busy doing what they could to prepare for the book signing, Mary was telling Mike that she would have to go to the General Store and get a newspaper. On her trip to the store she saw the sign promoting the book signing. She also saw the notice in the store. She decided to go; after all she wanted a good look at the famous duo.

During Mary's conversation with Mike about the book signing, Jessica overheard a few words like "Hawk's Landing," "Plaunt," "Tavern." It didn't do any good to know where she was because she couldn't escape now. She had little energy, she could sense the fluctuations in her blood pressure, and her heart was often skipping beats. As she drifted off to sleep, she didn't expect to wake up. She prayed the prayer she prayed as a little girl while kneeling at her bedside. Despair had darkened her eyes and paled her cheeks. She knew she could be murdered at any time.

♫

There was nothing to do in the afternoon. All of the flyers had been distributed, Ed Williams was on his mission, and the envelopes would be undergoing an analysis. With everything in place, I went fishing on Lake Mary. The day was perfect. The rain filled clouds had moved to the east. The sky was now a deep blue and the temperature was close to eighty degrees.

My rod and reel had been giving me some trouble but I was sure I could fix it once I got to Lake Mary. I arrived to find a family fishing off the dock in this remote setting. I parked, took out my pole and discovered that the line was all tangled up and the mess was probably more than I could handle. I put my pole back in Gavin's car and took a stroll down to the dock to see if the fish were biting.

"Having any luck?"

"Yeah, they're biting," an eight-year-old boy said with a smile. His younger brother kept quiet with his eyes fixed on his bobber.

"I was hoping to join you, but I've got no workable reel."

"Want me to take a look at it?" asked a gentleman about my age.

"Sure, if you don't mind. It's a mess and I'm not sure I can get it untangled."

He meticulously took it apart and put it back together again. "There you go. You can do a little fishin' after all."

"Thanks," I said putting out my hand to offer a thankful shake of his hand. "My name's Lou Searing."

"Joe Friday," he replied.

That's ironic, I thought. *Here I am, an investigator and a mystery writer, standing on a dock at an isolated lake on a remote island talking to a man by the name of Joe Friday.*

I took my pole, bait, and tackle box and headed to an opening on the dock. I said to one of the boys, "What's the secret to catching these fish?"

The same young lad didn't hesitate and answered, "Worms!" I knew I was in the company of some real fishing fans. Soon, Tammy, the boy's mother, got hold of a good-sized yellow perch, a keeper which probably would be in front of one of the boys at the dinner table later that evening. The boys caught some good-sized perch as well. Joe pretty much supervised, removed hooks that fish had swallowed, and offered advice for the distance from my bobber to the baited hook.

"This is one of the few lakes in Michigan where you don't see jet skis, cottages, boats, and water skiers," Joe said, looking out over the inland lake. "Think about it, Lou. An entire lake and absolutely no sign of human life."

"It certainly is nice and peaceful," I replied.

Joe asked what I did and of course I told him. He picked up on my investigating and writing my mysteries and his name being Joe Friday. We all had a laugh about the coincidence. I threw back each of the three little perch that decided to give me a few exciting seconds. It was mid-afternoon and I wanted to get back to the McRae's so I reeled in my line, gathered up my worms and tackle box. As I began to leave the dock, I told Joe, Tammy and the boys, Kyle and Brad, that I would add our chance meeting and fishing experience in my next story. They seemed pleased to realize that they would be in a mystery book. "I'm going to have a book signing at the Community Building tonight about eight. Stop in if you can."

"Just might do that Lou. Nice to meet you. Good luck with that next book."

As soon as I got back to the A-frame, I made it a point to talk with Gavin, Jenny, and Maggie to see if there was anything I should know or if there had been any action since I left. Nothing. All was quiet.

I called Deputy Sheriff Largent since I thought it was time to bring him up to speed with all that was happening. I wanted to meet with him but not in any public place where Mary might see us. The deputy told me he'd take the ferry to Bob-Lo and invited me to meet him at his parents' home in the Pointe Aux Pins area. He was coming over anyway to celebrate his mother's birthday. He also wanted to have his vehicle with all the communication technology in it.

A couple of hours later while we were sitting at the kitchen table, I told him all that I knew and suspected. I told him of our plans to try and follow Mary to her cabin by air after the book signing. I told him of the action I had taken regarding an analysis of the envelopes and Jessica's purse by the state police. Finally, I told him of the strange comments by the man on Mackinac Island.

"Hope you're okay with all of this," I said, realizing that Maggie and I probably should have involved him earlier on.

"Sounds like you and Maggie are doing a good job, Lou. What plans do you have now?"

"We may need a search warrant for Mary's cabin as well as her car. I suspect that Jessica, dead or alive, may be in or around that cabin. If Mary is in fact the person who kidnapped Jessica off Mackinac Island last Saturday night, then the DNA analysis should show that the three envelopes were licked by the same person. And I'm pretty sure that person is Mary Chandler. The clincher will be if the purse found at the transfer station has Mary's fingerprints on it."

"That makes sense. You're not going to get a DNA analysis done overnight, Lou. That will take some time. I can get a search warrant, but you don't know where we want to search at this time, correct?"

"That's right. We should know around nine-thirty or so tonight if Wags and Ed are successful spotting her from the air, assuming she comes to the book signing."

"Well, I'll tell you this, Wags is good. Nothing gets past him, Lou. You'll know where that woman is staying if Wags is looking for her."

I'll alert the prosecutor in St. Ignace that we may need a warrant. I'll explain the situation to him and with phone and fax we should have the paper work in order by the time we go in."

"Good. Thanks. Sounds like we're prepared for the next steps."

"When do you expect to go to this cabin, Lou?"

"Ideally we would go there tonight, but I don't like the prospect of trying to pull this off in darkness. I'd rather go in daylight in case we have people running off. I think an early morning surprise knock, talk and search would be best."

"Let me know where this place is. I'll work with the prosecutor to prepare the search warrant, we'll get the judge to okay it, and we'll be ready. Do you need me tonight?"

"I don't think so. You might come to the Community Center in plain clothes. I wouldn't want Mary panicking when she sees a deputy sheriff. We should be okay. We're only hoping to locate the place where she's staying.

⟡

Mary and Mike were plotting and planning how best to kill me. Once successful, they were convinced that Maggie would back off. After much discussion it was agreed that Mary would go to the A-frame about one o'clock in the morning and torch it. That evening Mike was to dig a grave out back and once Mary returned, the two of them would kill Jessica and bury her. Mary would take the Plaunt ferry to Cheboygan in the morning, get her boat and return to Bob-Lo to pick up Mike. The islanders would be focused on news of the fire and crisis at the west end.

The plan seemed to make sense. For once, the two of them were able to agree on a course of action that would complete their mission of killing Jessica and taking out the one detective who could foil their plan. The two seemed to relax a bit and for the first time since last Saturday evening, treat each other civilly. Perhaps the stress around committing the crime took its toll in their relationship. As the dinner hour approached, Mary and Mike seemed assured and comfortable with each other and their plan to end this killing mission.

⟡

Gavin and I went to the airstrip to welcome Ed and Erin and several boxes of books. They had enjoyed a good day for flying. I introduced Erin to Gavin and then briefed Erin on all we knew on the way to the McRae home.

As soon as we got in the door there was a call waiting for me. It was Jeff from the State Police Forensic Lab. "You're not going to like what I have to say, Lou."

"Give me what I need to hear, like it or not."

"Well, I had to take the material to East Lansing and they just can't get the analysis to you until morning."

"We'll take it when we can get it."

"They'll stay on it through the night because they know that one or more lives may be at stake."

"Thanks. I really appreciate all that you are doing for us."

"We can't have a DNA analysis finished, Lou. It takes too long."

"Fine. We'll take it when we get it."

"Any particular time to call in the morning, Lou?"

"Whenever you get the information, call me."

"Will do."

"Again, we appreciate all you are doing. I'm quite certain this information will be very instrumental in solving this case."

꒰ꙥ꒱

As Mary was about to go to the book signing, Mike took a shovel from the shed behind the cabin and began digging Jessica's grave. Mary wanted it deep so no police dog could smell the dead body.

"Good. That's a job that will be finished and all we need to do is drop her in."

"Yeah, I thought I'd do this later, but I might as well get it out of the way."

"I'll be back in a couple of hours," Mary said. "I want to see Searing and McMillan. Since they don't know me they might say something about trying to find Jessica."

"Makes sense that you go," Mike said.

"I guess I get some kick out of being the first to give them a case they can't solve and probably won't even live to tell about it," Mary said, with an eerie smile.

People began coming to the book signing and presentation early. Maggie and I greeted folks as they strolled into the Hoover Community Building in Pointe Aux Pins. I had no idea there would be this kind of response to our notices. Shortly before eight o'clock every seat in the place was taken and people were standing, not only at the back, but along the sides.

I asked for everyone's attention and began. "Thank you for coming. I had no idea there would be this much interest in the writing of a mystery, especially given the short notice of this presentation and signing."

Someone said, "The magician and an occasional visiting scholar is about all the entertainment we've got up here. When you're the only show in town, people will come."

"OK, thanks. I guess you've got a point there."

While Mary was getting a good look at the man she hoped would be dead in a matter of hours, it was time for Jessica to have her bathroom break. Mike opened the door, untied Jessica, and told her it was time for her to use the bathroom. He assisted Jessica in standing and walking to the bathroom. Although she was weak from her captivity, she wasn't as feeble as she pretended to be.

Once inside, she immediately went into the tool box and retrieved a small pocket knife that she had seen on the bottom of the box among a lot of scraps of paper and small tools. She took the small knife out of the box, and then using electrical tape, taped it on to her thigh. Her dress would hide the taped knife. She flushed the toilet signaling Mike that she was ready to return.

Mike escorted Jessica to the bed. Using an impassioned and weak voice, Jessica said, "Please don't tie my wrists to the bedposts. The pain, Mike. The pain is almost unbearable."

Mike could see no harm in granting her wish. She could hardly move as it was. So, he thought it only humane to agree. He tied her feet to the bedpost and after giving her some milk through a straw, left the room.

Jessica waited a few minutes and then slowly and in as much silence as possible began to remove the tape which exposed the small knife. She opened the knife and began, with all the muscle she could muster, to cut the rope from her feet.

In the meantime, back at the Community Building, I took the folks through the process of writing *Administration Can Be Murder*, an investigation of the poisoning of the special education administrator in Gaylord and all that goes into the creation of a novel. People were paying close attention and seemed to be interested.

I noticed Joe Friday and his family in the audience. I introduced them and told everyone how he had helped me with my reel and how much I enjoyed fishing with the family. There were several laughs when I mentioned that Lou Searing and Joe Friday were fishing on Bob-Lo's Lake Mary. Someone shouted, "Just the facts, ma'am, just the facts!" and everyone in the building laughed including Mary.

When I finished, I asked if anyone had a question.

"Are you here investigating and writing your next book?"

I wanted to be honest, but with Mary in the audience and not wanting the entire island to know that a murder may have been committed, I said, "Hey, every investigator and writer needs a little vacation. Carol and I are enjoying the peace and quiet of this island. We'll be leaving in a few days."

I then said, "I'd like you to meet my wife Carol. For any of you who have read the Searing and McMillan series, you'll recognize Carol in every book and she is probably best known for our walks on the beach behind our home in Grand Haven. She helped quite a bit in the last investigation in Gaylord." Carol stood and people gave her a nice round of applause.

"I would also be remiss if I didn't introduce you to Maggie McMillan. Maggie and I have been partners for about five years. She's the brains of our work. She sees patterns. She is the one our readers enjoy. In fact, I think I'll ask her to come up here and share some thoughts with you. You might have a question for her, too." The people applauded as she came forward. In fact, some gave her a standing ovation.

Mary remained seated and if I could have heard her thoughts, I would have heard, *Let's see if you can get this pattern. Your partner will be dead before sunrise!*

Maggie was not expecting me to ask her to talk, but rising to the occasion, shared some of our most frustrating experiences in solving murders and she told a couple of humorous stories. She got a question as well. "Do you realize what a marvelous example you are for people with disabilities and for people without disabilities?"

"Thank you. I'm simply living my life as independently as I can. I use technology and the many independent aids that are available now. I do what I enjoy doing and I'm not trying to be a role model. If I am, that's nice, but my message is to follow your dreams, do what you enjoy doing, and take advantage of all the people and technology that exists to help you adjust to your unique situation."

Since there were no more questions, I suggested that if people wanted to purchase a book to come to the front and Maggie and I would autograph it for them. I also said, "A portion of the sale of each book will go to the Bois Blanc Island Historical Society. Carol, Maggie and I value history and preserving our past. Thanks for coming. Good evening to each of you."

While I was autographing books, Mike Miles was outside the cabin talking on a cell phone. Jessica, almost free of wrist and ankle restraints, remained in her room trying to envision the best time to escape. She glanced out the window and saw the grave awaiting her body and Mike talking on the phone, but she could hear nothing of what was being said.

Mike was talking to a friend at the Pellston Airport, which was located about twenty miles from Cheboygan. "I need a helicopter with floatation capabilities."

"I can get that for you. When do you need it and where is it going to float, Mike?"

"I need it tonight at 1 a.m. And, I need it to land on Mud Lake which is at the southern end of Bois Blanc Island in the Straits. Look on a map to find it. It is almost directly north of Snake Island. Mud Lake is a big pond, but you'll have room to put the bird down."

"OK, 1 a.m. Mud Lake. You'll be there?"

"Yeah. There will be two of us, me and a woman. We'll need to get the woman some medical attention. She's been captive for several days. I can't say anymore, man, it's just that if we don't save her, she may be dead and buried by morning."

"OK, yeah, I can help you, but I'm leaving in the morning. Gonna be gone for four months. I'll be out of the loop, but tonight, yeah, I can be there. OK, two people, Mud Lake at 1 a.m."

"Yeah, and if for some reason we're not there, wait about fifteen minutes and then take off and go back to Pellston. I'll pay you for your effort."

"You'll have a flashlight or something for me to see you?"

"Yeah, we'll be at the southwest corner."

"OK, see you in a few hours."

"Oh, one more thing. If we don't appear, nothing is to be said about this call. Understand? No flight plan, no log book, no tracing the helicopter here, nothing. I don't like asking you to lie, but please do it if questioned by the Coast Guard or police or anyone. The helicopter never left Pellston and you never got this call."

"I'm a bit uncomfortable with it, Mike, but I'll do it for you. I told you in Vietnam that I owed you one for saving my life and I guess you're cashing in. OK, nothing said. Remember, I'm no good for you after 6 a.m. Gotta go for awhile."

"I understand, thanks. See you shortly after one. Don't come looking for us if we're not there."

"You can count on me, Mike. I'll be there for you and the lady." Mike put the small phone in his pocket and returned to the cabin. He knew this whole kidnap/murder thing was a mistake. He was in deep and he felt like he was in quicksand and slowly going down. Searing and McMillan would surely solve this thing. Mary was an amateur. With every minute, Mike was closer to being caught and having his life ruined. He would save Jessica's life. He knew he was a traitor in the eyes of Mary and there would be a price to pay, but that's the way it would have to be. He had a life to live and he was starting that right now.

Mike thought he might even explain to the police what happened on Bob-Lo in 1995 and take his chances. He simply couldn't live feeling like a fugitive, and now, almost being the murderer of a woman he really did admire. He took a beer out of the refrigerator, sat down, and for the first time in a long time, felt like things might work out for the best.

꙳

Back at the Community Building, Carol took the money and recorded each sale while Maggie and I autographed the mystery books. As this activity was going on, Jackee and John, Gavin, Jenny, Clara, and Erin were strategically positioned outside. Their job was to communicate via radio with Wags and Ed who were about to take off in the single-engine Cessna.

Jackee's eyes followed Mary as she walked to her car. She got in, started the engine and pulled onto the main road.

Jackee spoke into the radio, "Mary has turned south on the main road and is headed for the east end. Look for an "X" on the top." While I was speaking, Jackee had gone to Mary's car and with a damp rag had made a large "X" on it. She did this knowing that it would help Wags and Ed identify the car from the air. "She should be nearing the Main Dock about now."

Jackee listened and heard the return message. "We've got her. We'll follow her wherever she goes." It was getting dark but the headlights on Mary's car gave the impression of two hikers walking on a path with flashlights. Wags and Ed kept her in their field of vision.

They watched as Mary made her way along the main road until she came to Mud Lake Trail. She turned there and headed north a few hundred yards. She then turned into a winding driveway that went back into the woods. The area was desolate and isolated. The vehicle stopped and the lights went out. Wags knew exactly where she was. He also knew who owned the place - Doc Lemon, who rented it out to hunters. Wags banked his Cessna to the left and after activating the lights on the runway set the plane down to a perfect landing. Ed complemented Wags on the landing saying, "If I'd had my eyes closed, I wouldn't have known you put her down, Wags. Good job."

꒰ꕥ꒱

Within a half hour of the last book being signed, all of us, which meant the Williams, McRaes, Wags and Jacquilyne, Erin, Maggie, Carol and me, were seated around the McRae's living room. We patted each other on the back for a successful day. We had gotten important evidence to the Forensic Lab, we had managed to locate Mary's cabin, and we'd even caught a few fish and sold a few books.

I reported my discussion with Deputy Largent and his offer to get a search warrant for Mary's cabin. Wags mentioned that he knew the owner of the cabin Mary was renting and the Williams were anxious knowing that Jessica may be dead or alive a few short miles away.

We discussed the plan for the morning search. It would only involve Deputy Largent, Maggie and me. The deputy and I would go to the cabin, Maggie would monitor things from her van. Wags would stand ready if a plane was needed for any reason. He and Jacquilyne also stood ready to implement any procedures if they needed emergency medical action in terms of getting anyone to a hospital in Cheboygan. Cheboygan Police Chief Jones was alerted in case back up was needed. The others were to remain at the McRae's until a report came back from Maggie or me.

Even though it was getting late in the evening, Jackee and John suggested that Carol and I return to their home to experience a hollow log fire. They invited Maggie, but she was tired and declined the invitation. It was decided that Erin would stay in the east A-frame on the downstairs couch. Carol and I had our bed in the loft. We would join Jackee and John for a time and then be back in a few hours.

☙

Carol and I joined others around the campfire about twenty yards in front of the Miller home on the channel between Bob-Lo and Michigan's Lower Peninsula. The lights of the freighters could be seen slowly moving north and west. Above were thousands of stars. A three-quarter moon made the picture almost postcard perfect for a summer night in northern Michigan.

John took some kindling wood and created a nice fire on the shore. Once the fire was going, he placed a hollow log on its end. Soon the inside of the log began to glow and the fire channeled up.

Jackee dropped an empty aluminum can into the hollow log and the immense heat caused it to give off beautiful colors. The fire burned for a long time and was quite entertaining.

As Jackee promised, she had invited Jim Vosper over for a little history lesson. Also present were Joe and Marcia Lemieux and their dog Dexter. Joe and Marcia were teaching friends from Traverse City. The seven of us sat around the fire and listened to a few of Jim's memories. He recalled the logging era when his family owned a logging camp. He spoke fondly of his mother who was sympathetic to the lumberjacks and did nice things for them on their birthdays and other occasions. Jim told the colorful history of the Wilderness Club, a group of wealthy Detroit area folks who at the turn of the last century sought the same peace and quiet that we sought here at the beginning of the 21st century.

Carol and I asked a number of questions about education on the island. Jim explained that at one time the population of the island was such that there were three one-room schools operating on Bob-Lo. One was at Sand Bay, one was at North Shore, and one was at the site of the current school in the Pointe Aux Pins area.

As entertaining as the fire was and as interesting as Jim's stories were, we needed to call it a night. About one o'clock I said, "Well, we had better be going. We're planning to wrap this case up in the morning and we need to be alert."

Carol and I thanked our hosts for a marvelous fire and hospitality. We got on Gavin's Harley and headed to the West End.

CHAPTER EIGHT

Thursday, June 6
Bois Blanc Island

Mary left for the McRae A-frame a few minutes after midnight. Mike looked at his watch and decided that at about twelve forty-five, he'd tell Jessica his plan to escape the island. They would gather up a few things, get to the shore of Mud Lake and await freedom. Mike sat down with a beer but could feel his eyes getting heavy. He decided to set the alarm on a portable alarm clock beside his chair. A few minutes later he drifted off to sleep.

Unbeknownst to all of us around the hollow log fire, Mary was circling our A-frame, bent over and tipping a can so that a steady stream of gasoline would settle into the base of the small structure. Once satisfied that all was set to send the cottage up in flames and snuff out my life, Mary Chandler struck a kitchen match, threw it onto the back porch and then ran on the moonlit path to the road that feeds the west end cottage driveways. She could hear the crackle and see the flames shooting into the night sky as she got in her Ford and carefully drove down Lime Kiln Point Road. She didn't want to hit a deer or go off the road and be caught anywhere near the burning cabin.

The smoke alarm went off with a terrifying high-pitched shrill. Erin, who was asleep on the couch on the main floor of the cottage, instantly awoke and tried to comprehend what was happening. She acted quickly and took a towel, soaked it in water, opened the door and screen, stepped back about ten feet, put the wet towel over her face and hair and ran through the wall of fire. She couldn't see the steps and so ran headlong off the porch. She would find out later that she had broken her wrist trying to break the fall as well as her collar bone, but luckily the fire did not singe her body nor did she inhale sufficient smoke to cause any lung damage.

Dazed and outside the A-frame, she had no idea if Lou and Carol were in the loft bedroom. They could have come home, been quiet so as not to disturb her and then gone to bed. After all it had to be the middle of the night. She couldn't go back in, as much as she felt she needed to try and save them because the A-frame was engulfed in flames.

By this time, Gavin had awakened. The flames were seen by people at the Mission Point Resort due north on Mackinac Island. A call was relayed to the Island volunteer fire department.

Gavin looked anxiously outside to see his A-frame being swallowed by a huge fire. Without stopping to do more than pull on a pair of pants and shove his feet into some deck shoes, he ran outside. Jenny was right behind him. He saw Erin coming toward his home. "You okay, Erin?" Gavin shouted.

"Yeah, my wrist and shoulder hurt pretty bad, but I'm okay," Erin replied with a grimace as she clutched her arm to her side.

"Where are Lou and Carol?"

Panic touched her as she replied, "I'm afraid they're in there. I woke up when I heard the smoke alarm but neither of them came down from the loft and I heard no voices."

"Maybe they're not there. I don't see the Harley," Gavin said.

Maggie appeared and while the flames shot up hundreds of feet into the night sky, her fear that Lou and Carol were in the A-frame was so intense she could barely breathe. The vision of Carol and me gasping for air and succumbing to the heat and flames was more than anyone could bear. Jenny, Myrtle, and Maggie held each other realizing there was nothing they could do but pray that by some freakish chance, we were not in the fire.

After finding neither Carol nor me and not seeing the Harley, Gavin wasted no time getting the west end folks into action. He ran into his home and called neighbors who immediately put their west end fire alert into practice. They had prepared for such a disaster and now was the time to act on their plans. Gavin knew the volunteers and equipment from the other end of the island would arrive but not for several minutes.

The east A-frame was a gigantic bonfire, the efforts of the west end folks would be to contain the fire and keep it from spreading and damaging anymore than the cottage. Cars and trucks began pulling up and people were soon everywhere trying to fight the menacing blaze. Gavin got the hose and trailer and brought it to the scene of the fire. Two men pulled the hose down to Lake Huron and activated the pump so that the water would be brought up through two hundred feet of hose to try to contain the blaze.

Meanwhile Carol and I, on our way back to the A-frame, passed a car going in the opposite direction near the airstrip, about six miles from the McRae home. We heard and saw behind us, a fire truck followed by several cars. We pulled over to get out of the way having no idea that the focus of all of this effort was the McRae east A-frame.

⟑

At about twenty minutes to one, Jessica rose and slowly walked over to the door, cracked it to give her a view of Mike in a chair, his back to her door. He was either reading or napping. She didn't know which, but, it was clear that he was sitting still and did not know she was behind him.

Jessica cautiously and quietly went into the bathroom and opened the tool box where she had noticed a roll of wire. She made a large loop with the wire. She then stepped very cautiously behind the chair holding Mike. She looped the wire over Mike's head just as the alarm clock erupted in noise. Mike flew out of his chair as he felt the wire around his neck. Jessica, in desperation flew at him screaming and shouting to let her go. As he tried to pull away from her, Mike stepped back and one of his bare feet slipped in spilled beer and he fell over the end table. As he fell, his head cracked on the hearth. Suddenly all was quiet in the small cabin. Jessica could only hear her own breath as she leaned gasping against the wall. Mike was motionless and bleeding. Jessica could see the blood oozing from a large gash on the back of his head. He wasn't moving and she didn't take time to see whether he was dead or alive. She saw the door and her chance to escape.

As she looked out the front door, she sensed freedom. Gathering her wits about her, she hobbled away from the cabin and went down the dirt driveway toward Mud Lake Trail.

Jessica heard a helicopter and wondered why a helicopter was flying over the island this time of night. In desperation hoping it might be a means of escape for her, she shouted and waved her arms knowing full well it was useless in the dark.

Jessica, now at the point of exhaustion, collapsed to the ground and prayed she wouldn't die. She literally couldn't move, her arms and legs felt like lead, her chest hurt and her head was pounding. In the distance she heard the helicopter land. She knew she needed to conserve any energy she had left in her body. At least for now, she was out of the cabin and hidden.

After about twenty minutes, she felt she could stand up and try to walk. She stood slowly. Looking around she could see the lights of a car in the distance coming toward the cabin. Jessica quickly positioned herself behind a tree and watched the headlights go from low to high beam as the rays of light bounced all around her.

⌇

Mary drove down the narrow road approaching the cabin and thinking of what she would tell Mike. Her mission was accomplished. No one could have survived the fiery inferno. All that was left to do was to kill Jessica and vacate the island. The only remaining problem was getting off the island. The first ferry over to Cheboygan wouldn't leave until seven-thirty in the morning. They had no reservation, but there shouldn't be a crowd, after all it was midweek.

With all these thoughts swirling through her head, Mary just caught a glimpse of a fat raccoon scamper into the road. She felt the front and then the back tires go over the animal. *Oh well, at least it wasn't a skunk*, Mary thought. As she drove up to the cabin, Mary saw that the lights were on. Mike would be up, reading and tending to Jessica.

Just before Mary turned into the driveway, she caught a glimpse of something white near the base of a tree ahead several yards. A slight breeze had moved Jessica's dress from behind the tree. Mary thought it was a wayward piece of paper and continued on toward the cabin. She shut off the lights and got out of the car, took the empty gas can around back and put it in the shed.

Mary then walked into the cabin and saw Mike motionless in front of the hearth. As she got closer, she could tell that he was probably dead. She saw the bloodied gash across the back of his head. Her head swirled with panic. She immediately went to the bedroom where Jessica was being held captive. Her worst fears were realized when she saw that Jessica was gone.

She quickly recalled the glimpse of something white as she approached the cabin. She got her gun, attached the silencer, and grabbed her powerful flashlight. She went outside and walked down the road. In the meantime, Jessica knew she had to go as far from the cabin as she could. That meant leaving the road and walking deeper into the woods. Even though she had no energy, felt faint, and hurt all over her body, she knew that she was being hunted and she had to move away from the cabin.

Mary was a deer hunter and the only difference between hunting deer and Jessica was her intense anger. She felt no anger toward a deer, but there was great anger toward Jessica, not only for revealing her secret but for escaping and for all she knew, killing Mike. Mary moved the beam of her flashlight from left to right and back again to the left. She looked for any movement or anything in her field of vision that did not fit a deep forest and swamp area. She moved away from the cabin knowing that Jessica would move further into the woods trying to escape.

Jessica finally reached a point where she couldn't continue to move. She found a stack of wood in an area with a lot of brush. She knelt down and tried to be quiet. She could hear twigs snap and see the beam of the flashlight going over her head. The light got brighter and brighter and the wood snapping beneath Mary's feet became louder.

It was on the next pass of the flashlight that Mary saw a wisp of material near the ground by the wood pile. She turned off the flashlight and stopped in her tracks. She quietly moved toward the material while lifting her revolver.

Jessica knew that Mary was coming closer and closer and that death was seconds away. She couldn't see her life ending by being shot at point-blank range. Begging for her life was not an option. She took a deep breath and summoned all of her strength and decided to bolt toward the cabin using the lights ahead as a way to see the outlines of the trees. Her hope was that she could run in a zig-zag pattern so that the bullets Mary would fire might go astray or sink deep into tree trunks.

Jessica also hoped the surprise attempt to escape might catch Mary off guard for the few seconds she needed to get a head start. Jessica saw a small rock near her. She picked it up, flung it to Mary's left hoping it would startle Mary and cause her to glace in that direction.

The rock hit a tree and did cause Mary to quickly glance to her left as Jessica began to run, a run that occurred only because adrenaline was still within her body. Mary turned in the direction of the fleeting Jessica. She lifted her revolver and fired random shots at the blur caused by Jessica's light dress. She knew one of the bullets found its target, because Jessica screamed and fell hard to her right.

The medical examiner as well as the pathologist doing the autopsy would have a difficult call to make on the cause of death. The truth was that the trauma she experienced caused her to have a massive heart attack yet the bullet that would eventually be retrieved from her left side certainly led to her death.

Mary slowly walked over to where Jessica lay on the ground. She checked her for any sign of life, much like a deer hunter would inspect the kill. Jessica was dead. *Finally,* thought Mary, *the secret can be buried on Bois Blanc*.

Mary returned to the cabin and immediately went to the shed where she took a shovel, rake, and a pair of gloves. She walked back to Jessica's body and began to prepare a shallow grave. It took a long time to dig a grave and a lot of energy as well. She put Jessica in the grave and tossed in the gun. She then built a woodpile over the makeshift grave. She piled brush around the woodpile and covered the area with leaves. She then spread the displaced dirt in the forested area. Satisfied that her work was complete, she turned on her flashlight and inspected her work.

No one could possibly suspect that a body had been buried under the wood pile or anywhere in the area, she thought. *However, if anyone suspected that Jessica was buried in the cabin area, they might bring a dog in to hunt for her body.* Acting on this thought, she took the wheelbarrow back to the dead raccoon. She used her shovel to push the dead coon into the wheelbarrow and then brought the animal to the edge of the burial site. *Maybe,* Mary thought, *a dead raccoon would throw off a police dog. It might work.*

Mary was tired but the mission was complete. Jessica was dead, the murder she had planned for months was now history and Mary felt the revenge provided a feeling of satisfaction. I was dead, or so she thought, Jessica was dead and now all she had to do was get off the island.

It was now time to return to the cabin and figure out what might have happened to Mike and how best to hide the body. She entered the cabin and felt Mike's wrist. There was no pulse, no breathing. He was dead and blood was all around the hearth.

Mary knew she couldn't report this to anyone. How could she prove that she didn't kill Mike. No, she knew she had to get rid of Mike's body. It was as simple as that. She went outside and saw the grave destined for Jessica. Mike would have to be buried in Jessica's grave.

Mary had a difficult time with Mike's body. He was dead weight, literally, and while a relatively short man, he was all muscle. It took all of her strength to drag him by his feet from the hearth to the side door. Propping open the screen door and blocking the wheels of the wheelbarrow, Mary pulled him up into the wheelbarrow. This took almost the last bit of strength Mary had. But, she finally got him in the wheelbarrow and moved him out to the grave.

As Mary was about to tip the wheelbarrow so his body would fall into the grave, she heard a sound. A car was coming up Mud Lake Trail. She could see the headlights. Fear rushed through her entire body. She thought someone had seen her coming back from torching the A-frame and was coming to arrest her for arson or murder. She turned off the flashlight, leaving Mike in the wheelbarrow, and ducking, scurried toward the house, hiding from the lights but watching every move.

The car slowed and almost stopped. Mary hoped it was kids out to drink or lovers looking for an out-of-the-way place to express their passion. But, more than likely, it was probably the deputy sheriff coming to arrest her. Her thoughts jumped as she considered her alternatives. She could barely stay still.

Mary kept her eyes on the car lights. The car stopped. She could hear the engine even though the car was a good couple of hundred yards away. There was no other sound in the silence of night. Berating herself for having no weapon, Mary stole silently up to the back of the cabin. On her hands and knees she crawled to the side door and entered. Once inside, Mary moved quickly to get a large knife from the kitchen. She then went back outside.

Outside and armed, she felt a bit more powerful. She retook her position where she could watch the car and any movement of the occupants. She looked toward the vehicle and while she could still hear the engine, the lights were out and she couldn't see anything.

Suddenly the lights came on, the car turned around and slowly disappeared down Mud Lake Trail. Mary's heart slowly started to regain its regular tempo, but her hands still shook. She watched silently for a few more minutes to make sure the car was gone.

Mary returned to the wheelbarrow, lifted it up as high as she could, and slid Mike off into the grave. His body plopped head first and in a prone position. She would not have to reposition it at all. She put the wheelbarrow down and then began refilling the hole.

Mary heard a sound again. She stopped and listened, much like a deer would lift his head, frozen in stance, looking in the direction of the sound. She heard the sound again. She put her shovel down and walked back toward the cabin. Just as she reached the side door a German shepherd suddenly appeared on the porch. She froze, fearing he would attack her; but instead, he slowly approached her, wagging his tail.

Mary looked around wondering if the dog was alone. *It was nearly morning. There was not another cottage or cabin for more than a mile or two. He had not come around during the week. The dog had to have come from the car with the lights,* Mary thought. *Did the owner let the dog out to fend for itself or was this dog sent out to search for Mary or Jessica, and are there authorities in the woods ready to appear?*

The dog didn't seem to threaten her and there were no other sounds to indicate anyone was in the area, so Mary went back to her work. The dog actually took a liking to Mary and stayed with her, occasionally jumping up and putting its paws on Mary's shoulders while she rubbed his ears and told him he was a good dog. After covering the body, she took the excess dirt far into the woods and scattered it. She returned with a covering of leaves and twigs and scattered them over the area. Finally, she returned the wheelbarrow, shovel, and rake to the shed.

The German shepherd stood around and watched. He wasn't in the way and he wasn't a threat. He was quite friendly and once again put his paws up on her shoulders wanting his ears rubbed.

Mary figured he had been let out by the people in that car. She couldn't imagine that he couldn't find his way home, but maybe they were hoping that the people in Mary's cabin would find the stray and adopt him. There was no collar on him and therefore no tag. In fact, that's what Mary decided to do, adopt him. She'd take him back to Ludington. He'd like it on the *Stinky*, and she knew that the dog could keep a secret. She would call him Witness.

Mary was exhausted at this point. It was almost three-thirty and she'd been without rest for almost twenty-four hours. The stress of the last few hours was immense. It was all too much like a horror movie and so unreal.

Now Mary had to put all of her energy into cleaning the cabin and getting off the island. Mary sat down to rest for a few minutes. While she rested, she couldn't help but reflect on the way this perfect plan had been bumbled. It was all so simple; kidnap Jessica, dump her in the Straits or as a back-up, bring her to Bob-Lo, kill her, bury her, and go back to the Lower Peninsula to resume a life free of any rumor of her abortion. Now, Jessica was dead and buried on Bob-Lo, and so was Mike. She needed time to regroup.

CHAPTER NINE

Early Morning, June 6
Bois Blanc Island

The sun came up to a quiet east end and a weary west end. Few people on the east end knew about the fire twelve miles to the north. The McRae home was now the center of activity for many folks. The search operation with Deputy Largent was still planned, but a call to the deputy had moved the time to eight-thirty. Maggie, Carol and I had not gotten much sleep. The late night at Jackee and John's probably saved our lives. Had we been at the A-frame we very well may have been dead by now. Our arrival had been met with cheers and tears.

The acrid smell of smoke hung in the air. The burned-to-the-ground A-frame was a very sad sight. Not only was it a great loss for the McRaes but it left a very unpleasant feeling in their stomachs. The idea that someone would so violently try to kill someone they knew, shook them to the core. The events of the last few days were beginning to take a toll. Fear and anger were starting to fill everyone present. The phone had been ringing off the hook since Sunday morning. Now they had lost a major investment. It was time for all of this to end.

While the McRaes and others were inspecting the loss and standing around in wearisome states of minds, Mary was loading her Ford with leftover food, and other supplies she had brought with her almost a week ago. While putting the items in the trunk, Mary noticed the big "X" on her car.

Mary thought, *I didn't notice it yesterday and then I took it to the program last night. Someone could have marked it at the book signing. But why?* Mary wondered. *Probably so I could be followed*, she concluded.

If that's true then somebody knows I'm here, and if that's true, then the chances of finding the burial site have just risen substantially. On the other hand, maybe somebody just saw a dirty car and decided to make a big X.

This isn't good, she thought. *I'm a marked woman and I think my secret hideaway is no longer a secret. Well, in a few minutes there won't be any evidence of our being here so what difference will it make,* Mary glanced at her watch and thought, *I've gotta get going. The ferry leaves on time and I've got to get off this crazy island.*

Mary finished packing and once certain that the cabin was free of any evidence that she had lived there for almost five days, Mary, with Witness in the back seat, pulled out of the driveway and headed south to the main road.

When she arrived she was dismayed to see a lot of cars waiting to be put on the ferry. Mary got out, spotted Curt Plaunt and said, "Got room for one more?"

"Nope, all of these got reservations and we're full. Next crossing is at ten-thirty."

"I've got to get to Cheboygan. Can't you squeeze one more on?" Mary pleaded.

"Nope, packed. If you can get one of these folks to trade places, fine with me. I take seventeen cars max and I don't care who they belong to."

Mary approached a couple of people near the back of the line of cars. "I'll pay you folks your round trip fee if you would be willing to trade places with me. Gotta get to Cheboygan."

"Talkin' to the wrong people, lady."

"How about if I double the amount of money?"

"You don't understand," replied a tall and handsome gentleman. "All of us, or most of us on this crossing, have been at a watercolor painting workshop. We've been here for a week. This is a nice place, don't get me wrong, and I hope I don't offend you, but I gotta get to civilization."

Mary smiled to herself thinking, *You don't know the half of it.* He was still rambling on about wanting to drive on a paved road, when she turned and moved to the next people in line, but they didn't want to accept her offer either. Each seemed to have plans to get home and back to routines.

Mary said to Witness, "We're not going to get on this crossing."

This wasn't in the plan, Mary thought. She knew she needed to relax and be flexible, so she decided to take Witness to Hawk's Landing, get a cup of coffee and read the paper. First, she got a reservation from Curt so that she'd have a space on the next crossing. "You sure I'm all set for the ten-thirty crossing?"

"Right now, you're my only customer."

"Thanks."

꒜

Back at the McRae's, Gavin called a doctor living at the west end. "Doc, I've got a friend here who needs some attention."

"What's the problem?"

"I think she could have a few broken bones. I'd like you to see her. Can you do that?"

"Absolutely. Want me to come on over or is she coming to me?"

"We'll be over, Doc."

"I'll see you in a few minutes and I'll be ready."

Erin was in quite a bit of pain. She had ignored her injuries as best she could and had helped put out the fire. Although she had taken Tylenol and Gavin had put a splint on her wrist and put her arm and shoulder in a sling, her face was tight with pain and there were white lines around the corners of her eyes.

Gavin drove Erin to the end of the road where Doc was outside waiting to meet them. After gently and efficiently examining her, he was quite certain she had broken bones that would need to be set. His best advice was to get Erin to the hospital in Cheboygan.

"I think I can take the ten-thirty ferry," Erin said. "If you have something stronger than Tylenol for the pain, I'll be okay till I can get to the hospital." Gavin and Erin thanked the doctor and headed back to the house where I was about to take a call from Jeff Horner from the State Police Forensic Lab.

"Lou Searing, please."

"This is Lou Searing."

"Lou, Jeff here with a report from the lab."

"Great. What did they learn?"

"Well, we did a little more than you asked for. You're really getting your money's worth this time, Lou Searing."

"I'm all ears."

"First of all, we don't know if the DNA analysis on the licked envelopes will indicate that two of the envelopes, the invitation envelope, and the envelopes which you said were from a magic show were licked by the same person. That report will take awhile."

"Fine. I think it will eventually confirm our guess of who's involved. What else do you have?"

"The techs did a handwriting analysis and believe that the person who wrote the invitation and who wrote on the paper at the magic show are the same. The threatening letter is different."

"Good job. I didn't think to ask for that."

"This next thing is probably the most important information."

"Keep it coming, Jeff."

"Well, we did a fingerprint analysis and we found a good print on the invitation and on the purse that match."

"Good."

"We found another set. We ran them through our matching process but found nothing."

"What's that mean?"

"That means that whoever those prints belong to, we have no record of them and that means neither of these two have ever been arrested. But then, we found a print on the magic show paper and it matched what was on the purse and the invitation. So, while we don't know the person by name, you now have a select field of possible people."

"We sure do, Jeff. This is great information."

"We've got one more item. We found a good print on the threatening letter and we were able to find a match on that one. The print belongs to a man by the name of Mike Miles who lives in Lapeer."

"Interesting. That means he's been arrested in the past?"

"Yes. He was picked up for disorderly conduct several years ago. That's the only thing in our records, but it might help."

"It sure does. It sure does. I hesitate to ask if this is all, but I will."

"That's the whole story, Lou. We tried to do our best from what you supplied to us."

"Thank you very much. This is of tremendous help. I'll see if I can get you a promotion," I said with a chuckle.

"I could use one. Talk with you later, Lou." Immediately I went to Maggie and shared all that I had just learned.

"Guess that wraps it up!" Maggie exclaimed.

"Well, it certainly puts the two in our suspect pool."

"Enough to pin Jessica's disappearance on Mary, for sure."

"But, still no body, no witness, no evidence of a crime. We've a long way to go."

"We've got to get to that cabin, Lou. Every minute we're away interferes with our bringing closure to this case."

"You're right. Let's get in your van and meet Deputy Largent at the tavern so we can get inside and see what we see."

꒰ꕤ꒱

As we approached Hawk's Landing General Store Maggie said, "Let's stop here. I've got to get a paper. After awhile I begin to lose touch with the world."

As we pulled in, we noticed about five cars lined up in front of the store. Even the handicapper accessible spot was taken. "Look over there, Lou." Maggie said, pointing toward the car to the far right.

"That's Mary's car, right?"

"It sure looks like it."

"I'll go in and get the paper and see what I can see," I said.

"Be careful."

"Not a problem, people are all around, and it's broad daylight. Be back soon." I got out of the van, closed the door, and walked up to the store. I opened the door, walked in and looked left and right. There at a table on the right side was the back of Mary's head. I walked up to the counter.

"Got a *Detroit Free Press* or are they all asked for this morning?"

"Nope, got one here for you, Mr. Searing." Sheila said, taking the last paper in a stack behind the cash register.

The mention of my name caused me to wince a bit and I hoped that Mary didn't have an acute sense of hearing.

I bought the paper and walked out the door and climbed into Maggie's van. "I don't think Mary saw me. She's alone. Sheila mentioned my name but Mary didn't seem to turn in my direction."

"Well, if she's waiting to take the ferry off the island, she won't be leaving till ten-thirty. Since we know she's not at the cabin it seems like a good time for us to check it out. Let's get going."

Maggie pulled out of the parking lot. Her van, usually dark green with white trim was now practically tan. She couldn't wait to drive it through the car wash. As they drove down the main road they came upon a series of lawn sprinklers, shooting water out onto the road. The Lake Huron water was spread out over the road in front of a home. "Boy, there's some ingenuity," Maggie said. "If you want to keep your car and house from constantly being caked with dust from this road, you simply make dust into mud."

We continued on to the Bob-Lo Tavern parking lot. Deputy Largent was waiting there for us and we told him that we'd seen Mary and her car with a dog in the back seat at the General Store. Largent responded with, "I've got the search warrant. Let's go and see what we can see."

"Are we going to break in?" Maggie asked.

"It's hard to say. Most places on the island aren't locked, but you never know. We'll see." The three of us in two cars turned south onto the main road making our way to Mud Lake Trail. We turned off on the road where Wags and Ed saw the car turn in and bumped along until we came to a clearing and a small hunting cabin.

"Now I know where the phrase 'cabin fever' comes from. If I had to live in that postage stamp in the middle of nowhere, I'd go nuts in a matter of hours," Maggie said.

"No cars here. It doesn't look like anyone has lived here recently," I said.

"Wait a minute, Lou, look at this," Maggie said. "Footsteps, car tracks, bag of trash waiting for the coons, or a stray dog anxious to chew through it."

"Well, now that you mention it, yeah, there definitely has been someone here."

Maggie stayed in the van. Actually, she turned it around so she would be facing out in case we needed to be quickly on our way. She rolled the window down so she could hear as well as see any approaching vehicles. When she glanced in the rearview mirror, she could see Deputy Largent and me enter the cabin.

As she sat there looking around, Maggie's sixth sense, woman's intuition, or what made her a great detective and not just a good one, kicked in and she rolled her wheelchair over and positioned it on the lift. As she reached the ground, she drove off the lift and powered her chair around the cabin looking for anything out of the ordinary.

She glanced at the back of the cabin and noticed a leaf rake leaning up against the brick chimney. She thought that odd since it wasn't fall. She looked around to see what might have needed raking. No lawn with grass to cut and rake, no garden. She wrinkled up her nose with thought as she drove her chair over to the rake and looked at it. She carefully inspected the prongs and could see they were covered with dirt. There was also a twig caught between a couple of the prongs.

As she considered this, she noticed a small storage shed. She was curious about what might be inside. Opening the door, she saw a lot of tools, cans, a gas can, and an assortment of hardware items. It looked like a teenager's closet an hour after a mother ordered that the room be picked up and cleaned. Everything was jammed in the shed.

She did notice a shovel that, like the rake, had dried dirt on it. Maggie couldn't tell if the dirt was the result of digging a year ago or a day ago, but it had been used.

While Maggie was carefully looking around the cabin on the outside, Deputy Largent and I were looking around inside.

"Hey, Lou, come in here," Deputy Largent said. The tone of his voice indicated that he had found something.

"What ya got?"

"Well, look at this bed spread. Looks like some dried blood."

"Yeah, it does. Kind of hard to tell. It could be mud."

Then I looked very carefully at the top of the bed. If I had done a Sherlock Holmes imitation, I would have had a magnifying glass and a front and back brimmed cap. "Here are some strands of hair."

"Yeah."

"Of course, what would you expect to find at the top of a bed? But, it could be significant."

"Look in here, Lou." Deputy Largent had moved to the bathroom.

"Find something else interesting?"

"Yeah, this pane of glass has been cut. That's strange. See those fingerprints on the glass. We'll have the State Police come out and go over this place with a fine tooth comb. There's evidence all over the place. We better not disturb anything else."

I noticed a small alarm clock on the floor by the easy chair and end table. I picked it up and took it to Maggie's van. I knew I was tampering with evidence, but I had a feeling that the clock was a key piece of evidence and I wanted it. I decided to face a reprimand if one was to be forthcoming.

Maggie left the shed and drove her chair out a ways in several directions from the cabin. She didn't find anything abnormal except a lot of footprints in an area between a couple of trees. If it were deer hunting season it would make sense because the deer would be dressed and hung from the trees so there would be footprints all about from the hunters. But this was summer and there didn't appear to be a reason for this area to be covered with footprints.

We gathered outside the cabin and compared notes. Deputy Largent and I decided not to walk in back of the cabin because it would add footprints to those already on site and would make more work for the forensic technicians.

"I don't think we found anything that would give us any reason to arrest Mary. Looks like a cabin lived in for a few days."

"I'll give the State Police a call. Since we know Mary was here and since the lab work clearly puts her in position to have kidnapped Mike and Jessica, we need to have them thoroughly sweep through this cabin and the surrounding area. I'm going to ask them to take some photographs and casts of a few of these footprints. They might be evidence that might come in handy in a trial.

"I think I'll put up yellow tape around the place. It doesn't look like anyone is going to come out here for awhile, but you never know."

"Are you going to Hawk's Landing and arrest Mary?" I asked. "She's just sitting there drinking coffee."

"I can't do that, Lou."

"Why not? We suspect she's certainly involved in Jessica's disappearance."

"I can't arrest her, Lou. Think about it, no witness to any of this, no weapon, no body. We think she's involved and she probably is, but I can't go around arresting people based on what we've got."

"What about the McRae's burned A-frame?"

"Investigators are to be there today looking for cause."

"Cause? It was torched, Deputy. This was done to kill me and get us off the case. Surely you don't think it was some electrical short?"

"I know you two are frustrated, but we've got nothing to arrest her for."

"'Can we at least question her? Certainly there's justification for that?"

"Yes, there is. Do you and Maggie want to go along or do you want to remain out of the picture?"

Maggie thought a moment and said, "I think we should stay out at this point, Lou. Let law enforcement carry the ball."

"I disagree, Maggie. She knows that we're looking into this disappearance. I mean, she burned a building to kill me."

"What's your call, folks. I'm going to Hawk's Landing to talk to Mary."

"Let him go, Lou."

"You stay back if you want, Maggie. I'm going with the deputy. Gotta hear what she says."

⟡

Mary had been sitting in Hawk's Landing for quite a while. She went outside to allow Witness a stretch break and to drink some water. Then Mary went back in and sat at her table. Sheila had already filled up her cup with fresh coffee. A thought entered her mind. *I've committed the perfect crime. No one had witnessed anything; not the kidnapping on the boat, not the death of Mike, not the burial of Mike, not the killing or burying of Jessica, nor the arson.*

As crazy as this whole mess was and how botched up the plan had become, the fact was there was no way a jury would be able to convict me of anything. Reasonable doubt would be very realistic as she was certain the prosecution could produce nothing but circumstantial evidence, and her lawyer would easily say this is pure speculation or conjecture on the prosecution's part.

Mary had been on a jury in Ludington and she knew that the defendant did not have to testify, did not have to prove her innocence. It would be up to the prosecution to convince the jury, beyond a reasonable doubt, that she torched the A-frame, and had kidnapped and killed Jessica. And, with no weapon, no motive, no witnesses, and so far, no body, it was a simple case of circumstantial evidence, and not enough of that to convince a jury of her guilt. After all, the only witness was her new friend, "Witness" and he couldn't talk and even seemed to like her.

She knew, though, that if she were questioned she would have to say as little as possible and be careful about what she said. She would try not to outright lie, but to be as evasive as possible. She sat back in her chair and smiled to herself - proud that she'd actually pulled off something of this magnitude.

ک

We drove up to Hawk's Landing. Mary's car was still in its position on the far right side of the parking lot. Deputy Largent and I walked together into the General Store and strolled over to the table where Mary was sitting.

"Mind if we join you?" Deputy Largent said as he sat down. Mary really had no choice and she knew it.

"Nope. Did I get caught speeding out there on the main road, Officer?"

"Don't think so. We want to ask you a few questions."

"If one of them is how you get off this island, the answer is have a reservation!" Mary said, trying to make a joke.

"No, I know how to get off the island. I want to ask you about the disappearance of Jessica Williams and Mike Miles." Sheila appeared with a cup of coffee for Deputy Largent and asked me if I wanted something. She knew he liked his coffee black and as thick as she could make it. I declined.

"I don't know what you're talking about."

"Jessica Williams disappeared from Mackinac Island with her escort Mike Miles on Saturday night," Largent said.

Mary looked down at the table. She raised her head and said, trying to sound surprised, "Jessica Williams? I don't know anything about Jessica's disappearance. I know her, but haven't seen her for months. Mike? I know him too, but I don't know where he is."

"You're going to play your cards in ignorance and denial, I take it?" Deputy Largent asked.

"I don't know why you think I had anything to do with this. Why are you talking to me?"

"Have you got any idea how Jessica's purse ended up in a trash bag on this island?"

"No, how would I?" Mary said.

"You renting a place on the island?" Deputy Largent asked.

"Yeah, I had a cabin down on the east end."

"You just taking a few days to relax, is that it?"

"Yeah. This quiet island seemed a good place to relax for a couple of days."

I wanted to ask a question to put a bit of fear into the equation. "Any reason to be raking out back of your cabin, Mary?"

"Raking?"

"Yeah. The rake's out, not in the shed and twigs are caught in the prongs and dried mud's on the tips. Do you have an explanation for this?"

"All I can think is that the owner wanted to spruce up the place a bit, so he raked around the cabin." Mary added, "Why all the questions, Officer?"

"Well, let me put it this way, you're in kinda deep. We've already got evidence linking you to Mike and Jessica's disappearance. We're just giving you a chance to explain a few things."

"Well, I'm not responsible. That's for sure."

"Has your wound healed, Mary?" I asked.

"Wound?"

"Yeah."

"I don't have any wound."

"We found some blood on the blanket in the cabin bedroom along with some strands of hair. Just thought the blood was from some wound."

"The hair is mine. I slept on the bed for three or four nights. The blood? Must be from somebody who rented before us. Can't explain that one."

"You going to pay for the broken bathroom window? How'd you get such a clean break?"

"Again, previous renters, I guess. We sure didn't break any window."

Officer Largent interjected, "I take it you're going off the island."

"Yes, Officer. Time to get back to the real world."

"We'll need to know how to reach you."

"I understand. I'm either on my boat, the *Stinky*, docked in Cheboygan or at home in Ludington. Here is my card, all the information is there."

"Thanks."

We walked out and got into Maggie's van.

"Did she confess?" Maggie asked.

"Oh no, she had an answer for every question," I said, disappointed with the dialogue. "Actually, I've got to hand it to her, she was quick to respond to our questions."

"Had to have her fingers crossed behind her back," Deputy Largent said, shaking his head. "I've interviewed a lot of suspects over the years and many have good and quick responses, but after awhile, you can pick out the truth and we weren't hearing the truth."

"Well, come on, tell me what was said," Maggie replied, anxious to learn what excuses were thrown out.

"She denied knowing the whereabouts of Jessica and Mike, said the raking must have been by the owner, blood on blanket must be from the previous renter, and she's been staying in the cabin to relax," I said to Maggie.

"Lou, I've had a thought about this *Slinky-Stinky* thing. I think I know what happened."

"Deputy, this is very common in our investigations," I interrupted. "It will be Maggie who will see the one clue or the pattern that leads to the solution and I have a feeling she's done that now. Tell us what has occurred to you, Maggie."

"Well, the yacht *Slinky* was out that night. The owner and the harbormaster acknowledge that. The owner said he was down in Petoskey visiting some Chicago friends; we checked with the Petoskey Marina and they were there. Mary knew this was going to happen, somehow. If she didn't, she was incredibly lucky.

"Her boat is the *Stinky*. Remember at the magic show when Gary tried to read Mary's mind? He put down 'Slinky' but said something like, 'I didn't see the cross on the 'L.' That stuck with me. Now if you put some white tape over the two black portions of the upper "t" you then have 'Slinky.' Her invitation said to take a cruise on the *Slinky*. So, she goes to the marina in her yacht, the *Stinky* with tape over the "t" extensions. The *Stinky* just became the *Slinky*. The *Slinky* is where it is supposed to be as only a discerning eye would notice the difference between the boats. Jessica and Mike get on and the boat pulls out of the marina, into the breakwater and into the Straits. The real *Slinky* now comes into the harbor and goes into its slip.

"The boat was impersonated. Mary was able to use the slip for kidnapping Jessica off of the island and doing so in such a way that anyone would think her boat was the real *Slinky* and belonged where it was."

"Talk to me about the note that threatened harm to my family," I said.

"The note was written before the boat left the marina. Since the fingerprints were Mike's and the message said not to investigate the disappearance, it's obvious to me that Mike was in on the plan to kidnap Jessica and probably kill her. He was not a victim.

"So, for me, this was all planned out and seemed to be working until Mary made a stupid mistake about the purse and licked some envelopes. She probably had no idea of the technology available to the forensic scientist. These days if you lick something, you might as well sign it."

Deputy Largent added, "I've followed your reasoning and agree one hundred percent. But, we still have no body, no witness, no weapon, nothing to tell the prosecutor we have this thing solved."

I recalled a comment Mary had made a few minutes ago. "Deputy, remember when I asked Mary about the broken bathroom window and she said, 'We sure didn't break any window?'"

"Yeah."

"Who's 'WE'? She was with someone in that cabin."

"Humm, that's right. She did say 'WE,'" Deputy Largent admitted. "Good listening, Lou."

"For a guy wearing two hearing aids, it's a miracle I got that one, isn't it?" I said, quite proud of my picking up on that one error Mary made in her answers to our questions.

"You're like my grandfather, he always seems to hear only what he wants to hear. You probably wanted to hear that, Lou."

"I want to hear something that will break this case. I believe she's guilty."

"I know, but the bottom line is: I need a body, a witness, or a weapon. I don't even have a motive. If someone had evidence that Mary hated Jessica, it would give me a weak motive. In front of the judge, the prosecutor has to produce something that clearly points to Mary and right now, we don't have it."

"Have you got a bloodhound on this island?" Maggie asked.

Deputy Largent laughed, "We've got a lot of animals here, but I've never seen a bloodhound. Unless you can count old Claude Murray as a bloodhound."

"Who's Claude Murray?" Maggie asked.

"Claude Murray knows this island like it was the back of his hand. He can find a dime under a leaf."

"Really?"

"Oh yeah. We call on Claude whenever a hunter or a hiker is missing. Claude always finds the soul. Don't ask me how, either. We've had Wags looking down from his plane; search parties; every search technique known to man, and when all else fails, we call on old Claude Murray, and I'll be darned if he doesn't come up with the missing person every time."

"Let's call on him now," I said, eager to put Claude to work.

"If Claude can find a dime under a leaf, he sure can find two adults if they are on this island."

Maggie put the van in gear and pulled out of the parking lot. We drove to Claude's home. He was sitting on his porch, whittling a wooden chain. It passed the time and gave visitors something to talk about.

"You must be needing me to find somethin' or somebody, Deputy," Claude said.

"Well, we've got a mystery on our hands, Claude. We can't find a couple who's been missing since last Saturday night."

"Humm. That lady stayin' with the McRae's out on the west end?"

"Yes, her name is Jessica Williams. She and her date went out on a boat ride from the Mackinac Island Marina and never came back."

"That's what I heard. Who are your sidekicks here?"

"Oh, I'm sorry. This is Maggie McMillan and this is Lou Searing. They're private investigators from downstate. They're working on this with us."

"Well, it's a big island, you know. Can you give me some idea which half these folks might be on?"

I spoke up, "Mr. Murray, we think she..."

"Claude, call me Claude."

"OK, Claude, the suspects rented a cabin over by Mud Lake and I guess if Jessica was murdered, she'd be in that area."

"If she was dropped into Lake Huron or the Straits, I can't help. But, if she's on or buried on this here island, chances are I can find her or come darn close."

"We sure would appreciate your help," Maggie said.

"You folks want to get going on this now?"

"If you're ready, we're ready."

I looked at my watch. It was close to nine-thirty. I knew that Mary would be on the ten-thirty crossing. We'd be able to find her once she was off the island, but if an arrest could be made while she was confined it would be better.

Claude got into Maggie's van with the rest of us and we all headed to Mud Lake. We drove past the General Store and the Ford with the "X" on the top was still sitting on the far right side. We kicked up plenty of dust on our way as we pushed the speed limit up to around thirty.

We turned onto Mud Lake Trail and drove up to the cabin. On the way over, we briefed Claude on what we knew and what we suspected. He got out of the van and said, "You folks just leave me alone now. Don't talk to me or do anything. I need to be by myself and follow my instincts."

We stayed in the van while Claude just took off wandering. He ducked under the yellow tape marking the area and like a bloodhound, he'd stop here and there and look around. He'd kick a stick, he seemed to be smelling and listening to any slight sound. We did as he asked, simply left him alone.

About fifteen minutes later he returned and said, "I don't think she's around here. I get the vibes that she's in water and I wouldn't be surprised if she'd be in Mud Lake. It would be a logical place to throw a body if you didn't want it discovered, know what I mean."

"I thought for sure you'd find her buried around this cabin someplace," I said.

"Could be. I'm just saying I don't feel it, or sense it."

"You didn't think all those footprints out by those trees in the back could be a raked-over burial place, Claude?" Maggie asked.

"That place always looks like that. The guy that owns this place buried his dog out around there. He keeps it neat and picked up. I looked at the earth closely, looking for breaks. Didn't see any. Course a lot of the ground is covered with leaves, but I don't think anyone is buried here."

Once again I looked at my watch, a minute after ten. "Where do we go now, Claude?"

"Let me go further back into the woods. I think the deputy will tell you that my tracking is more accurate for a walking body than a dead body. Actually, I've got no experience finding someone dead. So, my batting average is zero."

Claude walked alone for a few hundred yards in all directions behind the cabin. As he was coming back toward the cabin he noticed something. "Lou, bring me a shovel."

I went into the shed and took out a shovel. "Look there, see that clump of dirt. Out of place. Wouldn't have seen it unless I was walking toward the cabin. Missed it strolling in the area. A clump of dirt like that doesn't just exist on property that's been lived on by folks. This means the ground, somewhere has been disturbed."

"Deputy, bring me that rake," Claude shouted back to Lyn who was talking to Maggie. Deputy Largent took the rake to Claude and stood there as Claude raked leaves and twigs to the side. About twenty seconds later he said, "Guess I was wrong, somebody's buried right there," pointing to a section of ground that looked perfectly normal. "Someone's right under there. Whoever disturbed this ground really took a lot of effort to make sure it looked just like it did when he or she began. The covering of leaves and twigs sure helped. But, the body's down there."

Deputy Largent began to dig into the soft, easy to move earth. He continued to dig until he hit something almost four feet into the ground. He moved the dirt around with the end of the shovel and quickly saw fabric from a pair of pants and then hairy skin. "I don't think we've got to do anymore. Let's leave this for the forensic technicians. I'll call St. Ignace and tell the sheriff a body has been buried here and leave the rest of the work to the pros."

"Looks like you got the evidence you need, Deputy."

"Well, at this point it's still circumstantial. I don't have proof that this body is Mike nor do I have any proof that Mary had anything to do with having this body buried there."

Claude said, "Notice how dry this is. The body's been put here since the last rain. If it had rained, the fabric and the earth would have been damp, and the earth is dry. So, you need to figure when it rained last and this body was placed here between then and now."

"Well, let's see, rained two days ago, I think."

"Then this body is pretty fresh. It was buried while this Mary was staying in this cabin," Claude said.

I looked at my watch and saw ten twenty-one. "That ferry leaves in nine minutes. If you want an arrest on suspicion of murder, we'd better get to the dock."

"Yeah, let's go," Maggie replied. I picked up the bag of trash that was resting beside the back door of the cabin. Never know what we might find in there. We got into Maggie's van and she put her shocks to the test over the rough gravel road as we sped off toward the main dock.

Deputy Largent got on his radio and contacted the sheriff. He communicated what he had seen and the facts as he knew them in the case. The sheriff said he'd get an arrest warrant from the prosecutor and the judge.

We pulled up to the main dock. Deputy Largent took a call on his radio informing him that the warrant for the arrest had been signed by the judge. He was legally empowered to arrest Mary Chandler on suspicion of murder.

The Plaunt boys were about to lift the ropes over the mooring which would free the boat and allow Curt to ease the ferry out into the Straits. Deputy Largent quickly got out of his vehicle and shouted to Curt, "Hold it, Curt. Hold it!"

"This thing always leaves on time, Deputy. What's your problem?"

"You've going to be a bit late crossing this time, Curt." The Plaunt boys put the ropes over the mooring and Curt came down from the pilot's house. Because the deputy was in uniform and was ordering Curt to go nowhere, Mary knew that she was about to be arrested. Mary also knew she couldn't act in any defensive way because it would be in contrast to her plan that she could be acquitted by a jury. By simply cooperating with the deputy, she'd not be committing any act that would be added to the list of charges no doubt coming to her.

"I'll be with you in a minute, Curt. Thanks." Mary and Erin were the only passengers on this crossing.

Deputy Largent walked up to Mary and simply said, "You're under arrest for murder."

"You're making a mistake. I didn't kill anybody!" Mary said with conviction but without much emotion.

Deputy Largent read her the Miranda rights and frisked her for a weapon. He handcuffed her and took her toward the car. He asked Curt to wait a few minutes as he planned to escort Mary over to Cheboygan and then drive up to St. Ignace. The Ford would be taken to Cheboygan and eventually taken to St. Ignace and impounded for an evidence search.

"Come with me," Deputy Largent said to Mary. "Don't resist me; walk off this ferry and get in the back of my cruiser," Deputy Largent said as he pointed at his vehicle. Mary did exactly as told and cooperated in every way. She looked over to Maggie's van where she saw Maggie and me standing by, watching the drama. Again she didn't say anything, but she knew I was alive and that the ordeal was over.

"Thanks, Curt. Sorry for the interruption," Deputy Largent said. "Your record of on time departures stands. Put my name and an asterisk by June 6. I'll take the blame for this one."

"Not a problem, Deputy."

෴

After Deputy Largent had Mary in his car, he moved over to Maggie's van to share some parting words before he accompanied Mary to St. Ignace for booking. Erin had walked off the ferry and joined Maggie and me.

"Thanks for all of your help, Lou and Maggie, and you too Erin. I think we can all sleep well tonight knowing this woman isn't out and about on Bob-Lo."

"Yes. My guess is the word of her arrest will spread over this island like a spring rain," I said.

"Any thoughts about what happened in summary form so I can discuss our best thinking with the sheriff?" Deputy Largent asked.

"This is what happened as far as I'm concerned," Maggie began. "There was a plan to kidnap Jessica. Mary couldn't have pulled this off alone. She needed an accomplice. It was Mike Miles. Mary must have done her homework, knew when the *Slinky* would be out of the marina, brought her boat in and picked up the two. They went over to Bob-Lo, then went to the Mud Lake Trail cabin. At some point Mary puts Jessica's purse in the trash, not thinking it would be discovered. I can't explain the delay in killing her, but there obviously was a delay. I guess they wanted to lay low for a while or maybe they learned we were on the case. Knowing we were on their trail, they burned down the A-frame and then for reasons unknown to us, Mike was killed. Whether that was Mary's plan all along or not we don't know. Where Jessica is right now, I haven't a clue! My hunch is that Jessica is dead too. We just haven't found the body yet."

"That's how I see it too," I replied, giving support to Maggie's theories.

"Could be," Deputy Largent said. "But, it's all speculation at this point."

"I have a request," Maggie injected. "When technicians are here later today to find a good footprint to cast, would you please see if they can get a footprint with a dog's print nearby?"

"Sure, we can ask for that. Where are you coming from?"

"That dog in her car is new and I've a hunch that the only witness to anything happening at that cabin several hours ago is that dog and we may need evidence of his being there as well."

"Sure, we'll have them take a cast of both, if two good prints are close together."

"Thanks," Maggie said with a smile.

"Well, I've got a suspect to book. We'll talk again soon."

Deputy Largent, with Mary handcuffed and in the back seat, drove his car onto the ferry for the trip to Cheboygan. The ferry and a very rare late departure pulled away from the moorings and began its forty-minute voyage to Cheboygan.

⊰⊱

As we sat in Maggie's van watching the ferry head out into the Straits, I told Maggie about the alarm clock I had found on the floor in the cabin. I showed it to her. She studied it and said, "Humm interesting. It was set for 12:45 a.m. and the plunger was never pushed in when it went off."

"Somebody wanted to be sure to be awake then."

"Yeah, but why then?" I asked. "Why not one-fifteen or one-thirty."

"Can't explain it," Maggie responded. "Maybe it'll be clear a bit later into the investigation."

⊰⊱

We did not realize it but as soon as the word of the arrest got around, so did the word that Jessica had not been found. A search for her would be conducted with all volunteers to report to the Volunteer Fire Department at nine o'clock in the morning. The Bois Blanc Island

Association would handle all expenses including a free dinner for all who volunteered to try and find Jessica.

Wags and Jacquilyne led the effort. All volunteers were assigned a section of the island and were asked to report back as soon as Jessica had been discovered or any clue of her having been on the Island was found.

Ed and Clara couldn't believe the turnout. It warmed their hearts to see such an outpouring of concern for their daughter. Most of the search took place between the Boathouse Motel units and a few miles southeast of Snake Island. Volunteers marched at about twenty yards apart back into the woods. People with ATVs volunteered to search, people with boats promised to cover every foot of shoreline, and Wags, Ed, and the Hoffmans promised to search from the air.

The State Police Canine Team was also involved. A dog, trained to locate a dead body indicated her presence in the cabin area and even outside the cabin. Ironically, the dog went to Jessica's burial site and clearly indicated something was to be found. The officer mistakenly thought the dog was responding to the dead raccoon and pulled the dog away and focused a search in an area on the opposite side of the cabin. Hours passed and no one returned to the base with any news of having spotted Jessica or any evidence that she'd been somewhere on the island.

While everyone gathered for a dinner at the firehouse, Jacquilyne got up and thanked everyone for volunteering. Ed Williams also got up and with his voice cracking a bit, thanked everyone for helping him and Clara try to find Jessica. He said they would never forget their help.

People ate and talked about the assumed murder as everyone was certain that Mary Chandler had killed Jessica Williams. They didn't find her, but to a person each would tell you that Jessica was murdered and buried somewhere on Bob-Lo.

When everyone had left, I talked with Wags and Jacquilyne. "Frustrating day, folks. I thought she'd turn up."

"She's not on the surface of this island, Lou," Jacquilyne said. "You don't get past Claude Murray, the eyes and ears of a hundred people, and a trained dog."

"She's either not on this island or she's buried deep on the island," Wags concluded.

"Yeah, I'm afraid you're right. Mike was buried so I'm sure Jessica is too. We just haven't found the spot," I said, nodding my head. "I'd like to think she's safely off this island, but I'm convinced that if she were safely off this island, she'd contact her parents or Gavin or would somehow make her status known to those who love her."

CHAPTER TEN

Friday, June 7
St. Ignace, Michigan

I t was time to leave Bob-Lo. There was no need for us to stay around. We gave hugs to the Williams expressing our sorrow for the way things turned out. We thanked Gavin and Jenny for their hospitality and help over the past five days. They had certainly gone the extra mile for us and for Ed and Clara Williams. Maggie and I knew we'd be back for the trial, a trial sure to find Mary guilty of at least one murder committed this week on Bois Blanc Island.

Carol and I were eager to get home. Carol had called our neighbor, Ben Logan, when she got to Bob-Lo last Sunday asking him to extend his taking care of our cats, Luba and Millie and our dog, Samm. He said he could continue to help but had to leave on vacation Friday. Maggie was eager to get home as well. So, the three of us took the 7:30 a.m. ferry to Cheboygan. Maggie drove Carol and me to Mackinaw City to get our car, where we had left it last Saturday when we originally headed over to Mackinac Island for the party. Once connected with our car, the three of us made our way to Battle Creek and Grand Haven, respectively.

༄

While Maggie, Carol and I were heading south on I-75, Mary was being arraigned in District Court. She stood before the judge who informed her of the charges against her. There were three: kidnapping, arson, and murder. He told her she had a right to an attorney and if she didn't have one, one would be appointed. A date was set for her preliminary examination and that it would be within the next two weeks.

Bail was proposed, but the judge denied bail. He felt there was sufficient evidence that Mary may have committed these acts. He felt she was a threat to society so directed that she be jailed. By denying bail, the rules of the court required that Mary not be jailed for longer than six months and the trial must begin within that time.

Mary would have preferred the family lawyer, but she really didn't want all of Ludington to know of this ugly event in her life. She decided to hire a St. Ignace lawyer who would be familiar with the county, procedures, jury selections and such things.

Mary hired a young and highly skilled attorney, Julia Sanders, to defend her. Julia was a relatively new attorney in Mackinac County, but a bright young lawyer eager to make a name for herself. Mary knew she was in a great deal of trouble, but she remained convinced that she would be acquitted.

Julia Sanders asked Mary to tell her everything she knew. "I've got to know the whole story, Mary. It sounds like they have enough evidence to put two murders on you. Give me the truth. I can't defend you unless I know the truth."

"I didn't kill Mike. I found him on the floor by the hearth, unconscious, bleeding to death. I felt helpless. I didn't call emergency or give him any first aid. I really sort of froze and on top of that I was furious at having Jessica gone. I left him to die if he weren't dead already."

"And Jessica?"

"I killed Jessica. I shot her and buried her on Bob-Lo. Her body is under a wood pile about a hundred or so yards west of the cabin."

"Tell me about the fire."

"I burned down the A-frame because I wanted Lou Searing to die," Mary said.

"From what we heard at the preliminary hearing, the evidence seems to be circumstantial," Julia said, looking at her notes. "Correct me if I am wrong, but I didn't hear a reference to a witness or even to having evidence of a murder weapon. Is that how you see it?"

"Yes. My dog, Witness, was the only one around."

"Tell me some details. You just talk and I'll listen."

"When I came back to the cabin from pouring gas at the base of the A-frame and setting it ablaze, I saw Mike on the floor by the hearth. Blood was all around. I saw a huge gash on the back of his head so I figured he fell and cracked his head on the hearth. I wasn't there, so I don't know, but that is what I think happened. If I called the cops, and they came out they would surely think I killed him.

"I immediately went looking for Jessica. She was so weak and exhausted, it was sort of like searching for a badly wounded deer. I found her, shot and buried her. Then I went back to Mike and I buried him in the grave he dug for Jessica."

"All of this information is critical for your defense, Mary."

"Have I got a chance?" Mary asked.

"Yes. I think so. I think I have a good case to put a lot of doubt into the jurors' minds about your having committed these crimes. We'll give it our best shot."

ॐ

The State Police Forensic Team spent the better part of a day in and about the cabin. Mike's body was removed from the shallow grave and transported to St. Ignace for an autopsy. In the cabin they found evidence of blood; Mike's was around the hearth area and they found dried blood on the bed in the small bedroom. Various sections of the cabin were dusted for fingerprints. Many photographs were taken both inside and outside the cabin. Several casts of footprint samples were taken for analysis. Finally, many tools, and the gas can were taken for study.

It appeared to the forensic team that someone had done a good job of cleaning up. They also thoroughly searched the Ford for any clues and did not find any evidence that Jessica had been in the vehicle.

At the other end of the island, the fire marshal had determined that the McRae A-frame was the result of arson. Gasoline had been placed around the baseboard of the cabin resulting in an even distribution of the fire. Investigators were unable to find any other clues. Because of the firefighters and neighbors fighting the blaze, footprints were undetectable and nothing was found that would be helpful to investigators.

The west A-frame rented by Jessica was thoroughly checked as well. The crime scene investigator found a couple of hairs in the shower stall and some Kleenex in the wastebasket. The hair and the tissue would provide a matching sample for the DNA testing.

While all of this drama was unfolding, another drama of sorts was underway in Ludington. Art Chandler, Mary's father and a long-time resident and wealthy entrepreneur was on the floor of his kitchen. Seconds ago he gasped, clutched his upper chest and fell forward. He couldn't reach the phone.

As luck would have it, this was the day for the Schwann's man to peddle his frozen foods. Art always ordered a half gallon of fat-free vanilla ice cream. The Schwann's man knocked on the door, but got no response. He looked through the small window beside the door and could see Art's feet on the floor sticking out beside the refrigerator. He immediately opened the door, rushed into the kitchen, assessed the situation, and called 911. Within a few minutes the paramedics were on-site. Art was taken to the Ludington Hospital where it was determined that he had suffered a massive heart attack and he was placed on life support.

The hospital attempted to reach Mary. A message was left at her apartment to contact the hospital. Mary never got the message.

CHAPTER ELEVEN

Monday, June 10
Bois Blanc Island

Ed and Clara Williams were beginning to accept the fact that their daughter was dead. They were convinced that Jessica was on the island, but with no admission of guilt from Mary Chandler and the realization that the all-day search failed to turn up her body, dead or alive, the Williams began to slip from hope into a realistic understanding that their daughter was dead. They thought it logical and a beginning of a healing to hold a memorial service at the grave site where her body would eventually be entombed if it were ever found. The day of the service was beautiful. Jessica's personal and professional friends from Traverse City and her colleagues from the CAUSE organization were making their way to the island. A greeting time was scheduled at the Hoover Community Building where people met with Mr. and Mrs. Williams, expressing their sympathy and sharing their sorrow with one another.

At approximately 4 o'clock, the procession left the Community Building and walked the five hundred yards to the Woodland Glade Cemetery for a short service at the site of Jessica's burial. This grave site was chosen by the Williams because Jessica so loved this island and because it was the last place she lived before her death. "I knew that if Jessica could be buried on this island it would make her happy," Mrs. Williams said to people walking toward the cemetery.

Woodland Glade Cemetery is set in nature. You don't see large markers, but instead you walk through a natural area and see flat, ground level markers identifying the deceased. Occasionally you see a natural rock and a plaque attached identifying the person and noting the dates of birth and death. It is without a doubt, the nicest and most naturally set-in-nature cemetery on the face of the earth.

When everyone had gathered, a circle of people formed around her grave site. Everyone took turns sharing a memory, mentioning a quality, telling a short story, humorous or serious about her life. The word that kept coming up was "advocate." She was an advocate for the profession of education, for all children, for teachers, for her community, and most importantly she was an advocate for children with disabilities.

After comments were offered, her minister from Traverse City offered a prayer. Following the short service, people lingered in the cemetery and then began to make their way back to the Community Building where refreshments had been prepared by several members of the Bois Blanc Island Association.

CHAPTER TWELVE

Thursday, June 13
St. Ignace, Michigan

While Mary was jailed in St. Ignace, she received a piece of mail with a Ludington postmark. It had been forwarded by her sister, Joy. A deputy had opened the letter to check for contraband and then presented it to Mary who sat on her cot in her orange prisoner outfit. The letter read:

> Dear Mary,
>
> My name is Laura Dilt and I am a nurse at the Memorial Hospital in Ludington. After your father's heart attack and before he died he asked me to write a message that he wanted you to have. He said such loving things about you. I wish you would have been here to hear them. His message was, My dear Mary, you were named after the Virgin Mother of our Lord and to this day you have been my example of an exemplary daughter. Your mother, God rest her soul, and I have loved you for you have followed God's commandments. You have honored your father and your mother. You have never coveted what belonged to others, you always valued life. You have

remained a loving spirit and your mother and I are so proud of you. I am not well and I long to see you, but if my wish is not granted, we shall see each other in Heaven. I love you always, Dad.

You must be a very special woman, Mary. Your father died peacefully. In writing you this letter I have done what your father asked me to do. Please accept my deepest sympathies as you adjust to your loss.

Very sincerely, Laura Dilt, LPN

Mary set the letter down on the cot in her cell. She broke down and cried uncontrollably. She had no idea that her father had suffered a heart attack and then died. She felt alone and in her grief was at last overcome by a tremendous sense of guilt and relief. Her father had died without knowing of the past few days. That was a blessing and about the only comforting thing Mary could think about in her grief.

Mary eventually learned that Joy had called the Chippewa County Jail to leave a message about their father's death. She had mistaken the name of the county where Mary was jailed. Consequently, she never got the message.

A few days later, an attorney visited Mary in her cell. He explained that the family fortune was hers. The will had been read and she had inherited all of the family's wealth. The amount was not immediately known, but it was reported to be in the millions.

CHAPTER THIRTEEN

Thursday, June 20
St. Ignace, Michigan

Today was the day for Mary's preliminary exam. The prosecutor had prepared information about the alleged crime, a list of witnesses the prosecution may call from to prove its case, and the maximum penalty of law allowed for each offence.

Mary was present along with her attorney. They listened as Kenneth Waring, the prosecuting attorney, put forth just enough information to convince the district court judge that there was probable cause for Mary to have committed the crimes. The fact that she owned a boat that looked very much like the *Slinky*, that her fingerprints had been found on Jessica's purse on Bob-Lo, and that she had rented a cabin where Mike was found buried convinced the judge that probable cause existed to charge Mary with kidnapping, arson, and murder." He informed Mary and Miss Sanders of the next step. He bound Mary over to Circuit Court where she would be arraigned.

The procedure was quick, clear, and businesslike. Mary was returned to jail and Julia returned to her law office realizing that she had a great deal of work ahead of her. Mr. Waring felt comfortable that he could continue to build a tight case for a conviction.

⤳

After Mary's preliminary examination in the 92nd District Court and before her arraignment in the 50th Circuit Court, Maggie and I met with Deputy Largent and the prosecuting attorney, Kenneth Waring. The meeting was to determine if there was sufficient evidence to proceed with a trial.

Maggie and I sat in a conference room with Deputy Largent and Mr. Waring. On an easel was a blank paper and a marker sat on the tray below it. The conversation began with Mr. Waring listing the evidence he had that would assist him in convincing a jury that Mary Chandler was guilty.

"I really don't think there is any evidence to support Mary Chandler killing Mike Miles," Maggie offered. "Mike was a partner, her strength, her ally. I mean, think about it. How was he killed?"

"The autopsy report said a massive head contusion," Kenneth responded.

"Would you say he had the strength to defend himself against Mary?"

"Oh sure."

"So, why would she kill him?" Maggie asked.

"I don't know. Maybe they got in an argument, disagreed about plans? The conclusion in the autopsy was that his neck snapped and killed him instantly," Kenneth said, looking at the report. "Even if we thought Mary killed him, we really couldn't prove it beyond a reasonable doubt."

"My guess is that it was an accident or perhaps Jessica may have tried to garotte him, wasn't a piece of wire found on the cabin floor?" Maggie asked.

"Yes, I think that was in the report."

"Mary couldn't have done it as she was burning the A-frame at the time. Also, the alarm clock went off at twelve forty-five so I assume Mike was alert and at that time Mary was gone. Neither Jessica nor Mary would have the strength to wound him like that. I don't think either woman killed him," Maggie reasoned, with myself and others nodding in agreement.

"OK, so we probably can't prove Mary killed Mike. But, do we have a case in the murder of Jessica?" Kenneth asked.

"I think it's clear that Mary killed her. After all she was in the cabin, we can prove that with the blood sample and the hair sample. We just can't find her. She might have been buried in Mud Lake or who knows where. This is a big island," Maggie explained.

"But, remember we have no witness to the murder, no weapon, and no body. I still haven't heard a good motive or any motive for that matter."

"We know Mary rented the cabin where the murder supposedly took place. And we've got that dog print near her footprint," Deputy Largent noted.

"Yeah, I think it's clear that we can prove that she was in the cabin or even outside, but I'm still bothered by no witness, no body, no weapon, and no motive, all key components of a high degree of probability for a conviction."

"I think if the jury sees the big picture, you'll get a conviction," I said, sounding quite assured

"Give me that big picture, Lou."

"The DNA indicates that she licked the envelope inviting Jessica to go on a cruise, and her fingerprints were found on Jessica's purse. A hair sample shows Jessica in the cabin rented by Mary. Jessica's blood was on the bed in the small cabin bedroom. So, it's clear she was being held captive in that cabin. Granted, we didn't find any evidence when we executed the search warrant allowing us to search Mary's car, but there is no question that she went from the yacht to the cabin in someway. Finally, there's no evidence that anyone else was in the cabin area."

"Talk to me about the fire."

"I'm certain that she was simply following up on the threat that was made to Maggie and me to stay off the case or harm would come to my family and Maggie would lose her two good limbs. Gavin McRae told us the night before the blaze a man called asking for me, saying he was a fan of my writing. My guess is that was a way to find out where we were staying. Gavin said he told the guy I was staying in the east A-frame next to his home."

"Not going to be able to have any credible evidence in the fire, are we?" Kenneth asked.

"The fire marshal said it was arson. He can testify to that. The forensic team found no fingerprints on the gas can they found in the shed behind the cabin. There was no gasoline in the can, but there was no way to tell how long it had been empty," Deputy Largent offered.

"Right, I know, but I'm back to the holes in my case, and they are the same with the possible murder of Jessica; no witness, no evidence she lit the match, and the lack of a motive. I don't think I can prove beyond a reasonable doubt that she torched the A-frame. About all I'm left with is the kidnapping and murder of Jessica and there is no body. Even so, I'm confident I can prove she's guilty of those two crimes."

"I would agree wholeheartedly," Maggie replied.

"Talk to me about the helicopter, Lou."

"Well, this remains a mystery. I heard that rumors were going around that the murderer could have flown onto the Island early the morning of June 6. A couple of home owners said they heard a helicopter flying low well after midnight and they also heard the helicopter take off fifteen to twenty minutes later. I checked with Wags and he's got no proof that a helicopter landed and took off. I checked with area airports and no flight plans included Bob-Lo. But, it is entirely possible that whoever was flying and or a passenger in that helicopter may have committed the murders."

"Couldn't have been, Lou," Maggie replied.

"I'm just saying that the thought hangs out there, Maggie. It's an unexplainable event that, as you say, is probably far removed from the events at the cabin, but it sits there as a possibility."

"It could give the jurors a reasonable doubt that Mary killed her," Kenneth said.

"I suppose it could," I replied.

"So, would you say we've got no case against Mary for killing Mike, no evidence strong enough to convict for the arson of the A-frame, but a strong case of circumstantial evidence that Mary kidnapped and killed Jessica."

"Very strong circumstantial evidence, I would say," Maggie replied.

"Her attorney, Julia Sanders, is an impressive woman. She has a reputation of capturing an audience," Kenneth said, a bit envious of her oratory skills. "She can very easily have people following her line of thinking. She's very convincing; if she'd decided to be a beach blanket salesman, she could make a living selling them to Yoopers in January. She's that good."

"But, the jury should see what's at play here," I said.

"No witness, but no one will disagree that both women were in the cabin that night and that one was being held against her will. No one will doubt that a murder took place. One person lived and one person died and well, it can't be any more obvious than that."

The arraignment in Circuit Court was based on the information provided in District Court. The prosecuting attorney officially charged Mary with three counts: kidnapping, arson, and the murder of Jessica Williams. The applicable Michigan statutes were referenced in the information document. Mary was not charged with the murder of Mike Miles. The prosecution didn't believe she killed him and felt that a kidnapping and murder conviction for Jessica was a better risk.

The judge, having completed his introductory remarks, asked Mary if she understood the charges.
"Yes, I do."

"How do you plead?" The Judge asked.

"My client will stand mute," Julia Sanders said, not wanting at this point to issue a plea of guilty or not guilty. She wanted her options open and this was the best way to assure that.

Miss Sanders did question having her client charged on all three violations of law at one trial thinking Mary should have more than one trial. The judge stated that he was convinced that the three were related and constituted a scheme or plan to the overall outcome, the death of Jessica Williams. The one trial decision would stand.

Julia Sanders knew she could appeal but didn't think it would do any good so kept silent.

༄

During the next four months, Mary remained in jail. The attorneys continued to gather evidence, study forensic reports, and to plan their comments before the Honorable John C. Ickes, Judge of the 50th Circuit Court.

During this time the forensic report from the State Police Lab became available to both parties. As I expected, the DNA analysis showed that Mary Chandler did lick the invitation envelope and the envelopes at the magic show in Barb's Tavern. The strands of hair found in the small hunting cabin did belong to Jessica and the dried blood on the bedspread in the cabin was Jessica's. Now, there was no question that Jessica had been held captive in that cabin and a conviction of kidnapping would have to be forthcoming.

༄

Julia Sanders poured over each report and found them most convincing that her client was indeed guilty. She kept going back to her major premise which would have to be the backbone of her defense: no witnesses, no weapon, no motive, and no body. She couldn't disprove that Mary had been on the island with Mike and Jessica. After all, she had rented the cabin and evidence placed her there. To a juror, the only way Jessica could have died was if Mary was the murderer. While she was deep in thought, the phone rang.

"Sanders and Harrison. How may we help you?"

"Are you the lawyer defending the lady who killed them folks on Bob-Lo?"

"We're defending the suspect, yes."

"I'd like to talk to you folks."

"We'd be glad to talk to you, sir. You have some information?"

"Can't explain the helicopter, that's all."

"The helicopter?"

"Yeah, I think your client there, did it. Don't get me wrong, seems pretty clear to all of us, but that helicopter had to have somethin' to do with it. Know what I mean?"

"No, I don't know what you mean, but I want to talk to you about this."

"That's why I called."

"I'll take a boat over to the main dock. Can you meet me there in an hour?"

"Yeah. We can go to Hawk's Landing for coffee."

"I'll be right over. I'm five-feet-five inches tall, blonde hair and I'll be wearing a light green Jacket," Julia said.

"I'll find you."

Almost to the minute, Julia was tieing up her boat at the main dock when she spotted an older man standing alone where the cars park waiting for the ferry to arrive.

"My name is Julia Sanders. Sorry, I didn't ask you for your name when you called."

"Name's Artie, Artie Otley."

"Pleased to meet you, Mr. Otley. Thanks for calling me."

"Let's go to Hawk's Landing."

Sheila took orders for two hot coffees. "You live here year round, Artie?"

"Yeah."

"You folks must enjoy the solitude. I couldn't handle it."

"Takes a certain type of character, I'm told. But I'm comfortable here, so it's where I live."

"Which is where, specifically, Artie?"

"I live in the Sand Bay area."

"Which is where exactly?"

Sheila had a map of the island on a wall and Artie pointed out the exact location of his home.

"OK, you mentioned a helicopter, Artie?"

"Yeah, late the night of that fire and when them folks supposedly were murdered, I heard this helicopter flying around, sort of buzzing the area I'd say and then it landed. I guess it landed. The noise stopped."

"You didn't recognize the chopper?"

"No. I don't think it was a Coast Guard helicopter. They make a higher pitched sound."

"You were up, obviously?"

"Yeah, couldn't sleep. I had a long nap that evening and it took the edge off, so I was up reading when I heard this helicopter. It wasn't natural that late at night and it flying low and buzzing the area."

"That's it? It lands and you didn't hear it again?"

"I heard it again and this time it come right over the house, flying low again."

"About what time was this?"

"When it come in or when it left?"

"Both."

"I didn't write it down or nothin', but if I was to guess, I'd say it came in around one, maybe. You see, when I heard about McRae's place being burned, that's what I thought might be a connection. Anyway to answer your question, I'd say it left one-fifteen to one-thirty. Again, I didn't write the time down. I'm just guessing."

"That's fine."

"Are you the only one who heard this helicopter?"

"No, believe it or not, other folks are up all hours of the night, too. A few other folks said they agree with me when I mentioned it. They thought it had something to do with the fire and the killin' too. They suggested I call you, but one said to stay out of it. You know, it seemed they got it all figured out and I don't want to be in any court or having some sick person recognizing me and torching my place. Know what I mean?"

"I appreciate your calling me, Mr. Otley."

"Had to do it. I mean, maybe this lady didn't do those things? I don't know, but I couldn't live with myself if I hadn't said somethin'."

"I'm glad you did. Thanks."

The two finished their coffee, talked about the fall colors, and dug deep into their pockets to get money for the coffee.

"I've got this, Artie," Julia said, putting a five dollar bill down on the table.

✧

Mary made a special request of her attorney. Mary asked to be allowed to make a videotape recording of herself before the trial. Julia thought this was an acceptable request and asked the sheriff to inspect the equipment she brought into the county jail. A room was set up for Mary and she took about ten minutes to complete the taping. No one listened to what she said. The taping went smoothly. Mary wrote her directions on a piece of paper, put them in an envelope, sealed it, and handed the recording and the envelope to Julia. Julia promised its safe keeping and to follow the directions Mary had written on the paper now in the sealed envelope, if she were ever directed to open it.

CHAPTER FOURTEEN

Monday, October 9
St. Ignace, Michigan
Mackinac County Court House

Courtroom drama would be absent during the trial of Mary Chandler. The media had her as guilty as a little boy with chocolate on his face, saying he hadn't been in the cookie jar.

Mary sat next to her attorney. She was not in prison garb when she walked into the courtroom escorted by two deputies. She had been granted a pretrial motion to appear in civilian clothes. Mary chose a simple print dress and a sweater. Julia was smartly dressed in a black tweed suit and looked very professional. The prosecutor's team sat at the other table. Mr. Waring was in his finest tweed jacket with dark slacks. Deputy Largent appeared in his freshly pressed uniform.

There were some spectators in the audience. The only one that was expected was Joy Chandler, Mary's sister. She sat behind Mary as a sign of support. Otherwise, the room was filled with media, including a crew from Court TV. All others were curious citizens from Mackinac County but mostly from St. Ignace.

A group of about one hundred potential jurors from Mackinac County were filing into the court room, taking their seats in the back half of the courtroom where theater style seats were lined up sixteen across and six rows deep. The potential jurors figured it'd have to be the trial of the lady on Bob-Lo who was accused of kidnapping, killing and then burying a couple of folks behind her rented cabin. There aren't many circuit court trials each year and with all the publicity around this murder, it would be safe to say this case was the Bob-Lo case.

Seated in the courtroom, potential jurors were reading paperbacks, newspapers, or magazines. Near the rear of the courtroom were two people: Lonnie McPhillips and Tricia Gonzalez. Both lived in St. Ignace and while they didn't know each other, they recognized one another.

"See you're on jury duty," Lonnie said.

"Yeah, the babysitting costs don't come close to matching the amount of money we get. I'm banking on not being chosen."

"Yeah, me too. My brother's a cop and we've talked a lot about that lady killin' those two folks. I've got her guilty walkin' in. I don't need to listen to nothin', let's get right to the sentencing."

"I agree. Seems like a waste of time to me. From what I've read, she'd better enjoy this courtroom because it's the last time she'll be around folks who aren't convicts or prison guards."

"You got a good point there," Lonnie said with a chuckle, a toothpick hanging out of the right side of his mouth.

Another potential juror was Priscilla Morris. Priscilla was one of the hearty year round home owners on Bob-Lo. Priscilla had followed this case by fact and rumor since word had gone throughout the island about the possible kidnapping and murder. She knew she wouldn't be chosen because she knew most of the involved folks on the island, as well as Deputy Largent.

Priscilla had been talking with other jurors while munching on tiny chocolate chip cookies she'd brought from home in a plastic bag.

"I've heard that the accused may not testify in the trial. If that's true, you can't help but pin a guilty verdict on the lady. If she didn't do it and then won't explain it on her own defense, she's putting the guilty stamp on the verdict as sure as I'm eating a chocolate chip cookie." Others listening nearby nodded in agreement.

ↄ

At 9:37 a.m., the potential jurors were seated and ready for the drama to commence. Some of the folks began to show some signs of nervousness. If their name got called, they'd be serving for quite a few days, listening to folks giving testimony, and having their lives disrupted all for what the majority thought to be a waste of time. If a poll could be taken, each prospective juror would probably say Mary Chandler killed the couple and should be in jail by four o'clock.

The sheriff asked all to rise as the Honorable John C. Ickes approached his bench. "The trial of Chandler vs. The People of the State of Michigan will commence," Judge Ickes offered with authority. He looked out at the sea of potential jurors and two TV cameras from Court TV. He glanced slightly to his left and saw Miss Sanders and the defendant, Mary Chandler, both serious and concerned. He looked across the aisle and saw the Prosecuting Attorney and Deputy Largent seated at the prosecution's table, closest to the jury. They looked confident.

Judge Ickes had much experience watching Kenneth Waring try cases and had always been impressed with his attention to detail and his quick mind. Deputy Largent has Judge Ickes's highest respect for integrity and honesty. Quite frankly, Judge Ickes believed the trial would be rather short and while he was to be unbiased, he did expect a decision to be rendered in favor of the prosecution.

He noted that his stenographer was ready to begin her work. To his immediate left, the sheriff had before him a box of names which constituted a jury pool. Both attorneys had juror profiles in front of them, plus law books, and notes needed to carefully lead the jury to thinking innocent or guilty.

To the judge's left, in front of the defense table could be found a large map of Bob-Lo island with numerous arrows pointing to the locations of some places expected to be mentioned in the trial. From the northwest to the southeast, these included the McRae home and two A-frames, the airstrip, Woodland Glade Cemetery, The Hoover Community Building, Hawk's Landing General Store, the Main Dock, the transfer station, the Boathouse Motel Units, Barb's Tavern, Mud Lake Trail, Doc Lemon's Hunting Cabin, the Miller home, and Lake Mary. In addition a large chalkboard was available should either party wish to use it.

Judge Ickes with his white hair, his bushy eyebrows, and his immaculate appearance sat fully in command of his courtroom. He leaned over and with his husky yet clear voice said, "Good morning, Jurors. Thank you for coming today to assist in this murder trial. The defendant, Mary Chandler, has been accused of arson, kidnapping, and murder."

The judge went on to explain the procedures to be used in his courtroom. He asked some general questions of all jurors and then the seating of the jurors began. The sheriff read off random names until thirteen citizens were seated, seven men and six women. As fate would have it, in seat number two was Lonnie McPhillips, in seat seven was Tricia Gonzalez, and Priscilla Morris was in seat nine.

The judge introduced the names of the lawyers, the defendant, Mary Chandler, Deputy Largent, and then read a list of witnesses and others who may be providing information during the trial. Jurors were asked if they knew any of these. Priscilla Morris was the only juror who raised her hand admitting she knew folks.

"Who do you know?" Judge Ickes asked.

"Well, I know Deputy Largent, I know Tom Wilson at the transfer station, Wags, Sheila, Artie, Mrs. Atkins, Gavin and Jenny McRae."

"How do you know them?"

"I mean I know who they are. They're not friends, but living on Bob-Lo everybody sort of knows everybody, so that's how I know them."

"Have you discussed this case with any of them?"

"Oh, no. Nothing like that. You asked if I know any of the folks on the list you read, and, I did, so I raised my hand."

"We appreciate your honesty. Thank you."

Neither attorney dismissed Priscilla Morris for cause. The prosecutor thought having someone from Bob-Lo on the jury would help his case. Defense Attorney Sanders thought a woman might be sympathetic to her client's plight. So, Priscilla stayed as juror number nine.

Another round of questions dealt with the chosen jurors' experiences with various crimes against them or their relatives. One juror admitted that he had been robbed and held a great deal of anger toward the thief. He was thanked and excused by Julia Sanders and replaced with another.

Kenneth Waring thought long and hard about dismissing juror number three. Her name was Joyce Shannon. She was a housewife and an aspiring lawyer who had returned to St. Ignace after growing up in the community. Joyce's father was living in a nursing home in town. She had a degree from Northern Michigan University and was enrolled at Cooley Law School in Lansing. She had successfully completed two years of study there. She married a lawyer in East Lansing who died in a tragic car-deer accident half-way between Lansing and Detroit. She was also six months pregnant with her daughter at the time of her husband's death. Her parents were aging in St. Ignace and with all of her grief, she decided to return to St. Ignace and care for her parents while trying to raise her daughter.

The life insurance policy of her husband was enough to give them a comfortable life, but the study of law fascinated Joyce. She continued her studies and was about six months away from taking the bar exam.

Someone with a background in law can be a good juror or she can be a poor juror. It's one of those 'a little information can harm you' scenarios. A waitress at the Big Boy, listening to the case might be quick to find Mary guilty, but someone like Joyce Shannon might get hung up on some technicality and bring a jury to a halt to debate some technical point. Waring was curious if Julia would dismiss Joyce for cause. She didn't, and so Mr. Waring decided, perhaps against his better judgment, that Joyce Shannon would be an acceptable juror.

Prosecuting Attorney Waring addressed the potential thirteen jurors. He was a large man having played linebacker for the Northern Michigan University Huskies and a year or two with the Green Bay Packers. He seemed to command respect simply by his presence. He wore a bow tie which also set him apart from most men in St. Ignace. He looked over the jury and began his remarks, "As you know this is a murder trial. I do have some questions that I'd like you to answer. Do any of you have a person with a disability in your family?" Three jurors raised their hands. Mr. Waring asked each to describe the nature of the disability and the relationship to the juror. He then asked, "The defendant is accused of murdering an advocate for persons with disabilities. Do any of you believe you would have trouble being objective in this trial because of your relationship to a person with a disability?" Each shook his or her head negatively.

Prosecutor Waring continued, "Have any of you earned a degree from Eastern Michigan University or a degree from any school majoring in special education?" Two hands went up. Mr. Waring interviewed each juror and discovered that one earned a degree from Eastern Michigan University in engineering in 1970 and another was a special education major at Northern Michigan University. Neither felt that having this in their background would keep them from being objective.

"I have no more questions, your honor."

It was Julia Sanders' turn to address the potential set of jurors. In direct contrast to Kenneth Waring, Julia was petite, slim, with short blond hair and pretty. What she lacked in size she made up in her ability to direct attention to the important points in her defense. It was hard not to attend to her attractiveness, but once you got past that, you would find yourself in her hands, following her way of thinking till she brought you to her conclusion. She was very convincing.

She asked each juror to look at Mary seated behind the defendant's table. "As you look at Mary, do you see a woman innocent of these charges? Because if you're thinking she's guilty, I want to know that now." No one raised a hand, including Lonnie and Tricia who only minutes before, told each other that she was certainly guilty of the crimes.

Defense Attorney Sanders also asked, "Will any of you assume guilt if I do not call Miss Chandler to the witness stand? As you know the defendant is not required to testify and I may decide not to have her testify. I would like to know now if any one of you feels that this decision means the defendant must be guilty." One hand went up. Julia asked the woman to explain her feelings.

"I just think she done it, that's all. From what I seen in the newspapers and from what I hear over the fence, she done it, and if she don't get up in the witness chair and defend herself, it simply tells me she's guilty." At the end of her questioning, Attorney Sanders would ask the juror to be dismissed for cause and another juror would be placed into the select thirteen.

Priscilla Morris sat in her chair emotionless. She did glance into the sea of unchosen jurors. Her eyes connected with one of the women who had heard her comment before being chosen. They communicated non-verbally, then Priscilla brought her eyes back to the front of the courtroom.

Eventually, Mr. Waring and Miss Sanders were satisfied with the thirteen people sitting in the jury box; eight women and five men.

Judge Ickes asked the jury, which was seated in two rows to his right and under a large photograph of Edward Fenton, a circuit judge from 1961-1974, to stand and take an oath. Once completed, the rest of the jurors were released, most of whom mentally heaved a sigh of relief in knowing they could get on with their lives and would only read about the verdict in a matter of days. There was no question that the case would be tried in every barber shop, beauty salon, and restaurant within a hundred miles of St. Ignace and that the outcome would be the center of discussion.

With the extra jurors excused, the courtroom held the media, several curious citizens, and many others who either knew Jessica, Mike, Mary or someone involved on the periphery of the case. The judge said to the jury, "The defendant is innocent until proven guilty. The defendant does not have to give testimony, and her attorney does not have to prove her innocence. It is up to the Prosecution to convince you beyond a reasonable doubt that Mary Chandler is guilty of the crimes she is alleged to have committed. We will now have opening statements which are simply expressions by both attorneys of how they expect to show guilt or innocence."

The jurors settled into their chairs as the court recorder prepared for long speeches, each word to be carefully transcribed. Judge Ickes looked toward the prosecutor, Kenneth Waring. "Counselor, your opening statement."

Prosecutor Kenneth Waring lifted his huge frame from behind the prosecutor's table. He walked around and approached the jury. He looked at each juror and when assured that he had everyone's attention he began, "Bois Blanc Island is a peaceful Island. It is known for its tranquility, its connection to nature, its welcoming of summer visitors coming across from Cheboygan to visit family and friends. But, during the week of June 1st, this island was the scene of much drama. By Thursday morning of that week, two people had died and been buried on the island, and in addition, an A-frame belonging to Mr. and Mrs. McRae was burned to the ground.

"This ugly and horrible series of crimes began on Mackinac Island. Jessica Williams, the victim, was attending a party at the Grand Hotel. She was a marvelous advocate for parents with disabilities, highly respected by all who knew her. She represented all that is good about serving others as a teacher, a principal, and as an advocate for those less fortunate. The evidence will show that she was lured from the Island and onto a boat named the *Slinky* and taken from the Island. She was at the party with a man named Mike Miles who evidence will show was a party to the crime of kidnapping. Mike quickly went from a friend and dance escort to a partner in crime, a partner of the defendant, Mary Chandler.

"Mary Chandler and Mike Miles took Jessica Williams to a cabin on Mud Lake Trail on Bois Blanc Island. Mr. Wilson will testify that he found a purse in a bag of trash at the Bob-Lo Transfer Station. Mr. Horner of the State Police will provide evidence that the purse held the fingerprints of the defendant and the victim. He will also provide evidence that the victim was in the cabin rented by the defendant.

"The disappearance of Jessica was immediately investigated by private investigators Lou Searing and Maggie McMillan. They will tell you of experiences in their investigation that led them to suspect

Mary Chandler and Mike Miles of kidnapping, arson, and murder. Because of the good work of Lou and Maggie, the evidence will show that the defendant burned the A-frame of Mr. and Mrs. McRae in an attempt to snuff out Lou's life.

"Early in the morning of June 6, two people died at the cabin on Mud Lake Trail. Mr. Miles was found buried approximate twenty-five yards from the cabin. While the body of Jessica Williams has not been found in the four months since this hellish week on Bob-lo, the evidence will show that the defendant murdered Jessica Williams.

"Perhaps the defendant and her accomplice saw their planning as leading them to commit the perfect crime, but through a few mistakes and the excellent work of Lou, Maggie and Deputy Largent, and the forensic techniques of the State Police, the evidence will show that their plan was foiled and you will clearly see the events leading up to her death.

"I would ask you to pay close attention in this trial as I will reconstruct this brutal murder on Bob-Lo and clearly show that the defendant did in fact kidnap, commit arson, and murder during the week of June 1. Thank you."

Judge Ickes looked at Julia Sanders, "Your opening statement, counselor."

"Thank you, Your Honor. I am pleased to represent Miss Chandler. I am very certain that at the end of this trial you will be convinced that Mary Chandler is not guilty of these crimes. My client and I are very aware of the rumors throughout our community and far beyond. We thought long and hard about requesting that Judge Ickes allow this case to be heard in some other part of Michigan because of all of the pre-trial publicity and the strong feelings of guilt in the minds of most. We decided to stay in this community because we felt that Mary could receive a fair trial and that the Prosecution will not be able to prove guilt beyond a reasonable doubt.

"I'd like to repeat what Judge Ickes has said, it is not up to us to convince you of Miss Chandler's innocence. Rather, it is up to the Prosecution to prove, beyond a reasonable doubt, that Miss Chandler is guilty.

"My defense will be quite simple. I will tell it to you now so that you can keep it uppermost in your mind as this trial progresses. I ask you to pay attention to anyone who witnessed any of these crimes. You will have no witness appear in this trial. I ask you to pay attention to anyone who talks about a motive for Miss Chandler to have committed these crimes. You will hear no motives. I ask you to pay close attention to any weapon that was used to commit these crimes. A weapon doesn't exist. I ask you to pay close attention to any facts, any evidence that proves that Mary Chandler kidnapped, killed, or set fire to an A-frame. You won't hear any.

"Finally and this is very important, I ask you to pay attention to a presentation of the body of the supposedly dead, Jessica Williams. You won't hear any because there is no body. This woman is on trial for the kidnapping and murder of someone who hasn't even been found dead.

"What you will hear is circumstantial evidence and as Judge Ickes will instruct you, circumstantial evidence is permissible. You will hear circumstantial evidence and I will, under cross-examination, emphasize how weak this is in helping you determine beyond a reasonable doubt that Miss Chandler is guilty of these crimes.

"As I close, I ask you to think about the phrase, 'two sides to every coin.' I'd like you to realize how easy it is to jump to conclusions because you think somebody did something or said something. We have incredible forensic techniques and the use of technology is immense now with DNA testing and other evidence that only a few years ago were unheard of. All of these avenues help prosecutors or defense attorneys convince you of the guilt or innocence of their clients. But, ladies and gentlemen of the jury, I caution you not to jump to a conclusion. I caution you not to assume guilt because of an appearance of guilt. Look for facts, hard evidence, witnesses, and you will not see or hear any that will cause you to believe beyond a reasonable doubt that my client is guilty of the three charges before her. Think instead of all of the possible things that could account for what you are about to hear. Think about the possibility of someone framing another, of believing something is there when in fact it is not, or seems to be.

"All of us look down the road on a hot day and swear we see water ahead, only to find nothing but dry and hot pavement. I caution you not to look ahead and think you see a guilty Mary Chandler, but when you get in the jury room, you'll see that these charges leave you with a lot of doubt, reasonable doubt that Mary Chandler kidnapped, murdered, and set fire to a building. I am hopeful and confident that you will determine my client not guilty. Thank you."

With opening statements complete, the trial was set to begin. The early part of the trial was very predictable. Witnesses were seated to the left of the judge. Betsy Bowers was the first witness for the prosecution. She explained Jessica's fear, watching Jessica and Mike get on the *Slinky* and then going to the police when the two did not return. Gavin McRae was next and told of going over to pick up Jessica and not having her be there to meet him. He explained that she hadn't felt well on the trip over. Tom Wilson said he found a purse in the trash, believed it to come from the Main Dock area and that he called the police to report it. The stage was set for the prosecution to move to begin attempting to prove that the defendant was guilty of the charges against her.

CHAPTER FIFTEEN

Monday, October 9
St. Ignace, Michigan

Mr. Waring called his next witness, Mr. Jeff Horner from the State Police Forensic Laboratory in Grayling, to testify. After establishing Mr. Horner's impressive credentials he immediately began to bring forensic evidence to the attention of the jurors.

"Did you find any blood in the cabin area?"

"Yes."

"Please describe this for the jury."

"We found Jessica Williams' blood on the bed in the cabin. We found a large blood stain near the hearth. The blood was from a massive wound to Mr. Miles' head."

"Did you find any fingerprints on the purse belonging to Jessica Williams?"

"Yes. We found Jessica's, Mr. Wilson's, and the defendant's prints on the purse."

"Did you find fingerprints of Miss Williams' in and about the cabin on Mud Lake Trail?"

"Yes, many fingerprints were found in the bathroom and in one of the bedrooms."

"Did you find any of Jessica's fingerprints on the boat, The *Stinky*?"

"Yes, and a few strands of hair belonging to Jessica Williams."

"Now, I'd like you to comment on DNA analysis of the invitation to Miss Williams from the defendant and the envelopes sealed by the defendant at the magic show on Bob-Lo."

"The analysis shows that all envelopes were licked by the same person."

"The defendant?"

"Yes, Mary Chandler."

"The handwriting. Comment about this as well."

"The handwritten invitation and the handwriting on the magic show responses are both from the same person."

"The defendant?"

"Yes."

"So, it appears that there's evidence that Mary Chandler and Jessica Williams are pretty much in the same area from the time Jessica leaves Mackinac Island the evening of June 1 to the discovery of Mike's body in a shallow grave the morning of June 6. Would that be a fair statement?"

"Yes, it would."

"Now, the dog's paw print. Tell the jury about your findings in this regard."

"We discovered a dog's paw print close to a footprint. It appears that the dog may have jumped up, putting his front paws on the person and stepping close to the human. We believe the hind paw print belongs to a German shepherd, and the footprint belongs to Mary Chandler."

"Thank you, Mr. Horner. No more questions, Your Honor."

"Miss Sanders, your witness."

"Thank you. Mr. Horner. Am I correct in stating that simply handling something doesn't imply guilt."

"That is correct."

"Jessica could have handed the purse to Mary and even asked her to put it in the trash or someone could have handed Jessica's purse to Mary and told her to put it in the trash. My point is that your testimony is that a print was on the purse, how it got there, may be quite a different story. Correct?"

"Correct."

"The dog print could have been any dog, couldn't it Mr. Horner? I mean do we have the capability of fingerprinting dogs and identifying a dog by a print and further wouldn't the dog's weight and the firmness of the ground determine the depth of the paw print?"

"We can't be absolutely certain that the paw print was from a particular dog."

"So, there is doubt. Is that a fair statement?"

"Yes. We are certain the print is from a German shepherd, but one could doubt it, yes."

"Concerning the DNA analysis. I don't doubt your findings, Mr. Horner. But is there any crime in licking envelopes?"

"No. My testimony was only that they were licked by the same person."

"I understand. Thank you for the clarification."

"Did your department do any analysis of evidence concerning the burning of the McRae A-frame?"

"We concluded that gasoline was poured around the base of the structure."

"Anything else? Footprints, match, car tracks, anything?"

"No."

"So, as far as the forensic scientists are concerned, the only thing you can tell us about this event is that gasoline was used to begin the burning of the structure."

"Correct."

"Were any fingerprints found on any tools at the cabin: shovel handle, rake handle?"

"No." Mary knew that would be the answer as both she and Mike used gloves. This was a part of their plan from the beginning.

"No more questions, Your Honor. "

"We call Deputy Largent," Prosecutor Waring said. The deputy approached the bench, was sworn in, sat down, identified himself by name, rank, and home address.

"Am I correct in assuming that you are the primary law enforcement official on this case, Detective Largent?"

"Yes. I am. The deputy assigned to Bois Blanc Island is Gerry White. He had an emergency family situation in the Detroit area so the sheriff assigned me to serve in his absence."

"There are a lot of details surrounding this case, Deputy, but I'll try to limit my questions to those areas of highest concern to the prosecution. Let me simply ask, do you have any evidence that the defendant Mary Chandler participated in removing Jessica Williams from Mackinac Island the evening of June 1?"

"Jessica was renting an A-frame belonging to Mr. and Mrs. McRae. In the wastebasket in the A-frame was an invitation to take an after-banquet cruise in the Straits on a boat named the *Slinky*. We believe she did get on this boat at approximately 10 p.m. And, the DNA evidence suggests that the invitation for this ride came from the defendant."

"I'd say it more than suggests, Deputy. It is obvious and now proven that the defendant invited the victim onto her boat the evening of Saturday, June 1." The deputy nodded.

"Please tell the jury about Jessica's purse."

"We did find a purse belonging to Jessica Williams. The purse was found in a trash bag by Tom Wilson, the transfer station worker on the island."

"Bob-Lo Island, correct?"

"Yes. It is believed that, as Mr. Wilson has testified, the trash bag came from the area around the Main Dock where visiting boats dock, but we can't be certain of that."

"Anything else?"

"Yes. A bit more about that invitation. The invitation was mailed from Chicago and delivered to the victim's home in Traverse City. The night of June 4, the defendant participated in a magic show put on by a guest on the island. As a part of that show the defendant wrote answers to some questions asked of the magician and sealed them in a set of envelopes. The Michigan State Police Forensic Lab in Grayling, as you just heard, ran DNA tests on the saliva from the invitation envelope and the envelopes at the magic show and has concluded that the same person licked the envelopes."

"Did Mary Chandler reside on Bob-Lo Island for a period of time in June?"

"Yes, it appears she rented a cabin, owned by Doc Lemon, on Mud Lake Trail from June 1 to June 8."

"Have you uncovered any evidence that Mary Chandler was in or around this cabin during this week?"

"Yes. In the first place, she readily admitted to us that she was at the cabin and resided in the cabin during that week. We have witnesses that her vehicle was seen at the cabin."

"Were the bodies of Michael Miles and Jessica Williams found near the rented cabin?"

"Claude Murray found Mike Miles, buried approximately twenty-five feet northwest of the cabin's back door. We did not find, dead or alive, the body of Miss Williams."

"So, in summary, we have evidence that Mary Chandler sent an invitation to Jessica Williams inviting her to go on a cruise in the Straits of Mackinac the evening of June 1, we have evidence that Mary Chandler resided at a cabin on Mud Lake Trail, and that the body of Mike Miles, Jessica's escort for the banquet and the man who boarded the *Slinky* with Miss Williams, was found buried near that cabin. Is that correct?"

"Correct."

"Your witness."

Julia Sanders got up from her chair and approached the witness. "Deputy Largent, do you have any witnesses to this alleged kidnapping of Jessica Williams from Mackinac Island the evening of June 1?"

"No, we do not. We do have a witness who saw her going onto a yacht on Mackinac Island and not returning. Miss Bowers has already testified to that, but we have no witness to a forceful kidnapping of someone against her will."

"Do you have any evidence that the defendant was present when Mr. Miles was buried near the cabin?"

"No, we do not. Well, as I said, we believe a person was there when the German shepherd put his front paws up on the person, but we have no evidence that the person was the defendant."

"Do you have any evidence that Mary Chandler was at the cabin the night the murders and burial were alleged to have occurred?"

"Yes, we believe that..."

"Hard evidence, Deputy - a witness, something besides evidence that she had been staying at the cabin."

"As I just said, we have a dog print that we think places the defendant at the cabin the night of June 6."

"A dog print?"

"Yes, ma'am."

"I don't think we need to pursue this line of questioning. So, correct me if I'm wrong, you are saying that nobody saw a kidnapping, nobody saw the defendant with Miss Williams or Mr. Miles at any time on the island or saw any interaction between the defendant and either Mr. Miles or Miss Williams?"

"That's correct. No witnesses."

"Let me now turn to a weapon. Do you have the murder weapon?"

"No, we don't."

"Let me turn to a motive. Do you have a motive?"

"No."

"You know of no reason why the defendant may have wanted either of the victims killed. Is that what you are saying under oath?"

"That's correct."

"So, correct me if I'm wrong, but it seems from my experience, that in any murder situation you need a body, a weapon, a witness or evidence that person is present when the murder occurred, and a motive. Would you agree, Deputy?"

"Yes."

"And, is it not your testimony that all you can say is that the defendant rented a cabin and was present at the cabin, and that Mr. Miles was buried near the cabin."

"Yes, at this point, all we know..."

"Simply answer the question, Deputy," Attorney Sanders interrupted.

"Yes."

"I'd like to ask about the yacht: was the invitation to go for a ride on the *Stinky* or on the *Slinky*? Because, if the invitation was to ride on the *Slinky* and the defendant owns the *Stinky*, it seems to me that we have a major discrepancy here and we may be putting a woman's life in danger when we're simply confusing the names of a couple of yachts. Is this correct?"

"It appears so."

"Thank you; your witness."

Prosecutor Waring approached the witness. "Deputy, is it your understanding that when someone finds a dead body they contact the authorities, call 911, call the police, get help from somewhere. Is this not the usual behavior for someone finding a dead body?"

"Yes, that's correct."

"The person finding a dead body usually doesn't take it upon himself to dig a hole and bury it like they might a dog or cat hit by a car. Am I correct?"

"Yes."

"So, one would have to wonder why the defendant would bury a body, wouldn't one?"

"Objection, Your Honor. My client has not been charged with Mr. Miles' death nor has she been charged with breaking any law concerning tampering with evidence or acting inappropriately."

"The defense brought Mr. Miles up, Your Honor. I didn't. Since it was brought up, I simply wished to ask the deputy for his experience with people reporting a dead body," Attorney Waring responded.

The judge pondered the statements made by both attorneys and then said, "The defendant is charged with the kidnapping and murder of Jessica Williams, not Mr. Miles. Your line of questioning is not relevant to the charges against the defendant. I will ask the jury to disregard the last set of questions by the Prosecutor. Objection sustained. Continue with your questions."

"Deputy, let's try to clarify this boat situation. Which boat is assigned to a slip at the Mackinac Island Marina?"

"The *Slinky*."

"And what boat is owned by the defendant?"

"The *Stinky*."

"Please describe the boats."

"They look very much alike: both are forty-six foot Tiaras with twin engines, off-white in color. The *Slinky* is out of Chicago, Illinois, and the *Stinky* is out of Ludington, Michigan."

"How do you suppose Miss Bowers could be wrong?"

"I believe someone took white tape and covered up the two ends of the "t" so it would look like an "l." There would be no suspicion of the boat being in the marina and the victims could have been easily kidnapped."

"I see. The *Slinky* was out of the marina?"

"Yes, the *Slinky* was to the west and had been in the Petoskey marina earlier in the evening."

"I see, so you believe that the *Stinky* impersonated the *Slinky* and allowed the victims to be kidnapped while any witness would clearly identify the boat as the *Slinky*."

"Yes, sir."

"Your witness."

Julia Sanders hesitated momentarily as she studied her notes. She came forward. "Thank you, Deputy. Let's go back to previous questioning. Did anyone see this white tape being placed over the "t" if that was in fact done?"

"No."

"Did anyone see the defendant in this boat, on the pier, in the marina, on Mackinac Island the evening of June 1?"

"No."

"So, correct me if I'm wrong, but once again, we have nothing but theory, nothing but, 'I think' or 'Probably, this is what happened.' Correct?"

"Correct."

"Your witness, Counselor."

"We have no more questions, Your Honor."

"The witness may step down."

The judge called a halt to the proceedings for the day. The trial would resume in the morning at ten o'clock.

That evening Mr. Waring was staying in his office, poring over the case, looking for anything that would assist him in convicting Mary Chandler. He was startled by the ring of the phone in a perfectly quiet office. "Mr. Waring, my name is Roger Wedel. I'm the man who flew that helicopter to Bois Blanc Island the night Mr. Miles was killed. Can we talk?"

"Most definitely. Where are you calling from?"

"Pellston."

"Can you meet me and a deputy at Audie's Restaurant in Mackinaw City in about an hour?"

"I'll be there. Thank you, sir."

Mr. Waring called Deputy Largent and asked him to accompany him to Mackinaw City. Deputy Largent immediately responded and said he'd come right over to the prosecutor's office. It was about 9 o'clock at night when the three men sat down over pieces of pie and hot coffee. Mr. Waring listened intently as Roger talked at great length about what he'd heard the evening of June 5.

Mr. Waring asked Roger why he had not come forth before now.

"I've been away for four months. When I returned I started to get caught up on local news and learned that Mike had died, and of course, the events of the night before I left came back to me. I felt I had to explain what I had heard. Mike asked me not to tell anyone, but I felt that I needed to speak out."

When the pilot had finished, Mr. Waring asked if he would be willing to testify at the trial the next day. He said he would. The three men shook hands and parted company. Mr. Waring thought as he reached the apex of the Mackinac Bridge on his way home, *If the jury has any doubt of the guilt of Mary Chandler, this locks up my case.*

CHAPTER SIXTEEN

Tuesday, October 10
St. Ignace, Michigan
Mackinac County Courthouse

Before the court was convened, Mr. Waring asked for a meeting with Miss Sanders and Judge Ickes. He explained that he wished to interview a new witness, the pilot of the helicopter expected to be presented in the testimony of Mr. Otley. Miss Sanders agreed to the new witness and Judge Ickes allowed the pilot's name to be added to the list of witnesses.

All rose for the entrance of Judge Ickes and eventually the jury as the thirteen members filed into the courtroom. All were seated. The judge asked for the Prosecution to call its next witness.

Prosecutor Waring then said, "We call Susan Atkins to the stand."

Susan Atkins calmly walked to the witness chair, took the oath, and completed her pre-testimony procedures.

"Mrs. Atkins. You have a cabin on Bob-Lo Island; is that correct?"

"Yes."

"Please tell us where it is located."

"The cottage is at the west end."

"That would be approximately how far from the Mud Lake cabin where the defendant was staying?"

"I'd say about fourteen miles."

"Is it true that you drove to Mud Lake Trail in the early hours of June 6?"

"Yes, that's true."

"Please tell the court why you were out driving at 3 a.m that morning."

"Well, this is kind of hard to talk about and I might get a little emotional, but it's the truth. We had this big German shepherd dog. His name was 'Berlin'." The people in the audience chuckled a bit at the name. "I know it isn't a very unique name but being a German shepherd and all and since we lived on Berlin Street in Adrian, Michigan, we thought the name a good one. Anyway, we decided that we could no longer keep Berlin. He was getting too rough with my young kids. I couldn't bring myself to have him put to sleep. No one would take him, so I figured if I let him out far from our cottage he might find someone to take him in."

"So, that's why you were driving around early that morning?"

"Yes. I turned down a road, I guess it was Mud Lake Trail. I wasn't looking for any road signs. I drove a bit and then I saw, in the distance, a light on in a cabin or a small house. So, I knew somebody lived there."

"So, you let the dog out?"

"Well, yes, but he wouldn't go which was very upsetting. I was crying and finally he got out of the car and stood there looking so mournful. I got back in the car, turned around and we took off. I was crying on the way home, but I had to do it. I just knew some kind soul would find Berlin and give him a home. He was a perfect watchdog here on the island, but we couldn't keep him."

"You said, 'We took off.' Who was with you?"

"Did I say 'we'? I didn't mean to. I was alone."

"OK, I wanted to clarify that. What time would you say this was?"

"Oh, about 3 a.m. We were taking the early ferry over to Cheboygan in a few hours and that's why I let him out, I didn't want to have him come walking back to our home. I just wanted him to go and have that be it. He's a good dog, just not around little kids and that's what I've got."

"OK, so you released Berlin around 3 a.m."

"Yes."

"Do you know if the dog went to the cabin?"

"I have no idea. I was just hoping he wasn't running behind me following us back to the west end."

"Your witness."

"I have no questions."

"We call Sheila Godbold."

Sheila walked up to the witness chair, identified herself, noted that she was co-owner, along with her husband, of the Hawk's Landing General Store."

"Sheila, did the defendant come into Hawk's Landing the morning of June 6?"

"Yes, she did."

"About what time?"

"It was about seven-thirty. She said she couldn't get on the ferry and had to wait until the ten-thirty crossing. She bought a newspaper and some coffee."

"Did she have a German shepherd dog with her?"

"Not inside my place. The dog was out in her car."

"You sure it was her car?"

"Sure am. She'd go out and give the dog some water and a biscuit or two."

"Did you recognize the dog?"

"It's Berlin, the dog that belongs to the Atkins."

"You're sure?"

"Yeah. He'd always come in with the family when they'd stop to buy this or that or to get ice cream cones. He was like one of their family." Susan Atkins broke down in tears and walked out of the courtroom to get a drink of water and get control of herself.

"No more questions."

"Do you wish to cross-examine, Counselor?" Judge Ickes asked.

"No, Your Honor."

"Next witness."

"We call Maggie McMillan," Kenneth Waring said. Maggie powered her wheelchair to the front of the courtroom and unable to get up into the witness chair, simply remained seated in her powerchair. She took the oath and identified herself as Margaret McMillan, a private investigator and an insurance claim investigator currently living in Battle Creek, Michigan.

"You've been investigating this murder with your colleague Lou Searing and with Deputy Largent?"

"Yes."

"I've called you as a witness to ask you about the footprint cast." Maggie nodded. "You discovered footprints in the area where Mr. Miles was buried, is this correct?"

"Yes, all about the cabin area actually. But, yes, the footprints were around where the body was buried."

"You checked out or examined the cast taken of the footprints by police technicians. Is that correct?"

"Yes."

"And wasn't it you who discovered a significant piece of information?"

"Yes."

"Please tell the jury and the court about that."

"While most of the analysis of the cast was concentrated on the footprint, I noted in the cast, the paw print of a dog. At first I thought nothing of it as the dog could be standing in front of the defendant or simply in the area and the print happened to be close to the footprint. But, on further reflection, I realized that this could be the hind paw print of a large dog and not the front paw print."

"How did you know this?"

"Well, it was sunken as if the weight of the dog were pushing down on it and the paw was spread which I've since learned from dog experts is what you'd expect with the hind paw."

"Objection, hearsay," interrupted Julia.

"Overruled."

"As you were saying, Mrs. McMillan," Kenneth stated.

"So, I believe the German shepherd let out by Mrs. Atkins approached the defendant in the early morning hours and as a sign of friendship, put his front paws up on the body of the defendant leaving the strong rear paws to sink into the ground."

"As an investigator, this, in your opinion, places the defendant at the cabin when Mr. Miles was being buried."

"Absolutely. There were no human witnesses, but there was a canine witness, and when Mrs. Atkins said she saw a light on in a cabin down the road, this was further evidence that someone was up and about. I suspect Mary Chandler was burying Mr. Miles."

"Objection. This calls for speculation, Your Honor," Julia Sanders bellowed.

"Sustained." The judge looked at Maggie and said, "Please do not draw conclusions from your testimony, but simply answer the questions." He smiled and Maggie nodded that she understood her error. The jury seemed to take note of this bold statement by a respected investigator.

"No more questions, Your Honor."

Julia Sanders approached the podium. "Mrs. McMillan, can you be certain that the dog print which you noticed near the defendant's footprints was, in fact, Berlin's back paw print?"

"Yes. We visited the humane society where Berlin was taken. We took a comparable cast and they are a perfect match."

"I realize you are not the dog expert or the forensic scientist who analyzed the cast, but I'm sure you admit that it is possible that the paw print belongs to another dog. I mean, nobody actually saw Berlin standing in front of the defendant."

"I suppose only the defendant knows the answer to that question, but my guess is that the chances are good that the back paw print belongs to Berlin."

"Thank you. No more questions."

"No questions, Your Honor."

"Mr. Waring, your next witness."

"Mr. Louis Searing, please."

I approached the witness chair and went through the pre-testimony procedures as everyone else had.

"Mr. Searing, I'd like to ask you about some conversations. The first is a conversation with Mr. McRae about a phone call he received the night of June 4. Do you recall his telling you about a phone call he received?"

"Objection, hearsay," Julia said, rising and making her point emphatically.

"Overruled."

"Yes, he said he got a call from a man who liked my books and wanted to talk to me."

"And, what did Mr. McRae tell him in response to that request."

"He said that I was staying in the east A-frame and could he give me a message."

"And?"

"The man apparently said not to bother me and he'd try to reach me later."

"What does this call mean to you, Mr. Searing?"

"It means that the caller learned where I was staying and having known that, it led to the A-frame being deliberately set on fire the next night." Julia Sanders wanted to fly out of her seat and object to my opinion, but for some reason she let it go.

"The second conversation took place at Hawk's Landing between Deputy Largent and Mary Chandler, the defendant. Do you recall that?"

"Yes."

"What was startling about that conversation?"

"We asked her about a broken window in the bathroom and she said something like 'We didn't break any window.' This was the only time she said 'We' which led me to believe that she was not alone in the cabin. I believe the 'we' refers to herself and Mr. Miles."

"Thank you, Mr. Searing; your witness."

"Mr. Searing, where were you after midnight on June 6?" Julia asked.

"My wife Carol and I were visiting with Jackee and John Miller and some folks at the east end."

"You left to go back to the McRae A-frame about what time?"

"I don't know exactly, but I'd say it was around one."

"You and Carol were on Mr. McRae's Harley-Davidson Motorcycle, is that correct?"

"Yes."

"Please describe for the jury the route you took to the west end."

"We took the main road to Pointe Aux Pins and then headed up to the west end on Lime Kiln Point Road."

"Did you pass anybody during the ride? By that I mean, anyone coming toward you?"

"One vehicle."

"When you say, 'vehicle' you mean a car?"

"It had two headlights so it wasn't a motorcycle or an ATV."

"Where was this?"

"It was south of the airport."

"Did the vehicle come from the airport?"

"I don't know. I recall it was near the airport, because you come around a good curve near the airport and either the car was coming from the airstrip or simply following the road south from the west end."

"So, this car could be transporting someone from the airstrip?"

"Could have. I really don't know."

"Can you identify the driver of this oncoming vehicle?"

"No."

"Can you tell us how many were in this car?"

"No, the lights were too bright. I can't be absolutely certain, but I think the brights were on and it was all I could do to see the road and stay clear of the vehicle."

"You and Carol rode on to the McRae's?"

"Yes. We had to move over to allow the fire fighting folks to get past us."

"So, the fire had been set before you arrived?"

"Yes, when we got there, it was a huge bonfire."

"Let me summarize for the jury. You and Carol were visiting with the Millers on the East end. You left on Mr. McRae's Harley after one o'clock in the morning. You passed one car as you approached the airstrip but you couldn't identify the car, tell how many were in the car or who was driving. Have I accurately summarized your testimony, Mr. Searing?"

"Yes."

"Thank you. No more questions, Your Honor."

"The prosecution rests, your honor.

"Miss Sanders, your first witness."

"Your honor, I wish to make a motion for a Directed Verdict and ask that you throw out this case, because in our opinion, the evidence, even in a light most favorable to the prosecution, is insufficient to meet the elements of the charged offense."

Judge Ickes pondered the request and in a silent courtroom leaned toward the microphone and replied, "Counselor, on the contrary, the evidence is sufficient to address the charges in this case. The trial will continue. Please call your first witness."

Julia dropped her head in disgust having failed in an important attempt to win this case for her client. She looked up and said, "The defense calls Mr. Artie Otley." Artie, wearing suspenders and a nicely ironed shirt, rose from his chair and made his way to the witness stand. He raised his hand to take the oath and then was seated. He stated his name and address for the record.

"Mr. Otley, I've asked you to testify because I understand that in the early morning hours of June 6, you not only heard a helicopter but went outside and saw it hovering over the island. Is this correct?"

"Yes."

"Please tell the jury about this."

"Well, I couldn't get to sleep after a long nap early in the evening and I heard this helicopter sort of buzzing the island and flying low and all. I went outside and looked up and seen it."

"Then you also heard it again, correct?"

"Yes, I heard it about fifteen minutes later. I didn't go outside, but it was the same chopper, I'm pretty sure of it."

"Am I correct that you weren't the only one who heard this helicopter?"

"Others heard it, too, and I think whoever was flyin' it killed those people on Mud Lake Trail."

"Objection, speculation, Your Honor," bellowed Mr. Waring.

"Sustained." The judge looked at Mr. Otley and said, "Please only answer the questions and don't draw any conclusions from your observations."

"Yes, sir. I'm sorry if I did...."

"Mr. Otley," Judge Ickes interrupted. "It's just that witnesses are to only answer questions as directly as they can." Artie nodded and looked back at Julia Sanders.

"So, I think what you're saying is that this helicopter is not commonly seen around Bob-Lo. Is that a fair statement?"

"Yes. Once in awhile we see a Coast Guard helicopter but that's about it."

"Thank you, Mr. Otley. Your witness."

"I have no questions."

"Miss Sanders, next witness," said Judge Ickes, peering over glasses perched near the end of his nose.

"The defense calls Joy Chandler."

Joy, pretty, slim, and stylish was a contrast to her sister. She approached the witness stand, took the oath, stated her name and address for the record and took her seat.

"Joy, you are the sister of the defendant, correct?"

"Yes. She is my younger sister."

"Would you say Mary has any violent tendencies?"

"Oh, absolutely not. Mary has always been compassionate about people, her work, and her community."

"You mentioned her work."

"Yes, Mary has been an advocate for people with vision problems all of her life. She works tirelessly to see that children have a quality education. Mary got her degree at Eastern Michigan University in Special Education. I've never known Mary to be upset or assertive to a point of anger. No, the charges are not about a sister I know."

"Did you know the victim, Jessica Williams?"

"No."

"Did you ever hear your sister talk about her?"

"I vaguely recall her mentioning her as a roommate for a short time when she was at EMU, but that's all I can recall."

"Could you imagine any reason for your sister to be upset or angry at Miss Williams?"

"No."

"Thank you. No more questions, Your Honor."

"Mr. Waring. Your witness," Judge Ickes said.

"Thank you. Miss Chandler, are you close to your sister?"

"I wouldn't say 'close.' Our parents were very religious people, straight and disciplined. I rebelled as a teenager and left home. Mary was the apple of our father's eye and she was their shining example of the perfect daughter. I was always a bit jealous of her. She was adored by the family, she went to college and got a degree to help people less fortunate, and she was successful. But, because I left home, I was not particularly close to Mary."

"So, while you testify that she isn't an angry or violent person or you can't imagine her being accused of these crimes, the fact is, you really don't know Mary do you."

"Of course I know her. She's my sister. We grew up together and we've stayed in touch over the years."

"Before she was accused of these crimes, when was the last time you saw her?"

"We live in the same town now, have for the last few years, and we see each other at Christmas for a few minutes or we bump into each other in a store in Ludington on occasion."

"My guess is there's a lot about you that Mary doesn't know, and a lot about Mary that you don't know. Would that be a fair statement?"

"I guess so. That can be said about any two people, family or not."

"Precisely my point. No more questions, Your Honor."

"Mr. Waring do you have any additional witnesses to call to the stand?" Judge Ickes asked.

"Yes, your honor. I call to the stand Mr. Roger Wedel."

"Mr. Wedel. Please state for the record your name, address, and occupation."

"My name is Roger Wedel. I live at 1627 Blueberry Road in Pellston. I am the owner of Wedel's Helicopter Service in Pellston."

"You've heard the testimony of Mr. Otley?"

"Yes, I have."

"What do you wish to add?"

"I was the pilot of that helicopter."

"Why were you flying it around Bob-Lo Island at approximately one o'clock the morning of June 6?"

"I was there to help a friend, Mr. Mike Miles. We served together in Vietnam in the early seventies. He saved my life and I promised him that if he ever needed me for anything to let me know. He called the evening of June 5 and said he was ready to cash in."

"What did Mr. Miles say?"

"He said he needed me to fly my helicopter with floatational capability to Bob-Lo and to bring it down on Mud Lake. He said he'd be there around one with a woman who needed some medical help."

"Jessica Williams?"

"He didn't mention a name. He said he was saving her or I would be saving her and that if we couldn't get her off the island that night, she'd probably be dead and buried by morning."

The entire courtroom stirred and gasps and mumblings could be heard. The jury was especially taken aback with this testimony. Mary was emotionless with her eyes fixed on Mr. Wedel in stunned disbelief. It was the first time she realized that Mike had betrayed her.

"Dead and buried by morning?"

"Yes, those were his exact words. He said she had been held captive for five days."

"Why did you come forth, Mr. Wedel?"

"Mike told me that under no condition was I ever to tell anyone about all of this, but he is dead now and I have to live with myself. I want justice to be done. Plus, I felt that Mike would be okay with my stating the facts. So, that's why."

"Obviously, Mike and Jessica did not appear at Mud Lake?"

"No, I saw no one. I used my spotlight to try and see anyone along the shore, but saw no one. He directed me not to go looking for him but to leave after fifteen minutes and so I did. I took the chopper up and flew to the west before heading back to Pellston."

Thank you, Mr. Wedel. Your witness, Counselor."

Julia Sanders was stunned as well. She wasn't expecting the witness to admit that Mike had said that Jessica may be dead and buried that night. This didn't look good now, but the fact still remained that there was no body, no witness, no motive, and no weapon. She rose and approached Mr. Wedel.

"Mr. Wedel, did Mr. Miles say anything else to you that evening? Did he mention Mary Chandler or Jessica Williams?"

"No."

"Did he suggest how this woman might die?"

"No."

"Is it possible that she could die of natural causes and not be murdered?"

"I suppose so, but I thought he meant she'd be killed."

"I realize that is what you thought, but Mr. Miles didn't say she would be murdered. He said, if I heard you correctly, she may be dead and buried by morning. Is that your testimony?"

"Yes."

"Is it possible that Mr. Miles was less than serious?"

"No way. Once you've been to Vietnam and you're fighting alongside a buddy, you learn to trust his word, your life could depend on it. Mike didn't play games with me, in Vietnam or here. I believe that woman was to be killed and buried. There is no question about that."

"Mr. Wedel, why did you wait until this last minute to come forward?"

"I left the morning following Mike's call for a four month contract out west. I got back a couple days ago. While getting caught up on local news, I learned of Mr. Miles' death and called the Prosecutor's office."

"No more questions, Your Honor."

"You may step down, Mr. Wedel," Judge Ickes said, realizing that Mr. Wedel's testimony was very significant to this trial.

Julia Sanders rose. "Your Honor. I request a short recess so I can confer with my client."

"Granted. Court will reconvene in fifteen minutes."

Julia huddled with Mary. "As we've discussed often, we now need to decide if you should testify. Is that something you might consider?"

"Why do you think it's necessary?" Mary asked.

"The testimony of the helicopter pilot is very damaging. His statement that she may be dead and buried by morning doesn't help our case. Since her body hasn't been found, everyone naturally assumes she was murdered and buried and you are the obvious killer."

"I can't get up there. The questions I'd have to answer. It would be obvious that I am guilty as all get out because I did kidnap her and kill her and I did torch the A-frame."

"Well, I think I can still drive home the point that I've been doing since the beginning; no witness, no motive, no body, no weapon and see if they'll go with that reasonable doubt, but we've just lost the possibility that someone in that helicopter did the killing. He was too credible a witness for that to continue to be an excuse."

"I can't testify. I can't"

"OK, we'll keep you off the stand."

Judge Ickes rapped his gavel on the wood block. "Court is now in session. Counselor Sanders, your next witness?"

"The defense rests, Your Honor."

There was immediate reaction of surprise that the defense had decided not to have Mary Chandler testify. That could only mean that they feared the cross-examination of the Prosecutor or that Mary's vow to tell the truth, the whole truth, and nothing but the truth would be incriminating.

It was time for closing comments by both attorneys. Mr. Waring was first. "Ladies and gentlemen of the jury. Mary Chandler has been accused of kidnapping, arson, and murder. The judge allowed three charges in the same trial because they may constitute a pattern, a scheme or a plan. We have shown through the testimony of experts and reports from forensic scientists that Mary Chandler did write and seal an invitation to Jessica Williams to take an ill-fated cruise in the Straits on Mackinac in the evening hours of June 1. She was kidnapped by Mary Chandler and Mike Miles. These two took the boat *Stinky* to Bob-lo Island docking at the Main Dock. Mary then discarded Jessica's purse by putting it in the trash, not suspecting it would be discovered by the man working at the transfer station on the island. The three went to the cabin on Mud Lake Trail. Jessica was held captive there until her death in the early morning hours of June 6. Mary Chandler learned that Lou Searing and Maggie McMillan were looking into Jessica's disappearance. She took steps to kill Louis Searing by burning the McRae's east A-frame where Lou was staying; they knew this from a phone call to Mr. McRae the night of June 4.

"Mary came back to the cabin to find Mike dead. She knew she couldn't call the police or she would be suspect of kidnapping and murder so she buried him. Since no body has been discovered in the past several months and there's been no word from Jessica, we can only assume that she is dead and buried on Bob-Lo. The defendant is the only logical person to commit this crime. I can't make it more convincing or obvious than that.

"I trust you will see the pattern. As you heard in testimony from Mrs. Bowers, Jessica was not herself the night of June 1, there was some evil lurking in her life and now only the defendant knows why she is dead. Now you, ladies and gentlemen of the jury, have the responsibility to the citizens of Michigan, to the citizens of Mackinac County, and to the citizens of Bob-Lo Island to see that justice prevails and find her guilty of kidnapping, arson and murder. Thank you."

Defense Attorney Sanders was slow to rise. She knew that Kenneth Waring had outlined for the jury exactly what happened on Bob-Lo. The jury seemed to be with him as they listened intently and took notes. The defense for her client lay clearly in reasonable doubt, so she would play this card to the best of her ability.

Miss Sanders stood before the jury and paused for a moment. She raised her head and said, "All of you will remember my opening statement to you a few days ago. I asked you to look for evidence of kidnapping, arson and murder. I asked you to look for a witness, for a motive, for a weapon, and even for a body. Here we are at the end of the trial and I remind you, ladies and gentlemen, that you still have not heard from a witness, someone who saw the defendant kidnap Jessica, someone who saw the defendant burn down an A-frame, someone who saw Jessica murdered, if in fact she was murdered. In fact, the call to Mr. McRae came from an unknown man and certainly not my client. I asked you to look for someone who saw a murder and all you've been told is a murder may have been witnessed by a dog and then we can't even be certain that the dog is the dog we've come to know as Berlin.

"Doubt. You must have doubt. Remember Mr. Searing said that the vehicle that passed him as he went toward the McRae home early on June 6 was a car that passed him south of the airport road? Well, that car could have been holding occupants who carried out this crime. Reasonable doubt.

"As was pointed out in this trial, my client is not charged with the murder of Mr. Miles. Don't you have doubt in that whoever did kill him most certainly killed Miss Williams, and I will state again, if Miss Williams was in fact murdered? Reasonable doubt.

"You've heard about the helicopter and even though Mr. Wedel is a most credible witness, could it be that someone in the helicopter, so close to the cabin on Mud Lake Trail, might have appeared and killed two people or at least Mr. Miles? Doubt, doubt, doubt!

"You are about to make a decision about a person's life and it will be very difficult to commit a person to prison for life when you can't point to one witness, one weapon, one motive, or I repeat, even a body that tells you beyond a reasonable doubt that Mary Chandler is guilty of one, let alone three, crimes." She looked deep into the eyes of the jurors. It was so quiet you could hear a pin drop.

After an effective pause that caused everyone in the courtroom to seriously ponder her point, Julia Sanders concluded her remarks. "Thank you for your attention during this trial. You've been a jury who has listened to much detail and a very confusing case. I admire you and I know Miss Chandler is thankful for your attention. This trial determines her future and I only hope that in the jury room, you'll talk about the lack of a witness, a weapon, a motive, a body, and you'll all have to agree that the evidence needed to find a woman guilty isn't there. It simply isn't there. Mary and I ask you to return verdicts of not guilty. Thank you."

Judge Ickes looked at the Prosecuting Attorney. "Your rebuttal, Mr. Waring?"

Kenneth rose and walked to the front of the jury. He paused, collected his thoughts and said, "Thank you, Your Honor, and thank you, Jurors. Miss Sanders has repeatedly told you, 'No body, no witness, no motive, no weapon,' and I readily concede that, but the circumstantial evidence is overwhelming. I ask you to recall the words of Mr. Wedel, a respected veteran of the Vietnam War, a man of integrity and honor. He testified that Mr. Miles told him that the woman he'd have with him may be dead and buried by morning. Mr. Miles and Miss Williams did not show up for the rescue and Mr. Wedel was obviously unsuccessful in saving Jessica's life.

"The next morning, the body of Mike Miles is found in a grave, several feet from the cabin rented by the defendant. There are now two bodies, one dead and buried as my evidence presented in this trial shows. The other, Jessica Williams, has never been found and it has been more than four months since these crimes occurred. There is a secret buried on Bob-Lo and it rests in the mind and soul of Jessica Williams. The fingerprints, the DNA analysis puts Jessica in that cabin, the threatening note to Mr. Searing, the burning of the A-frame where he was staying, clearly points to the defendant as the kidnapper, the arsonist, and the murderer.

"The only words you heard in this trial that give you any clue to the interaction between Mary Chandler, Mike Miles and Jessica Williams comes to you from a helicopter pilot who told you and listen carefully to his words, 'If we don't save her, she may be dead and buried by morning.' Well, she wasn't saved so it's logical to assume that she was murdered and buried on Bob-Lo. It was not of Mr. Miles doing, I can assure you of that.

"Yes, no weapon, no motive, no body, and no witness, but a man with sterling credentials told you the plan was for Jessica Williams to be and I quote, 'dead and buried by morning'. Mike Miles is dead and buried and that leaves only one person to commit the murder and burial and she is in this courtroom. She is the defendant, Mary Chandler."

As with the concluding statement of Defense Attorney Sanders, the room was quiet. Prosecutor Waring had made his point and made it emphatically. From almost all of the jury, the people in the audience, and surely those watching on Court TV, a collective mental "Amen" could be heard.

⊰⊱

It was time for the thirteenth juror to be dismissed. The judge asked jurors to take a small piece of paper and write their juror number on it. He reminded jurors six and nine to put a line underneath their number so as to be able to tell which was the six and which was the nine. All numbers were put into a small box, shuffled and the judge pulled out number ten. This juror took a deep breath, shook her head, gathered up a few things and left. She seemed to have two conflicting emotions, relief for not having to continue with the case but a sense of frustration in listening to all of the testimony only to be told to go home and not offer an opinion.

The remaining jurors were given instructions by the judge and then led by the sheriff to the jury room. The sheriff reminded them to knock if they needed anything. The door closed and the twelve were finally together with a job to do. It was time to make a decision. It would be safe to say that all twelve came to the courthouse to begin serving on the jury believing that Mary Chandler was guilty of all charges. Now, they would listen to each other and confirm their pre-trial hunch, become hopelessly deadlocked, or they would find her not guilty of all charges.

The group quickly decided upon Joyce as the foreperson. The choice was easy because no one volunteered to take the job. Tricia seemed impressed with Joyce's interest and knowledge of law.

"I think Joyce would make a good foreperson. I suggest her," Tricia said.

Others seemed agreeable and Lonnie said, "Guess that settles it. You're elected."

Joyce sat in her chair, inwardly pleased to have the responsibility and outwardly humble and hoped she could do a good job. She began her responsibility by saying, "Well, I guess it comes down to us, doesn't it?"

"I say let's vote it up or down on each charge and get out of here," Les Gier said. The rest of the jurors were surprised at his lack of patience in discussing each charge. He loudly told everyone that he didn't want to be there in the first place. This was taking him away from his work and he was losing dollars for every minute he sat on this jury. The woman was guilty and they should just vote and get on with life!

"It sounds like a simple solution," Joyce replied. "But, I really think in fairness to the judge, attorneys and the defendant that we discuss each charge and then take a vote to see if we are in agreement." The body language around the table seemed in agreement with Joyce's thought.

The next hour or so was a discussion with everyone taking a turn to say what was on his or her mind. Joyce made sure that everyone had a chance to comment and for all members of the jury to question one another.

The feelings of the jury seemed to be encompassed in the statement made by one of the quiet jurors who said, "It seems that what we all think is there isn't sufficient evidence to convict her of the arson charge, but the evidence seems overwhelming that she kidnapped and killed Jessica." Most heads nodded affirmatively.

"OK, now can we vote this thing up or down and get on with our lives?" Les asked impatiently.

"I think that's a good next step." Joyce replied being courteous. "Let's take a straw vote on each charge and see where we stand. If you don't feel comfortable voting, don't do it. We're just seeing where people's heads are at the moment."

"Are we voting for the final vote now?" Priscilla asked.

"No. This is just a straw vote to see where we stand at the moment," Joyce responded.

"OK, I'm ready then."

"On the charge of arson, how many vote guilty?" Joyce asked. Three hands went up. "Not guilty?" Nine hands were raised, including

Joyce's. "It looks like the majority see her not guilty of the arson charge. On the charge of kidnapping, how many vote guilty?" Eleven hands went up. "Not guilty?" Only Joyce raised her hand. "On the charge of murder, how many vote guilty? Eleven hands went up. "Not guilty?" Joyce raised her hand.

"Looks like our leader sees an innocent woman over at the defense table," Les remarked. "Looks like we've got a little convincing to do here."

"Let's let Joyce tell us why she is voting like she is. Maybe she's got a good point that the rest of us haven't considered," Priscilla said.

"Well, I found myself agreeing with the defense attorney when she said there is reasonable doubt in this case. She kept saying, no witness, no weapon, no body, no motive and I'm not sure I'm ready to put a woman in prison for life without at least one of those things being clear."

Joyce's comments caused eleven other people to feel like they had to defend their vote and with each seeing that everyone else thought like them, it simply fueled a lot of negative looks and comments at Joyce. The psychology of the thing got to Joyce as well. She felt cornered. She thought she had to defend herself against the others and so she dug in her heels a bit more. It was on the verge of becoming ugly when Joyce's cool head prevailed. "I think we could use a break. We need to get some fresh air, and take a moment to relax."

"I say we call it a day. Let's ask the judge to dismiss us," Lonnie said. Everyone agreed. A note was passed to the judge and permission was granted.

CHAPTER SEVENTEEN

Wednesday, October 11
St. Ignace, Michigan
Mackinac County Courthouse

The jury met at 9:30 a.m. in the jury room. People appeared fresh, coffee cups were filled and they were ready to get back to trying to make a decision. After they came together, Tricia commented, "Last night, I thought about what Joyce had said and I think she has a good point. If I were going to doubt, it would be the story about the car going south of the airport. Maybe whoever was in that car had something to do with the murder."

"The woman doesn't even take the stand to defend herself. What is going on here?" Les asked. "She won't get up there 'cause she's got to raise her hand and swear to tell the truth and her attorney knows that she done it and putting her on the stand brings all the truth out. She's not stupid. That's why she asked us at the beginning, if we'd think she was guilty if she didn't call her as a witness. Of course she wanted to know that. Well, what are we supposed to think? She won't even get up there and tell us what happened. If she's innocent, why doesn't she tell us her story?" Several heads were nodding in agreement. Joyce's wasn't.

"She doesn't have to defend herself," Joyce responded. "The judge said that it is up to the Prosecutor to convince us beyond a reasonable doubt that she committed these crimes. The burden of proof is on the Prosecution."

"Burden of proof. There you go with that legal mumbo-jumbo. She killed the lady, burned the guy's A-frame. That pilot set it in stone for me. Who else would it have been? It had to have been Chandler. Let's vote this through and get on home," Les demanded.

"We can't do that. Looks like we're hung, we've either got to convince Joyce or the rest of us have got to change our minds," Lonnie said.

"We're not changing our minds. Are you nuts? Sure the evidence is circumstantial, but for cryin' out loud, what do you need to have a crime be more obvious. The evidence has her kidnapping that Jessica Williams, bringing her to Bob-Lo, keeping her at a cabin, killing her and gettin' rid of the body. I'll give you that nobody saw her, but the evidence is overwhelming against her," Les said with emotion. He knew he was speaking for the majority.

"Can you folks open your minds for a minute and look at this another way. Try, just try for me, OK?" Joyce said, getting a little emotional herself. "Let's say the cruise after the banquet was legit. Can't you see Jessica handing her purse to Mary when she gets on board the boat? Or maybe, Mary takes it and moves it below since it may get wet, for example. Then let's say they arrive on Bob-Lo so Jessica doesn't have to go all the way back to Mackinac, and she'll arrange to send her friend the shawl or whatever was borrowed. Then let's say she's kidnapped by someone on the island who wants to frame Mary. This guy kills Mike and Jessica and then Mary isn't guilty of anything and we'd send her to prison for life."

"If your version of what happened really happened, then why doesn't Mary Chandler get up in that witness chair and tell everyone the truth, how she was being framed and that she is the hero and not the criminal?" Les asked. "We could go around this table and concoct all kinds of 'what ifs' and all of the stories would make sense, but we have to base this case on the evidence, albeit circumstantial, but based on that, this woman is as guilty as they come."

Joyce responded emotionally, "The 'what if' I have to live with for the rest of my life is what if someone in that car came to the cabin and killed those two people. Mr. Searing said he saw a car coming south on Lime Kiln Point Road and he said it was before he got to the road going to the airport. There was no witness, no weapon, and no clear motive and I have doubt, that's all. I have a doubt that Mary killed Jessica. She obviously didn't kill Mike or she'd be on trial for killin' him. So whoever did kill him probably killed Jessica. I'll not change my vote to guilty."

"I can't believe you're thinking this way. Look at the total picture! How can someone rent a cabin and have a guy buried out back and not be involved? I can see where the evidence is not there to convict her of burning the guy's cabin, but kidnapping and murder. She's as guilty as they come. How else can you explain it?" Les asked.

"Framed for one. We don't know what's going on in the lives of all these people. Sure it looks like Mary is involved, but in this country we don't lock people up for life because of people thinking something happened. There must be evidence and a jury has to make a decision that a person is guilty beyond a reasonable doubt, and I, for one, have a reasonable doubt. If someone witnessed it, if there was a weapon with fingerprints on it, if I knew of some deep-seated hatred or something like that, my doubt would be decreased and I could agree with you folks, but the Prosecution has not made a case that takes away my doubt."

The rest of the jury sat and watched this two-person dialogue and everyone seemed to be ready to vote guilty or not.

"Are we ready for our final vote?" Joyce asked. All nodded.

"OK, all those who vote guilty of arson, raise your hand." No hands were raised. "All who vote not guilty, raise your hand." All twelve hands were raised. "All those who vote guilty of kidnapping, raise your hand." Eleven hands went up. "I guess that makes me the only one to vote not guilty. And, finally, all those who vote guilty of murder, raise your hand." Eleven hands were raised. "Once again I will vote not guilty. I'm not changing my mind and I doubt eleven of you will see this the way I see it, so we'd better tell the judge we're deadlocked." Joyce wrote a note to the sheriff saying they were deadlocked. Lonnie knocked on the door to get his attention.

Judge Ickes directed the jury to come into the courtroom. When all were seated he said, 'I want to thank you for your deliberation in this case. Reaching a consensus is sometimes difficult. Each of you has spent three days listening to testimony and trying to reach a verdict. I'm going to ask you to return to the jury room and continue to deliberate. I ask you to listen to each other, to consider all of the evidence, and try to come to consensus. If you have any questions which, if answered, will help you reach a decision, please do not hesitate to ask me. Thank you."

All the jurors rose and in single-file, returned to the jury room, each taking the seat they had occupied before going into the courtroom.

"Is there anything we can say to help you, Joyce?" a juror asked.

"Yes, you can tell me who killed Mike Miles, because, whoever killed him probably killed Jessica. If Mary were on trial for the murder of Mike, I'd be with you folks—no doubt—guilty, but why isn't she charged with the murder of Mike? Why?"

"Maybe Mike killed and buried Jessica?" Priscilla asked.

"No way," Les bellowed. 'You don't call for a helicopter to come and rescue you and then kill the person to be rescued."

Joyce saw in Priscilla, the first glimmer of doubt. "Yes, Priscilla. Exactly, maybe Mike did kill her and maybe he called the helicopter as a decoy to fool everyone into thinking he would save her when the plan was for him to kill her and maybe he did."

Discussion continued until it was time for lunch. The jurors were taken as a group to a local restaurant where they were directed not to discuss the case with anyone. Following lunch the jury returned to the courthouse and sat down to a few hours of talking and thinking and trying to convince others of an opinion.

A break in the deadlock occurred mid-afternoon when a juror said, "Remember when that Mrs. Atkins used the wrong pronoun? She said 'we' or 'us' in referring to going back to her cabin. Maybe Jessica was rescued by her and that slip wasn't a slip."

"Right!" Joyce said, picking up another possible doubter.

"Or, maybe she was rescued by the helicopter pilot and he's back now to get revenge for killing his friend, Mike. Maybe Jessica is alive and was taken off the island in the helicopter," Lonnie said coming up with yet another possible outcome in this mess.

"Right again!" Joyce said. "You see, I'm not alone. You're beginning to see what I'm saying. There is doubt. We weren't convinced beyond a reasonable doubt."

Les stood up. "Listen, folks. This is getting out of control here. We're straying from the evidence. We're simply going crazy with our imaginations. I can do the same thing. How about a spaceship coming down and whisking Jessica off to Mars. See, I can play this game too." For the first time in three days, some folks smiled and a few even chuckled. Les had broken the trend of thinking of possible reasons for Mary not to have killed Jessica. Les continued, "Let's get back to using common sense and draw from the testimony. I say we vote this up and get her in jail where she belongs!"

Joyce could tell she had lost her hold on the thinking of her fellow jurors. "OK, Les, let's do it. Is there anybody with me in thinking she is not guilty of kidnapping and murder?"

"I will vote for kidnapping, but not for the murder," Priscilla said. "I agree with you, Joyce."

"OK, Priscilla. Anyone else?" No hands were raised and no one spoke up. "I assume everyone votes not guilty in the charge of arson but everyone but me votes guilty for kidnapping and everyone but Priscilla and me votes guilty for the murder charge. Have I got it right?" All nodded.

"When we get in there, we'll probably be polled, and..."

"What does that mean?" Tricia asked.

"After I give the verdicts, one of the attorneys may want the sheriff to ask each one of us how we vote and I assume you'll all vote consistent with my summary a moment ago. Correct?" Everyone nodded.

"OK, let's tell the judge we're ready and get this over with. One last time for anyone to speak up." Silence.

๛

It was about 4 o'clock in the afternoon of October 11, a cloudy and cold day. Word had gone throughout the courthouse and community that the jury was about to re-enter the court room. The media, the prosecutor's team, Mary, Julia and Joy took some deep breaths and slowly made their way to the defense table. The judge walked into a standing-room only crowd.

The door at the side of the courtroom opened and the 12 jurors filed in. Everybody looked at a stream of faces. There were no clues to the verdict based on facial expression. Most of the jurors looked down as they walked or looked straight ahead. They looked like they had been through a very stressful situation. The jurors stood in front of their chairs until the judge said, "Please be seated."

The air of anticipation was higher than it had ever been in Judge Ickes' courtroom. Mary sat in her simple print dress. She had prepared herself for this moment, when her future was delivered to her by twelve people she didn't even know. A guilty verdict would put her in prison possibly for life. A not guilty verdict would allow her to live a normal life once again. But she would never be free of the torment in her mind. What had once been an overwhelming need to exact revenge was now seen as another failure to live up to the life of obedience to God's laws. She could only be thankful her parents had never known the truth about her. She sat quietly with hands clasped and waited.

Prosecutor Waring was fully expecting a not guilty verdict. A guilty verdict would come from a quick decision. The fact that the jury took so long and couldn't reach a decision told him that someone or perhaps several jurors didn't think Mary was guilty of at least one charge. And, if they doubted one, they could very well doubt her guilt on all three charges.

He had prepared a statement for the media no matter what the verdicts. If a not-guilty verdict came forth, it would be a crime. He believed Mary Chandler killed Jessica Williams and for a just society to determine otherwise would make the justice system the laughing stock of citizens throughout Michigan.

Julia Sanders fully expected a not guilty verdict. The length of deliberations and the hung jury prior to Judge Ickes' plea to keep working let her know that she'd be victorious. She knew her client was guilty but the court system allowed for the decision to be made by peers after an honest debate by both attorneys. She was proud of her performance. A guilty verdict would definitely be a surprise.

Judge Ickes had enough experiences as an attorney, as a prosecutor, and as a judge to know that once twelve people begin to discuss a set of facts backed with emotion, it was very difficult to predict what the verdict might be. The judge expected a guilty verdict because he felt Mary did kill Jessica on Bob-Lo, and because he thought Prosecutor Waring did a good job of presenting the case. But, he had to admit that Julia Sanders put forth a convincing argument for reasonable doubt.

With everyone seated and silence so deafening you could almost hear people's thoughts, Judge Ickes said, "Ladies and gentlemen of the jury, have you reached a verdict?"

"We have, Your Honor," Joyce replied.

"In the matter of first degree murder of Jessica Williams, how do you find the defendant?"

"We were unable to reach a verdict, Your Honor."

Mary Chandler took a deep breath with her eyes closed. At least she was not guilty. Mary felt her heart pounding in her chest. She had just heard the words that meant there was some hope after all. The entire courtroom erupted in comments of surprise at the verdict Judge Ickes banged his gavel and demanded that order be restored in his courtroom. In a matter of seconds, all was quiet.

"Your Honor, I wish a poll taken of the verdict," Kenneth Waring said. The request was granted and all but Joyce and Priscilla voted guilty.

"In the matter of kidnapping of Jessica Williams, how do you find the defendant?" Judge Ickes asked.

"We were unable to reach a verdict, Your Honor."

"I request a poll of the jury, Your Honor," Kenneth Waring said, realizing the worst was probably yet to come. The poll was conducted and each juror except Joyce Shannon stated, "Guilty" when asked.

"In the matter of arson of property belonging to Mr. and Mrs. McRae, how do you find the defendant?"

"Not guilty, Your Honor."

"I request a poll, Your Honor," Prosecutor Waring stated. The poll was conducted and each juror said, "Not guilty."

Everyone in the courtroom once again began to talk and shake their heads in total amazement at the verdicts. Judge Ickes again slammed his gavel down and demanded that order be restored. Everyone complied and silence was once again present in the courtroom.

Mr. Waring made note of each vote and since an overwhelming majority voted to convict Mary of kidnapping and murder, he felt he would request a retrial.

"Your Honor, I hereby request that bond be continued and I hereby petition the court for a retrial."

"Your request is granted," Judge Ickes replied. He turned to the jury and said, "I wish to thank the jury for their time and their hard work in this case. I ask you to return to the jury room as I wish to have some words with you. Each attorney is invited to join me if you wish. This trial is adjourned."

Once inside the jury room, Judge Ickes again thanked the jurors for their hard work. He repeated that he had hoped a verdict would have been reached, but he understood that in this case that was not the outcome. He explained that since the defendant was not found guilty of kidnapping and murder, she could be tried again if the prosecutor wished. This is not double jeopardy as no verdict of guilt or innocence was rendered by the jury.

Each attorney then had time with the jurors to ask questions so they could understand the thinking behind the verdicts. Jury members were quite vocal about the strengths and weaknesses of the defense and prosecution. Both attorneys thanked the jury for their candid observations and then went out to face the media. They were joined by those jurors who didn't mind talking with reporters and the folks from Court TV.

When the lawyers and a few jurors walked out of the jury room, the media quickly pounced on them to get reactions and quotes so that their stories got to the newsrooms in time for the 6 o'clock news.

The reaction on Bob-Lo was met with despair. Justice had not been done. Most were sure of Mary's guilt and this hung jury stuff only led many to continue their disbelief in a just system for handling criminals. It was as if the curtain wouldn't come down quietly on this tragedy that unfortunately had occurred on their jewel of an island. These folks did not want to draw attention to their island and the whole matter was a huge embarrassment to the people who lived there. From now on, visitors to the island would want to see the cabin on Mud Lake Trail where the murders supposedly took place and too much attention would be given to a horrifying event, and not enough to the pristine beauty of the island.

Joy took a moment to thank Julia for her work to defend her sister. Mr. Waring was explaining to reporters his reactions to the verdicts. He didn't want to come across as a sore loser, but he was convinced that Mary was guilty and not to have the verdict go his way, or rather, the way of the people, was disheartening to say the least. He thanked his staff for tirelessly gathering information in the case.

The most attention was being given to Joyce Shannon who chose to come to the back of the courtroom to be questioned by the media.

"What was the deciding factor in having a hung jury?" a reporter shouted above the noise.

"Doubt. It was possible that Mary was framed. We couldn't totally agree that she had murdered Jessica. We didn't doubt that she was at the cabin, but without a witness, a weapon, a body, and a clear motive, it was doubt. We, or I guess two of us simply had a reasonable doubt."

Within a half hour, the courtroom was vacant and quiet once again. All the players in the drama were getting on with their lives, the jury went home to finally talk about the case with family and friends, the attorneys went back to their respective offices. Judge Ickes had a racquetball game early in the evening, and reporters went scurrying to call in stories or whisk film to television studios.

"Well, how about that?" I said to Maggie.

"She's a guilty lady, Lou. I hope some justice comes in the retrial. And, I guess we now know why the alarm was set for 12:45. He planned to take Jessica to a helicopter that would carry them safely off the island. My guess is he didn't tell Jessica his plan in time. Jessica saw a chance for escape, and in the struggle he slipped and died."

"I agree. It all makes perfect sense now, doesn't it? The puzzle parts are all set and each part now gives us the whole picture."

"But why? I still don't know the motive," Maggie said in frustration.

"My guess is there will always be buried secrets of Bois Blanc. We may never know."

ॐ

When the court proceedings were concluded and interviews with the media were complete, two planes came back to Bob-Lo. Maggie and I flew with Ed and Clara while Gavin and Jenny flew with Wags and Jacquilyne. Maggie left her power chair in her van in St. Ignace. Wags and I helped Maggie get in the plane. We'd find a pushable chair on Bob-Lo.

The people on Bob-Lo had been glued to their satellite dishes and one had been fed into the Community Building where several people gathered to watch. When it was all over, people felt frustrated because they collectively thought that Mary Chandler had gotten away with murder. Time would probably heal and people would have a sense of being able to get back to normal once again.

Erin had been in the Community Building watching the end of the trial when she spotted, across the room, the strange man from Mackinac Island. When she saw him she instantly recalled his prediction of magic revealing the murderer. He wandered in her direction.

"Told you. It was in the magic," he said, with an eerie smile.

Erin shook her head and wondered if the man was okay. "Yeah, I guess you were right," Erin said, walking away to greet others in the building.

Jenny approached Erin, "Fred's okay." He's quite eccentric, but all of us know he's harmless."

"I saw him on Mackinac Island and he recognized me as someone working with Lou and Maggie on the case. He said Jessica was murdered and the solution was in the magic."

"Well, that's easy to explain. He's Mrs. Henderson's son, the bed and breakfast lady you interviewed. She no doubt told Fred about your looking into the disappearance of Jessica and Mike. He mentioned to his mother that he overheard the people visiting with Mike late last Friday night talking about a kidnapping and murder. She didn't believe him. Seems that Fred often makes up far-fetched stories. Apparently, this time, he was right and nobody would listen to him.

"The line about magic. He has long been fascinated with magic and attributes everything to magic. So, telling you the solution was in the magic was just his way, once again, of relating everything to magic."

"But, he was right. It was rooted in the magic with Gary bringing Mary to Lou and Maggie's attention."

"Coincidence."

"But what's he doing here on Bob-Lo?"

"Oh, he likes it here. Wags brings him over about once a month to give Mrs. Henderson some time to herself. He seems strange and people often feel uncomfortable around him, but we old-timers have grown accustomed to Fred and his strange ways."

I greeted Erin and thanked her once again for all of her work. "You played a key role in this, Erin! Thanks a lot."

"I enjoyed it, Lou. I may switch careers and get into forensic science. It's a fascinating field."

"They can use good people, I'm sure. You saw how their work was instrumental in solving this case."

"By the way, what did they do with Mike's body?" Erin asked.

"Handed it over to a relative in Lapeer. I think he had an uncle in the area."

"Whatever happened to the three people on Mackinac Island?" Erin wondered.

"They were questioned by the authorities. It seems that Mike had asked them to help him with a problem. Mike explained that I would probably investigate Jessica's disappearance and they promised Mike that they would monitor my comings and goings. They assured Mike that I'd be off the island.

"Mike wrote a note that they were to go to the hotel and leave me a message late Saturday night. Then they were to monitor the ferries and marina to see that I left the next morning and if I didn't, to locate me and report to Mike. They were simply friends who did what they could to help, believing that I was an enemy of their friend.

"They were arrested for abetting in a criminal activity and destruction of property."

"Did they go to jail for their role in this?"

"You know, I don't know. I wasn't involved in the trial and never heard the outcome."

Before Maggie and I were to be flown back to St. Ignace, the McRaes decided to host a get together of all the people who had helped us with the investigation. They arranged for the reception to be at the Hoover Community Building. Present was Tom Wilson, the man at the transfer station who spotted Jessica's purse; Curt Plaunt, the captain of the *Kristen D*; Gary Grayson the magician; Doc and Annie Heckstall. Barb from the Bob-Lo Tavern, and Sheila from Hawk's Landing were on hand. Wags and Jacquilyne were there. Vanessa Redhawk was present taking lots of photographs. Jackee and John Miller were there talking about the honey business. Claude Murray and Buck Ramsey were chatting and enjoying some coffee. Doc Edwards, who helped Erin, was there. Deputy Largent stopped in to greet folks, but didn't stay long. Bunker was there writing an article for the *Bob Lo Tattler*, the Association's newsletter. Joe Friday and his family stopped in for some cake and coffee. Jim Vosper could be seen talking with friends and neighbors while munching on a piece of cake. Gavin had taken his boat over to the island to pick up Tony Adams, Bob Brockington, Mrs. Henderson, Fred Henderson, Leo Little and the owner of the *Slinky*, Bert Richards. Even Jeff Horner from the State Police Forensic Lab in Grayling made a trip up to see everyone.

Guests were milling about, discussing the trial, the verdicts, and expressing their frustration with the whole ugly mess that like a cancer had come to their island and wouldn't go away. Into the room walked Julia Sanders, Mary's attorney. She approached Gavin McRae and the two conversed for several seconds. Gavin seemed surprised by whatever Julia was saying. Gavin then got everyone's attention when he tapped a spoon on a glass repeatedly. "Could I have your attention. This is Miss Sanders, as most of you know. She has brought a videotape that she wants us to watch, or rather only those of us here who are residents, full or part-time. In addition, Mr. and Mrs. Searing, Mrs. McMillan, and Mr. and Mrs. Williams are invited to watch it as well."

There was a buzz of conversation as the people were curious about what they would be viewing. In a few minutes the equipment was ready, the videotape inserted, and after a few seconds, Mary appeared on the screen. Gavin adjusted the volume. All residents gathered round the monitor and listened. Non-residents went outside and remained curious, never to know what was seen or heard.

"As all of you on Bob-Lo now know, the jury has made their decisions regarding my guilt or innocence for the charges of kidnapping and killing Jessica Williams. I am making this tape recording before the trial so I do not know what the outcome will be. I will tell you the truth and the truth is that I did kidnap Jessica, I did burn down the A-frame and I did kill Jessica. Following the trial I will inform my lawyer of the burial spot, and release her of the client/ attorney privilege so Jessica's body can be given a proper burial.

"My message to you has nothing to do with the outcome of the trial. I do have several things to say and I thought the use of this videotape would be the best way to communicate with you. I would rather simply come and talk to you, but I'm sure the authorities wouldn't allow it and all of you would probably feel very uncomfortable being around me given the crimes I've committed.

"If Mr. and Mrs. Williams are viewing this, I am truly sorry for what I did. I ask your forgiveness, but I understand if you can't forgive me for taking the life of your daughter. If the McRaes are viewing this, I am sorry for burning your A-frame. I felt I needed to get Mr. Searing out of the case and fully believed he was sleeping in the A-frame when I set fire to it. I'm sorry, Mr. and Mrs. Searing and Mrs. McMillan, for threatening you and for attempting to take your lives. I am very thankful you are alive. I understand that a woman was injured escaping the fire and I'm thankful for her life as well.

"Beyond asking for forgiveness and expressing my sincere remorse for the crimes I committed, I want to talk to the people on Bob-Lo Island. If these people are not viewing this videotape now, I will ask my lawyer to see that people who live on the island have the opportunity to see and listen to my words.

"I have inherited millions of dollars from my parents. I am giving the majority of this inheritance to the people of Bob-Lo Island. However, there are conditions to receiving this money. These are as follows; the cabin owned by Doc Lemon must be totally destroyed, the Mud Lake Trail must be closed and allowed to be wild land once again. There must never be any mention made of the tragedy that took place here. There must be no media, no mention in *The Bob-Lo Tattler*, no answers to questions asked by people coming to the island. My name and the name of the victims must never be mentioned. Nothing must be written in any account of the history of the island. Nothing built with this money is to have my name associated with it. In fact, the name Chandler must never ever be found in the papers related to the island. I will have an independent source monitor my request and if any violation of our agreement can be documented, the money and any interest will be given to a collection of charities that will be known to the executor of my estate.

"The money will save your school, will provide any community needs, will maintain the pristine existence of your island or you can compete with Mackinac Island for tourists. How you spend the money or not spend it is totally up to you, but the condition is that not a word be said about what happened here. The issue is now whether or not you can keep a secret, whether or not you can bury the secrets of Bob-Lo. From this moment on, the name Mary Chandler or any reference to what happened on Bob-Lo from June 1 to June 7 must never be spoken.

"You probably wonder what it was that caused me to kill Jessica. It was a secret once shared between us—a secret never to be revealed. But it was and it devastated me so that taking her life, though wrong, was the revenge I sought.

"I did not kill Mike Miles. Mike and Jessica also shared a secret until Jessica told another. Mike needed revenge as well. Together we plotted and planned Jessica's death, her price to pay for breaking our trust.

"Jessica and Mike and their secrets are buried on Bob-Lo. If you keep your end of our agreement, all of our secrets will forever be buried, if only in our minds. I seek your forgiveness. Good bye."

A blanket of silence descended over the people at the reception. Gavin McRae broke the silence when he said, "Thank you for coming. May we all begin to heal. I'm sure the Island leaders will be in touch with us soon to discuss this development. Have a good day in peace."

Many left the Hoover Community Building and quietly walked to their cars or homes. All of a sudden the judgements of the people came to rest in a test of their character for they knew that if anyone violated the terms of the agreement, the entire island would suffer the consequences.

⁓

There were still several folks in the Community Building when I received a call from a producer in Hollywood. He had seen the Court TV show and after listening to all the drama thought the tale would make for an exciting movie. "Once you get that book written, Lou, contact me and we'll talk about a movie."

I was floored by the opportunity. I didn't even think about all the implications and consequences of having a movie crew on Bob-Lo for several weeks. I simply said, "Sure. Thanks."

I got everyone's attention, "Hey, listen to this. That was a movie producer in Hollywood. He saw the Court TV program and sees a movie coming from all of this. As soon as I finish the book, they'll want to talk about a movie."

The people were of many different minds. Some could see the excitement, the fun of having movie stars walking around on their island and others saw a disturbance of their peace and quiet. Some thought the attention to Bob-Lo would be good. They'd be a famous place. Others felt like they had just lost their island.

The offer was put to rest, when Jackee Miller spoke up, "I think that whatever any of us might think about this offer for Hollywood to immortalize our island, the offer for millions in exchange for never saying a word about the week of June 1 or to ever mention the woman's name, seals this offer. We can get back to living our lives on this island we love. Offer is rejected!" Everyone cheered with sustained applause.

As the reception was about to end, Jacquilyne asked, "What's the title of your next book, Lou?"

"Oh, how about, 'Buried Secrets of Bois Blanc: Murder in the Straits of Mackinac?'"

"Sounds appropriate," Jacquilyne said with a smile.

CHAPTER EIGHTEEN

Wednesday, October 11
Bois Blanc Island
Later That Evening

Wags took us back to St. Ignace. We thanked him and Jacquilyne for all of their help during the investigation. We waved to him as he took off and headed southeast to Bob-Lo. We got into Maggie's van and with Maggie at the controls, began the long trip south.

As we were going across the magnificent Mackinac Bridge, Maggie looked to the left and right and noting a few yachts in the Straits said, "I think I'd like a yacht someday, Lou."

I was surprised to hear her say that. Not because I didn't think she liked the water, but because I thought it would be practically impossible for her to navigate on and off easily - let alone get about once on board. I should not have doubted my friend, Maggie McMillan.

"There'd have to be some accommodation. But, I've found over the years that if I decide to have an experience, and if it is humanly possible to accommodate the desire, I'll have it."

"Well, you've certainly lived your life as an example of that, Maggie."

"It would take building some kind of a device to put me down into the yacht and to take me out, but that shouldn't be a problem. I may have to get a good craftsman to renovate the insides, maybe even redesign it."

"What would you name it, Maggie."

She thought for a few seconds and said, "Sea Legs." I didn't know whether to laugh or not. While I took a second or two to orchestrate a reaction, Maggie burst out laughing. "It seems that when any of these boats pull away from the dock, the boat goes where it is steered. I can steer a boat with the best of them. The boat will take me where land legs can't take me. When I get right down to it, the only legs I've got are my "Sea Legs."

I thought about it for a second and it made perfect sense to me. "Tell you what, when you are ready for your maiden voyage, Carol and I will buy a bottle of champagne, crack it over the hull, and we'll enjoy a sail into the sunset."

"It's a deal."

CHAPTER NINETEEN

Saturday, October 14
Spring Lake, Michigan

Our son Scott, his five-year-old son Benjamin, and I were sitting in a rowboat on Spring Lake trying to coax a fish or two to take our bait. We were celebrating Ben's fifth birthday with the present he wanted, fishing with his dad and grandpa. After an hour of not having much luck, Scott said, "Guess that's why they call this sport 'fishing.' If we catch any, they'd call it 'catching'." Ben and I laughed.

Seconds later Ben said, "Grandpa, I got one. I got one!" Ben reeled in a nice looking smallmouth bass and I scooped it up with the net.

A few minutes later, Ben had another worm on the hook and the three of us, three generations of Searings, were sitting in a boat with peace and quiet.

All of a sudden Ben said with excitement, "You got one, Grandpa. You got one!"

I pulled it closer. Scott got the net ready. Ben watched in great anticipation. I pulled it left, then right and kept on reeling in the line. As the fish arrived alongside the boat, I said, "OK Ben, Grandpa's going to pull it close, you get that net ready. If it doesn't fit in the net, your Dad'll have to grab it with his bare hands."

"OK, Grandpa, I'm ready."

I pulled the line up and the sunfish flew up out of the water. "You don't need a net for that little one," Ben said with a laugh.

"I thought I was bringing Moby Dick home for dinner. He fought me like a hammer shark!" We all enjoyed a good laugh as I removed the hook from its mouth and tossed the little fighter back into the lake.

The moment was special. "You know, Ben, it doesn't get any better than this. Fishing with you and your dad. I'm a blessed man. I've got my health, I'm in love with your Nana, I enjoy investigating and writing my stories, and if I'm not mistaken, the biggest fish in the lake is right this minute looking at my worm and thinking it will be his dinner!"

"Silly Grandpa," Ben said, as his bobber quickly dropped out of sight.

Epilogue

Mary Chandler was re-tried on the charges of kidnapping and murder. On a very cold day in November, she was found guilty on both counts. She was sentenced to life in prison without parole. There was no mention of her confession at the trial. All islanders had kept their word.

The McRaes used their insurance money to build a two-story cabin in front of the original east A-frame. They made an arrangement with the CAUSE organization to have their cottage available, free of charge, to an advocate and family for a week each summer.

In the cottage library can be found an autographed copy of **Buried Secrets of Bois Blanc**. The inscription reads, "To Gavin, Jenny, and 'Grandma Down the Hatch' with gratitude for kindness and assistance in solving the murder on Bob-Lo, Lou Searing."

Erin O'Brien's bones healed and soon she was back to perfect health. Erin found the investigation of crime so fascinating and challenging that she quit her job at the Michigan Department of Education and sought graduate training in forensic pathology. She is due to graduate in 2003.

Mr. and Mrs. Williams returned to their home in Traverse City. They had been through a nightmare but hoped that time would heal the pain of having lost their daughter.

Jackee and John Miller finished their retirement home on Twin Lakes. They both plan to retire a few years earlier than expected. The honey business was thriving and the peace, quiet, and living with nature seemed to fit them better than the fast-paced life in the Lower Peninsula.

The People of Bob-Lo Island used their money wisely. Not one word, to anyone's knowledge, was ever said about the murder on Mud Lake Trail. The money was invested and only the interest was spent. A community committee was formed to receive suggestions from the people on Bob-Lo. A democratic process was used to prioritize projects to be funded.

Joy Chandler never saw her sister after the trial. Mary did see that she received a million plus dollars to be comfortable for the rest of her life. After all, some of the inheritance rightfully belonged to her.

Witness was turned over to the Humane Society and ironically enough was adopted by the Waring family.

Carol, Maggie and I went back to Bob-Lo in early July. We wanted to see the friends we had made during the investigation of the murder. Wags took me up for a ride around the island. Carol got a Mackinac Island Fudge ice cream cone at the Hawk's Landing General Store, and Maggie dreamed of owning a yacht, a dream that was sure to come true.

Carol and I returned to our home on Lake Michigan, south of Grand Haven. We enjoyed our walks along the beach with Samm, our golden retriever who was chasing sticks thrown in any direction. Carol made quilts for soon-to-arrive grandchildren, practiced her Tai Chi on the beach, read all those books she never had time for when she was teaching, and dedicated herself to being a wonderful Nana to Ben, Nick, Jack, Hannah, and Thomas.

I reached for a few M&Ms, while Samm and our cats Luba and Millie slept peacefully at my feet. My computer keys began to dance with the telling of my next story.

The End

A PARTING THOUGHT

"The joy is in the doing."

J ack Kammeraad, a former junior high school teacher of mine, now a good friend and a fine artist, once told me, "Rich, always remember, the joy is in the doing." Initially, the meaning of his wise thought was unclear. Upon reflection, I soon discovered that his comment held much truth. The joy is truly in the doing, in the creation of the work at hand. As I look back on the books I have written, I have found that there is great joy in "listening" to the imagination, developing a story, talking to the many folks who contribute to the story, and attending to the numerous chores that must be completed to have a book take form to pass from a vision to reality.

I suggest to you that you think about Jack's comment. I suspect you will see that the joy is in the creation of a meal, in the tilling of the soil, in the painting, the sculpting, in the development of a project, in the sanding of the wood or whatever your passion.

It is not that joy ceases upon completion of the vision. There is joy in seeing the fulfillment of a dream, but I have come to understand Jack's wisdom that the joy is in the doing. May you find immense joy in your doing.

Richard L. Baldwin

RICHARD L. BALDWIN

COMING SOON

A body is found under a dock at the Grand Haven Marina. Lou and Maggie investigate and soon find themselves tracking a serial killer who is terrorizing boaters along the Lake Michigan shoreline. You won't want to miss *The Marina Murders*, coming in 2002.

RICHARD L. BALDWIN

BUTTONWOOD PRESS ORDER FORM

To order additional copies of *Buried Secrets of Bois Blanc: Murder in the Straits of Mackinac,* or earlier mysteries, *Administration Can Be Murder*, *The Principal Cause of Death* and *A Lesson Plan for Murder*, visit the website of Buttonwood Press at www.buttonwoodpress.com for information or fill out the order form here. Thank you.

Name_____

Address_____

City/State/Zip_____

Book Title	Quantity	Price
Buried Secrets of Bois Blanc ($12.95 – Softcover)		
A Lesson Plan for Murder ($12.95 – Softcover)		
The Principal Cause of Death ($12.95 – Softcover)		
Administration Can Be Murder ($12.95 – Softcover)		
TOTAL		

Rich Baldwin will personally autograph a copy of any of his books for you. It's also a great gift for that mystery lover you know!

Autograph Request To:

_____

_____

Mail Order Form with a Check payable to:

Buttonwood Press   Fax: 517-339-5908
PO Box 716   Email: RLBald@aol.com
Haslett, MI 48840   Website: www.buttonwoodpress.com

Questions? Call the Buttonwood Press office at (517) 339-9871

Thank you!